BEYOND THE DISTANT HILLS

SEQUEL TO A DISTANT HORIZON

ANNEMARIE BREAR

BEYOND THE DISTANT HILLS

AnneMarie Brear

The Woman from Beaumont Farm

Distant Series
A Distant Horizon

Beyond the Distant Hills

Contemporary
Long Distance Love

Hooked on You

Short Stories
A New Dawn

Art of Desire

What He Taught Her

CHAPTER 1

*B*errima, NSW, Australia. July 1853.

EMERGING from the shadow of the bark hut, Ellen Emmerson stretched for a moment, then shivered slightly. Here in the British colony of Australia, July meant the middle of winter, whereas in her native Ireland it would be summer.

The breaking of dawn and the rising of the sun cast an opaque pink light over the frigid silver-green land. Frost sparkled on the grass as birds chirped and sang in the eucalyptus trees. The odd rabbit hopped about until disturbed by the waking activity of the workmen, and then they quickly disappeared into holes in the ground.

Ellen paused for a moment, thinking of her homeland, the undulating green land that rolled down to the sea on the coast of Mayo where she'd been born and raised. Where she had married Malachy Kittrick and despite the odds nurtured four children until the famine struck, ruining their lives.

The death of her third son Thomas and her father was the

first of many events that tore at her soul. Malachy lost his way from being a happy, successful farmer to an out of work drunkard. He died in a fight, leaving Ellen to forge another road alone as a widow. When the landlord's agent burned down her cottage because of unpaid rent, Ellen knew she had to make a decision that would change her life.

Looking around the land she owned with her new English husband Alistair, she felt a deep sense of belonging in this wild and untamed country. Their land boundary began on top of a high ridge and extended down into a valley and stopped at the river's edge. In the valley, a herd of long-horned cattle grazed contentedly.

At the edge of the ridge, on ten wide flat acres, a hive of industry was waking up to a new day.

Ellen watched as teams of men climbed out from their tents and stirred campfires to boil the billycan for a cup of tea. Carpenters, stonemasons and labourers, forty men in total, would continue the building of the fine bungalow made of locally quarried sandstone, and which would have a verandah wrapped around all sides of the house, giving Ellen and her family sweeping views of the valley below. The house was close to finishing. Another six weeks or so should see it done. It had taken over a year to build so far, and after living in a bark hut for nearly the same length of time, and giving birth in it, she was ready to be in a proper house furnished with the very best furniture that Alistair could import from England.

Behind her she heard the stirrings of Riona, her sister, and the whispered tones of Bridget, her eight-year-old daughter. In the cot by the bed slept baby Lily, her five-month-old daughter, a child not sired by her husband but secretly by his best friend, Rafe Hamilton, the man Ellen had loved since first meeting him in Ireland two years ago.

As much as she admired, respected and cared for Alistair, he'd never had her heart, but their marriage was good. He didn't know the true parentage of Lily, and Ellen believed she made the right choice not to tell him. Rafe was in England and unlikely to ever return to the colony. Alistair adored Lily and Ellen's two sons, Austin and Patrick, as well as Bridget, treating them all as his own. So, she and her sister kept the secret to themselves and focused on the future, a future Ellen was determined to make as successful as she possibly could, and that meant becoming one of the country's most profitable landholders.

Land, something she'd been denied in Ireland, was the measure of success. With land, a person had security. Land offered endless ways to provide for a family. Land would remove the tarnish and stigma of being the poor Catholic Irish peasant that she once was.

Heading towards the chicken coop, Ellen waved to some of the men who were loading the cart with axes and saws in readiness to fell some more trees. Timber was needed for the building of not only some parts of the house, but the other buildings needed for the fledgling estate. The plans included stables, barns, a dairy, laundry and servant quarters.

Ellen unlocked the coop and the two-dozen hens happily roamed out onto the grass. She checked the nesting boxes and collected eight eggs and noticed a broody hen sitting on newly hatched chicks.

'Good girl. Keep them warm. You've had them too early,' Ellen soothed, throwing the hen some grain from her apron pocket.

'Morning, Ellen.'

Strolling back to the hut, Ellen acknowledged Moira, her widowed Irish friend who'd come over on the same ship as Ellen. 'Morning. Eight eggs.' Her breath was visible in the chilly morning air.

'Grand.' Moira stood by the water barrel and removed the lid before dipping a jug into it. Moira, dark haired and older than Ellen, was like a sister to her.

Behind the hut was the cooking area. A crude brick fireplace stood alone away from the hut so as not to be a fire danger. A tree slab table and stools were positioned under an awning made from tree saplings with a bark roof. This outdoor kitchen was Moira's domain, where she cooked for the family.

'Mama,' Bridget called, coming out of the hut, carrying the baby. 'Lily has a tooth.'

'My, isn't that exciting news?' Ellen grinned, taking Lily from her. She stared into the sweet round face of her youngest daughter and her heart swelled with love. Rafe's blue eyes stared back at her, reminding Ellen of the man she missed so desperately.

'She'll be gnawing on bones before you know it.' Moira laughed. 'Until then it's porridge.'

'I'm hungry,' Bridget said, sidling up to Moira as she stirred the fire.

'And so you should be a growing lass like you. Now set out the bowls for me and we'll get started on breaking our fast.'

'You've your lessons to do this morning,' Ellen told Bridget.

'I want to go riding, Mama.' Bridget pouted. She'd lost her Irish accent and spending time with Alistair gave her a more English cultured tone. He'd instructed her to call Ellen Mama and himself Papa, not the Irish mammy and da.

'Only once you've done your lessons.'

'Aunt Riona said I could.'

'I don't care what Aunt Riona said. I'm telling you lessons first, my girl.'

Bridget stormed off to set the table.

Ellen watched Bridget for a moment, noticing her daughter's black hair now reached her bottom. It needed plaiting to make her look presentable, but her daughter was want to be a little wild. Everyone who met Bridget commented on her young beauty and Ellen knew her daughter's headstrong ways needed to be curbed, or the two together could lead to trouble. She had plans for Bridget to grace the highest society in Sydney, but to reach those lofty ambitions, Bridget needed to be brought up as a lady, which was difficult to do on a building site in the country away from polite society.

However, returning to Sydney to Alistair's house on the harbour wasn't something Ellen planned to do anytime soon.

On marrying Alistair, she had mixed in the upper society of Sydney and been on the receiving end of gossip due to her being a poor servant. She wasn't one of *them* and didn't particularly want to be, which was why she'd moved to Berrima to oversee the estate here. But she did want her children to be part of the social scene, to befriend sons and daughters of the colony's elite. She wanted them to marry well, to be safe in the knowledge that no one would look down on them because of their inferior Irish background. She'd even turned her back on being a Catholic and became a Protestant to help pave their way into prestigious houses.

Alistair's English pedigree and wealth would give them an advantage she never could, and to expand on that, she encouraged Alistair to grow his business and his circle of rich and influential friends.

'Good morning.' Riona came to stand beside her. 'You're deep in thought.'

Ellen jiggled Lily in her arms as the baby began to grumble. 'I need to go into Berrima and collect the post. Hopefully, Alistair has written about the new land for sale in Moss Vale.'

'Why worry about that land? You've more than enough here.' Riona shook her head.

Before Ellen could answer, Mr Watkins, the carpenter working on the house, walked over to her from the men's quarters.

'Mrs Emmerson, may I have a word, please?'

Ellen passed Lily to Riona. 'Give her some porridge. She can have some milk from me when I return.' She turned to the older man. 'How can I help?'

He unrolled the plans of the house. 'We've hit rock here at the corner of the verandah on the east side, facing the proposed gardens. We can't break into the rock. It must be over twenty feet wide and probably just as deep.'

'That is bad luck.' Ellen studied the plans. 'We'll just have to build over it, then. Extend the verandah over this rock and out a few yards until you hit dirt.'

'But that won't work, Mrs Emmerson, as the roof line stops directly above the rock.'

She glanced at the house. 'Extend the verandah, Mr Watkins, and make it a shape like this.' She bent and using a small stick she drew a six-sided shape in the dirt. She didn't know the name of the shape, but she liked it. 'Then build a new roof over it to match that shape.'

'But that won't be following the lines of the house walls. It'll jut out like a… like a pier.'

'I agree it'll not be conventional, Mr Watkins, but it'll make a nice seating area, won't it? We'll plant trees or vines, yes vines, to grow over that sitting area.'

'Are you sure, Mrs Emmerson?' He didn't sound convinced.

'Definitely.' She knew he wanted to wait and ask Alistair's opinion, but with her husband in Sydney, Watkins knew that Ellen was in full charge and her opinion was the only one he needed.

'Very well. I'll instruct the men. There's a wagonload of cedar arriving today. It should be the last of the flooring to go down.'

'Excellent. And the cedar doors, Mr Watkins?'

'Being sanded and hung today. The mill will need paying.'

'I instructed them to send the invoices to my husband in Sydney.'

He let out a breath. 'Good, and the men's wages?'

'I'll give the money to you this afternoon to pay them.' She took a step, then stopped. 'Mr Watkins, I'm aware the men need to go into Berrima and drink themselves stupid for a day or two, especially after being paid, but there'll be no repeat of the fighting and arrests of last month, is that understood?'

The builder reddened. 'I can't apologise enough for what happened last month, madam. It won't happen again.'

'If it does, you and your men will be dismissed. The house is nearly finished. I can hire someone else to do the remaining work. You must understand that my husband has a reputation to uphold. To have five men arrested and placed into the stocks in front of the courthouse is a mark on my husband. He'll not stand for it happening again, and nor will I.'

'It won't, Mrs Emmerson. However, the men need to let off some excitement after working hard all month. It's a difficult job keeping them here when the goldfields beckons them like a lusty woman, if you beg my pardon.'

Smothering a smile, Ellen nodded. 'The temptation to dig for gold is hard to resist. I'd like to go myself—'

'You would?' Watkins asked incredibly.

'Of course. Why wouldn't anyone want to try their luck?' She chuckled. 'I may be small and a woman, but I'd like to see the gold diggings for myself. But as my husband has said to me many times, there are a lot of gold finds and an equal lot of men driven to madness when they find nothing but dirt.'

'I've heard the same, yet it doesn't stop men following their shadows across the country to search for gold.' Watkins replaced his hat and nodded towards Ellen before walking away.

Entering the hut, Ellen brushed her hair and wrapped it into a bun at the back of her head and tied on her bonnet. She took her blue wool shawl from the trunk, which matched her blue dress. With her gloves on and her reticule over her wrist, she left the hut thinking of the gold diggings that were springing up all over the country. Alistair told her ships were doubling in numbers coming to the country, all filled with eager men looking to strike it rich down south. The new city of Melbourne at the very south of the mainland was expanding so rapidly with new buildings that there were rumours it would overtake Sydney soon as the superior city.

'You're going now?' Riona asked, sitting at the outside table, where she fed Lily porridge.

'Yes, I'll take the buggy.' Ellen kissed the top of Bridget's head and then Lily's. 'Moira, do we need anything added to the list?'

Moira, bent over the smoking fire, didn't look up. 'No, I don't think so. Though a decent kitchen wouldn't go astray.'

'Six more weeks and we'll be in the house, and you'll have a large kitchen.'

'And help? I need help in a large kitchen.'

'I'll find you some help.' Ellen left them and went across the open space to the stable area, which in fact was nothing more than a fenced off yard where the horses were kept. A small hut where Douglas, the groom, slept also housed the tack. The two-wheeled buggy Ellen used to get about rested under a tree nearby.

'Morning, Mrs Emmerson.' Douglas, a young man in his late teens, brought out Betsy from the holding pen.

Ellen had only been driving the buggy for six months. Once Lily had been born, she'd insisted on learning to drive to give her the freedom to travel around the district. Alistair had bought the old mare from a farmer and taught Ellen. She'd revelled in the liberty of going wherever she wanted. All her life she had walked to get to places. In Ireland, in the snow and fog, the heat of summer or the cold rain, she had walked. Now she felt a true woman of means by being able to drive her buggy into Berrima or any of the other villages.

One day she would have her own carriage, but for now, the one they owned was in Sydney with Alistair. However, the little buggy brought her great joy. She preferred it to riding a horse, which she was learning to do. Bridget, an excellent rider already, laughed at her feeble attempts, but she was slowly adapting to riding a horse.

Once on the dirt track towards the village, Ellen sat back in the seat and enjoyed the clip clop of Betsy's gentle gait. She passed several bullock teams, all heavily loaded with wheat, timber or family possessions.

Down the hill she admired the two-storey red-brick house belonging to the Harper family, a fine elegant house which overlooked the village.

In Berrima, Ellen was surprised to see so much traffic in the sleepy village. A large group of people were gathered in front of the impressive sandstone courthouse, and she assumed the court sessions were taking place. Further down, past the intimidating gaol and outside of the Surveyor General Inn, another party of men were mounting their horses, and across the road were several burgeoning carts.

Ellen slowed Betsy next to one of the horsemen. 'Has something happened?'

'Bushrangers, madam.'

'Bushrangers?' She shivered a little.

'They have held up an inn near Murrimba. Some of us are going to see if we can apprehend them. A small contingent of soldiers have already left for Hanging Rock.'

Ellen gripped the reins, a little alarmed. Bushrangers, notorious armed men who robbed people, had held up Alistair's carriage on the road near Bargo Brush when he first showed her his property before they were married. She had talked to the dangerous men and when the Irish leader had heard her accent, he'd let them go without injury, except to their pockets.

She wondered if the same gang had held up the inn. 'Do you know the name of the bushrangers?'

'An Irishman named Eddie Patterson and his gang.'

Eddie. The same first name of the Irish leader who held up Ellen last year. It had to be the same person. She remembered him wearing a red handkerchief over his face. 'Have they killed anyone?'

'No. But they are causing a lot of trouble. Stealing horses and money and food.'

'And they are still in the area?'

'We think so and if they are, we will find them.'

'Let's hope you do. And the others?' Ellen nodded to a bigger party further along the road, consisting of carts filled with equipment.

'Gold diggers. They are off to a place called Braidwood in the south.'

'I've never seen the village so busy. If gold is found closer to here, we may be overrun.'

'Indeed, and what a distasteful idea that is, too. Melbourne is having all sorts of problems with miners fighting the licence fees and then there are bushrangers robbing coaches carrying gold. We want none of that here, Mrs...' The gentleman on the horse eyed her with a tilt of his head. 'I do not believe we have met before, madam?'

'No, I shouldn't think so. I'm Mrs Alistair Emmerson, Ellen.'

'Oh, I've heard of you, Mrs Emmerson. I am George Riddle from Elm Lodge, Sutton Forest. You are building a fine house on Oxley's Hill, I'm told.'

Ellen bristled. 'Our land is our own, Mr Riddle, not Mr Oxley's. We are not his tenants. His property is further east, overlooking Bong Bong. We share a boundary.'

'It was a mere figure of speech, Mrs Emmerson. I meant no offence. Mr Oxley and his family own much land hereabouts.'

Ellen took a moment, mentally slapping herself for being too quick to bite at his mention of the Oxleys' property. She needed to remember not everyone was judging her because of her poor Irish background. Some were happy to make friendships based on who she was now. 'Perhaps when our house is finished you may wish to visit us and see the property for yourself?' Ellen invited, injecting warmth into her voice. 'And your wife, of course, if you have one?'

'I do, and thank you. Mrs Riddle and I would be delighted. Do you have a name for your property yet?'

A name... Ellen panicked. She and Alistair hadn't spoken of a name yet. All the properties in this area had names for easy identification. 'It'll be called... Emmerson Park, Mr Riddle.' Fingers crossed, Alistair would approve.

'Emmerson Park. Excellent. Good day, Mrs Emmerson.' He rode off with the other men with much holler and excitement.

Ellen flicked the reins, urging Betsy on until they reached the other side of the green, and stopped before the White Horse Inn. Outside, several farmers had stalls selling produce.

She entered the inn, the place where she collected her mail, and was surprised to see a large parcel for her from Alistair, as well as several letters all tied in a bundle with brown string.

'Your husband is still in Sydney, Mrs Emmerson?' the landlord asked from behind the counter.

'Yes. He hopes to journey here next week and bring the boys home with him. They have two weeks break from school.'

'You'll be happy to see them.'

'I can't tell you how wonderful it'll be to see my boys.' The thought of seeing Austin and Patrick filled her with much joy. She missed her boys dreadfully while they were at school in Parramatta.

'Your house is coming along well, I hear.'

She smiled. Little managed to get past the landlord. 'It is. We are very pleased with it. Another six weeks should see it completed.'

He slid a pamphlet across the polished bar. 'Your husband might be interested in this.'

Ellen picked it up and read the advertisement for acreage plots of land being sold north of Goulburn. 'Goulburn is to the south of here, isn't it?'

'It is, Mrs Emmerson. Good grazing land, especially for sheep. I thought it might interest your husband. A fellow brought it in yesterday on his way to Sydney. The plots will be advertised in the newspapers next month. So, if you want pick of the best plots, I'd not waste time.'

'Thank you for showing this to me. Good day.'

Depositing her parcel into the buggy, Ellen nodded to a woman walking past, who she knew worked in the bakery up the road.

Having lived in the area for over a year now, she recognised a lot of faces and was slowly being welcomed into the local society after spending time at home giving birth to Lily and not accepting invitations.

On impulse Ellen decided to visit the bakery and buy fresh loaves of bread to save Moira from baking them in the temperamental outside fireplace.

'Mrs Emmerson?' a lady called to her across the street.

Ellen waited until a wagonload of sawn timber passed before crossing over to Mrs Dawson. 'Good day.'

'I'm so pleased to see you, Mrs Emmerson,' the other woman gushed. 'I had every intention of visiting your property to invite you to a tea party I'm hosting next Saturday at three o'clock. I do appreciate it is short notice, but I've only just this morning returned from Sydney and decided upon it. I do hope you will join us?'

'I'd be delighted, Mrs Dawson.' Ellen was genuine in her response. She'd met the Dawson family twice before and liked them. 'Alistair is due to arrive here on Friday.'

'Splendid. Do bring along your sister and children. It's an informal affair.'

'Thank you. Was your trip to Sydney a success?'

Mrs Dawson sighed dramatically. 'Yes, mainly, though in some respects it was not. I fear the fashion is still rather lacking. I receive advertisements for the new dress and hat styles being made in England. My sister who lives in Highgate near London sends them out to me as often as she can, but I despair of ever being on top of such things in this country. We are so out of touch, don't you agree?'

'I'm afraid fashion isn't something that interests me terribly much.'

'No? Well, there is no point out here, is there? We are bound to fail, Mrs Emmerson. London is such a long way away. Still, I shall remedy my wardrobe once we arrive in England at the end of the year.'

'You're leaving the colony?' Ellen's eyes widened in surprise.

'Only for a year or two. My eldest son, Frederick, is going to start Eton in September. We are all going on the voyage. I shall be so happy to see my sister again. We leave at the end of August, which is why I wanted to host a tea party before we close up the house and leave. It gives us the chance to say goodbye.'

'I don't know how I'd cope not seeing my sons for years on end. It's bad enough with them only at Parramatta.'

Mrs Dawson's eyes dimmed with sadness. 'It will break my heart. However, I must do the right thing by Frederick. My husband is insistent Frederick attends Eton as he did. Fathers make the decisions and mothers must adhere to them, mustn't we?'

Ellen was about to argue the point, for she had total say over her children. Alistair was a good stepfather, but he would never take control over her children without her consent.

'Oh, there is Mathers.' Mrs Dawson grimaced. 'I have hired a new maid, Mrs Emmerson, and such a creature you ever did see. The girl is so lazy, but I shall train her up and hopefully succeed in making something out of her.'

Ellen eyed up the slip of a girl who came down the road. The thought of servants made Ellen cringe. She needed to engage some for the house, but after being one herself she was loathed to suddenly become a demanding mistress. 'I best go, Mrs Dawson. I shall look forward to the tea party on Saturday. Goodbye.'

Strolling on up the road towards the bakery, Ellen side-stepped a mangy dog snuffling in a pile of rubbish. The cool day didn't deter children from playing outside cottages or women from hanging out washing.

She entered the brick cottage that was the bakery. The smell of fresh bread made her hungry. A man stood in front of her, arguing with the serving girl. With his back to Ellen, she couldn't see his face, but his Irish accent alerted her to a fellow country-man, though his belligerent tone annoyed her.

'Jesus, girl, will you listen to me!' he shouted. 'Sure, and I don't want to buy your bloody bread. I just want to ask you some questions.'

'I said I can't help you, mister.' The girl glared back at him. 'I haven't a clue who you're talking about.'

'I was told the woman I'm looking for lives around here. How many Irish women are there in this god forsaken place? She has dark red hair, blue eyes, pretty and—'

'I don't *know* her, sir. Go ask at one of the inns. I've customers to serve.'

The man slapped his cap against his leg and spun on his heel straight in front of Ellen. For a moment, she was about to apologise and step to the side, but instead she stared straight into the face of Colm Kittrick, her brother-in-law. Shock rendered her immobile and wordless.

Colm recovered first. 'Ellen! Sweet Holy Mother of God. It's you!'

She blinked several times. Colm had lost weight and reminded her so much of Malachy that she stumbled a little.

He took her elbow to steady her. 'I can't believe it, so I can't.'

'Colm... What... I...'

'I knew I'd find you.' He guided her outside as another customer entered the bakery. 'I should be so angry with you, and I was for a long time, but seeing you now, I can't be anything but pleased to see you.' He looked her up and down. 'My, you're a stunning woman, Ellen. This country suits you.

Look at you. I've never seen you so finely dressed. You look like a lady!'

Ellen took a step back. The skirts of her sapphire blue dress swayed at the sudden movement. 'Why are you here?'

'To find you and the children.'

'Why?'

He frowned and slapped his hat onto his head. 'Because you're my family. You left without a word, so you did. You promised to bring the children to me and say goodbye. Then I heard you'd left in the night like a band of thieves.'

'Our cottage was burnt down by Major Sturgess and his men!'

'Why didn't you come to me?'

She gave him a look of contempt. 'Because you wanted more than I was willing to give, Colm, and you know it.' Her brother-in-law had always wanted her for himself, something that she found abhorrent.

'I would have saved you all from crossing the seas to a strange land. You should have trusted me.'

'Trusted you?' she mocked. 'With all your secretive ways?'

'I'd have taken care of you. You shouldn't have run away, Ellen. You should have come to me when they burnt down your cottage. I'm your family.'

'I didn't want to go to you, Colm,' she defended, starting to feel more herself. 'Major Sturgess threatened to send me to jail. He would've taken the children from me. My family would've ended up in the workhouse.'

'Sure, and I'd not let that happen if you'd just come to me.'

She shivered in the cold as the memories of that awful night returned. The night when not only had her cottage burned but her uncle, Father Kilcoyne, had been shot and murdered by the major's men. The major had blamed her for the death and told her to run and never return to her village. Seeing no way out of the ordeal, she'd gathered her children, her mammy and Riona and walked through the night to Wilton Manor where she worked. She knew the servants there would help her, and so did Mr Wilton when he learned of her fate. Mr Wilton's generosity helped to get her family to Liverpool, England, to his friend Rafe Hamilton and his ship, which brought them to Sydney.

Now Colm had found her, the one man she never wished to see again. He brought nothing but painful memories. She'd not gone to him for help because he wanted her in his bed. Even before his brother had died, Colm had made it clear he wanted her. She'd never liked him and didn't trust him.

Her eyes narrowed at him. 'How did you find me?'

'It's the longest story, Holy Mother, so it is.' He grinned. 'But I did it. I knew I would find you once I got to Australia.'

'You shouldn't have come all this way, Colm,' she told him.

'Of course, I had to. I needed to know you were alive. Kathleen, the maid from Wilton Manor, told me that you had emigrated to Australia. She said you wrote a letter to the manor's cook, Mrs O'Reilly. As soon as I heard I bought a passage to Sydney on the first ship making the journey.'

Ellen closed her eyes. She'd written once to her old friend Mrs O'Reilly, telling her she'd made it safely to Sydney. Obviously, Mrs O'Reilly had shared the news with the staff at the manor. Ellen couldn't be mad at her for doing so. She never expected that Colm would learn of it.

Colm stared at her. 'You don't seem pleased to see me?'

'I'm surprised. I never expected you to come here.'

'Louisburgh was no longer home for me without my family. I was alone and, well, the state of the place was becoming more grim, so it was. So many people have gone because of the potato blight. They've died or emigrated or ended up in workhouses. It's bleak back home because of the British. The famine destroyed the country at the hands of the British.'

'Keep your voice down,' Ellen hissed. 'This is a British colony, it's not America. You can't shout your mouth off here!'

'Shame. It needs its independence from Britain just as America did. Why didn't you cross the sea to America?'

'I wanted to come here.' She said no more, not wanting to explain her reason to him. He must never know about Rafe Hamilton and his help.

Colm gazed around the little village. 'This place reminds me of home a bit. It's green. Is that why you decided to leave Sydney and come here? It's a devil of a journey on bad roads to get to this area.'

'I came here because this is where my husband's property is.' She waited for his reaction to her words.

His eyes stretched wide. '*Husband?* You're *married* already?'

'I am.' She raised her chin in defiance. She knew he'd judge her.

But instead of being angry, he seemed to fold into himself. Before her eyes, his height seemed to diminish. He no longer scared her, and the relief was immense.

'Did you think I'd stay a widow for the rest of my life?' she queried harshly.

'No... Yes... I'd hoped you were still free...'

'So, you could marry me?'

'Aye, and what is wrong with that?'

'Because I didn't want you back in Ireland, Colm, and I'd still not want you now even if I was *free* to choose you.'

He took a few steps backwards, his mouth moving as though to speak, but after a moment he hung his head as though in defeat. 'I've always wanted you, Ellen.'

'You should have moved on when we were young, Colm. Got yourself a wife of your own.'

'Can I see the children?'

Instinct begged her to say no, but she ignored it. Although in the past he had tormented her with his lusty looks and suggestive hints that she should be his woman, he'd been a good uncle to the children. He'd helped feed them through the hunger when the potato blight had destroyed their crops year after year. 'Very well.'

In silence, she led him back to the buggy. She steered Betsy back through the village and up the hill away from prying eyes who'd wonder who sat beside Mrs Emmerson in her buggy.

'How did you find out I was in Berrima?' She finally broke the tense atmosphere between them as she turned Betsy into the tree-lined track leading to the homestead.

'In Sydney, I met a man who'd been on the same ship as you. We worked together for a couple of weeks. He knew through his wife that you were working for a fellow named Emmerson. I asked about in some of the inns for days, but no one had heard of Ellen Kittrick. I found the offices of Emmerson Imports and Exports down by the harbour and hung around them for days, but never saw you. The office was closed each time I called there. Then one night by chance I met a bullock driver who said he'd hauled some stone for a gentleman named Emmerson in the country down south. So, I headed down here and started to ask about. Yesterday, I stopped at the Prince Albert Inn north of Mittagong, and they told me to go to Berrima.'

'You've come a long way for nothing, Colm.'

'I've come for my family, so I have.'

'What do you mean?'

'I can take you back to Ireland, Ellen. We can live in Dublin. I'll work hard for us.'

'I'm *married*.'

He swore under his breath.

Ellen reined in Betsy near the hut. For a moment she sat and simply stared at the men working on the house. When leaving this morning to collect the mail, she'd never thought for a second that she'd return with the brother-in-law she loathed.

It took all of her effort not to turn the buggy around and whisk him back down the track, head north towards Sydney and take him out of their lives. But it was too late now.

'Is that Bridget?' he asked in awe.

Ellen turned her head to where he pointed. Bridget stood watching the stonemason work, her white dress contrasting against the backdrop of green trees. 'Yes.'

'She's so big,' he murmured. 'She was such a wee little thing last time I saw her.'

'Starving will do that... stunt growth. Here she's adored by her new father and wants for nothing. She's happy, Colm. Don't upset her with stories of the past. She barely remembers Malachy. He was gone from home so much before he died.'

'My poor brother didn't have what it took to survive.' He climbed down from the buggy's seat.

'Don't start, Colm. I'll not talk about Malachy and all that happened back home. It's done. Over.'

Douglas came to take Betsy's bridle as Ellen retrieved her parcel and headed for the hut.

At the door she hesitated and then pushed it open.

Riona sat at the table, sewing in the light from the glassless window. She glanced up with a smile. 'You're back quicker than I expected.'

'Yes.'

'What's wrong?' Riona stood and then stared at Colm as he ducked his head to enter the hut. 'Colm Kittrick?'

'Good day to you, Riona O'Mara.' He took his cap off.

'Holy Virgin Mother.' Riona's gaze flicked from Colm to Ellen and back again. 'I never expected to see you here.'

'He's come to see the children.' Ellen strode to the table and put down the parcel. She faced Colm. 'I should have mentioned that the boys are away at school. A wonderful school which will turn them into gentlemen like their stepfather.'

'They aren't here?' he asked amazed. 'I want to see the boys.'

'No. Only Bridget is.' Ellen stepped to the cradle. Lily slept soundly. 'This is my daughter, Lily.'

Colm's eyes widened. 'You have another child?'

'I do.' She again felt the need to be defensive. 'My husband is in Sydney.'

They all turned as the door opened and Bridget came in holding a small piece of sandstone. 'Mama, look what Mr—' Bridget's words dried up as she stared at the man.

'Do you not remember me, Bridie?' Colm asked.

Ellen moved to her daughter and put an arm around her shoulders. 'This is your uncle Colm, from Ireland.'

'I remember.' Bridget tilted her head and studied him.

'You've grown into such a fine young lady, so you have.'

Bridget glanced up at Ellen. 'Can I have my riding lesson with Douglas now?'

'Yes, go on.'

Bridget ran out of the hut and Ellen folded her hands together. 'Life has changed for us. We aren't poor Irish peasants anymore.'

He glanced around the hut. 'Still living in a cottage though.'

'Only until the main house is built.'

'The main house... Is it rich you are now?' He glanced around. 'I'm pleased for you for sure, but the children are still my family. I want to see them.'

'Then what? Are you staying in Australia?'

'My only thought was to see you all,' he replied not meeting her eyes.

Instinct told Ellen he was lying. Colm had always been as slippery as an eel and as sly as a fox. 'There's nothing for you here, Colm. My children will be brought up in a different society to the one we knew. The past belongs in Ireland.'

'Are you saying that I have no role in their lives?' His lips thinned in anger.

'You don't have a say, no. They have a father, a good one. He's a gentleman who can give them everything they need. They don't need reminders of what we left behind back home.'

'You're ashamed to be Irish?'

'I'm not ashamed of anything, Colm Kittrick,' Ellen said hotly. 'But I want only the best for my children after all we've been through. *My* husband will provide for them. *My* sons will be gentlemen. *My* daughters will marry gentlemen. They will all have the chance to be successful. Never again will they go hungry or go without proper clothes or boots. Never again will they know what it's like to be treated worse than animals. Ireland is in the past and that's where it will stay.'

'Me included?'

She nodded.

'You've become English then?' he snarled. 'Married to an Englishman and your sons will be brought up as *Englishmen*.'

'It's a better alternative than being poor Irish living in a bog.'

'You should have trusted me. You'd still be home in Ireland if you'd only come to me! I'd have kept you safe.'

'From Major Sturgess and his lies? How could you have kept me safe? And what would have been the price I'd have to pay?'

'You make me sound like the devil.'

'Weren't you? For years there were rumours about you being a part of the Young Irelanders Movement, but then you were also known for being friendly with the English soldiers. You played both sides, didn't you? Were you a spy for the English?'

'No!'

'Then what were you doing? For the soldiers never came to your farm and harassed you, did they?'

'That's because I could pay my rent so I could. I didn't rely on bloody potatoes as Malachy did. I told him to sow other crops, but of course he didn't listen to me.'

'It was more than you not planting potatoes, Colm, and you know it. You never went short of anything.'

'If you want the truth, I'll give it to you,' he snapped. 'I was a runner for the movement. I took messages back and forth in the outlying areas. I was never caught because I paid off soldiers and anyone in authority who looked too closely into my business.'

She folded her arms across her chest. 'So, it was all true. And now? Why are you really here? Are you on the run?'

'No.'

'I don't believe you. Who wants you? The British or the Movement? What have you done?'

'I'm not a wanted man. I swear on all that's holy, that I'm not. I've simply come to take my family back home.'

'We aren't your family and Ireland isn't our home. Australia is our home, our future.'

He huffed. 'Ireland is what runs through our blood, Ellen. It made us. You are the woman you are because of Ireland.'

'I am the woman I *am* because of my *own* strength of purpose, because I wanted to survive against the odds.'

'The children need to understand where they come from,' he declared. 'They aren't English! You can't make the boys Englishmen. It's not right! They should be home and fighting for our freedom!'

Ellen narrowed her eyes in thought. 'My God, you're still part of the Young Irelanders, aren't you?'

Colm stiffened, his cheeks flushing. 'You know nothing. All that is done with.'

She didn't believe a word he said. 'What was your plan once you'd found me?'

'To take you home where you belong. Ireland is our home, the children's home.'

'It's not only about taking your family back. You're here for other reasons, aren't you? *Tell me.*'

His cheeks reddened. 'Ireland needs its sons and daughters to fight for its freedom from the British yoke. Austin and Patrick need to be a part of it. There are men here in the colony who advocate the cause. I have met them.'

'There is a rebel group in Sydney?'

'They are good men. True Irish! They were sent here as young men, ripped from their country by the British. Men who wish to fight but are now too old to do so. They can't return to Ireland, so they help in other ways.'

Realisation dawned on Ellen. 'They have money and arms which you will take back for the fight. Arms, money and my *sons*.'

'Yes, but—'

'Ahh...' She guessed correctly. 'The *cause* wants recruits. Too many men have left Ireland's shores.'

'The English have starved us off the land, forced us to live in foreign countries. The sons of Ireland need to take back what is *ours*.'

'It's a war you can't win, Colm. They tried a rebellion in '48 and it failed.' She felt sorry for him. 'The British are too mighty. Ireland's sons are too poor and downtrodden after years of the blight.'

'We can rebuild. We must rebuild!'

'Not with *my* sons you won't,' her bitter tone made him flinch.

'They were Malachy's sons too, my nephews. They are *Ireland's* sons.'

'Austin and Patrick are *mine*!' She growled like a cornered dog.

Lily began to stir. Riona jumped forward and scooped her up and left the hut without saying a word.

'Perhaps your sister might make me a good wife...' Colm murmured. 'I suspect she'd make a suitable substitute for you.' He grinned evilly.

'You stay away from my sister and my children.'

He chuckled. 'I could take her in the night, and you'd be none the wiser until morning.'

Ellen stiffened angrily, but a tingle of fear shivered down her spine. 'I think you need to leave now. I'll have someone take you back to the village or wherever you want to go.'

'I want to see the boys.'

'You won't be seeing them. They are away.'

'I'll find them.'

Her blood turned to ice. 'You touch my sons and I'll hound you unto death, I swear to the Holy Virgin I will.'

'I want *my* nephews, Ellen. They are my *blood!* They have the *right* to be in Ireland with me. Ireland needs them to fight against British rule. It's what Malachy would have wanted, so he would.'

'Malachy is *dead*, and so will you be if you go anywhere near my boys.' She stood very still. 'Now get out.'

He ignored the command. 'They are at school in Sydney, yes? A toff's boys' school... It'll be easy enough to find. I found you, didn't I?' He taunted. 'And I'll find them and when I do, you'll never lay eyes on them again. Your sons are lost to you, Ellen, and now you'll see how it feels when your family is stolen away from you!' He pulled his cap down low and stormed out of the hut.

Shaking, Ellen stepped to her secretaire and pulled out a sheet of paper and began to write.

ALISTAIR, *Colm Kittrick is here and threatens to take the boys back to Ireland with him. Please collect them from school and take them away. Perhaps to your cousin Robin in Melbourne? Write when you are safe.*

Your wife, Ellen.

SHE HURRIED out of the hut, scanning the men building the house for Mr Thwaite, the overseer. By the horse yard, Colm stood talking to Bridget, while he was distracted Ellen hurried over to the builders in search of Mr Thwaite. She found him talking to one of the stockmen hired to watch the cattle now Mr Thwaite had been elevated to the position of overseer of the estate.

'Mr Thwaite.' Breathless, Ellen thrust the envelope into his hands. 'Find a trusted man or go yourself to Sydney, but give this to Mr Emmerson as soon as you can.'

'You seem upset, madam.'

'That man over there talking to Bridget is her uncle from Ireland. He's threatened to take Austin and Patrick back to Ireland with him.'

'No!' Thwaite's chest swelled with disbelief and anger. 'I'll go for the constable!'

'There's no time for that and he'd only deny it and I have no proof. My husband must be informed to take my sons away from Sydney.'

'I'll go myself, Mrs Emmerson, this is too important a task to give to another. I'll take two horses and ride swiftly. I'll leave Mick Jones in charge, with your permission?'

'Thank you, yes. Please hurry.'

He tugged his hat to her. 'You can rely on me.'

He strode away and Ellen sighed in relief. She knew Mr Thwaite would reach Alistair before Colm learned where the boy's school was, travel there and find them. Austin and Patrick would be happy to see their uncle and whatever lies he told them they would believe and leave the school grounds none the wiser of his real intentions.

Lily's crying reached her. Riona carried the baby about the building works, trying to soothe her. Colm still stood talking to Bridget as she sat astride Princess.

Ellen seethed. How dare that man arrive here and bring threats and disharmony to her new life! She had survived too much for him to ruin it now.

A red mist of rage filled Ellen and she marched over to them. 'I told you to go, Colm.'

He gave her a cool look. 'I'll go when I'm ready, Ellen. You don't order me around. I'm not your lackey.'

'I might not have had any power back home but here it's very different,' she snarled. 'This is my land! I want you gone. I have a dozen men who will happily throw you off the place. Do you want a fight?'

'Isn't Uncle Colm staying, Mama?' Bridget asked innocently, dismounting.

Ellen tried to calm down in front of Bridget. 'No. He has other plans.'

'The boys won't get to see him.' Bridget led Princess to the fence.

Colm patted her on the head. 'Don't be worrying about that, me darling. You and your brothers will see me again.' He sauntered away with a wink to Ellen as he left.

Ellen bent and held Bridget's shoulders. 'What was he asking you?'

'He was asking about Papa and the boys.' She shrugged, unconcerned. 'Douglas says the farrier needs to put new shoes on Princess. Can I go with him to the village?'

'You're not going to a blacksmith's. It's not what young girls do. You are to practice your drawing and painting. You're to stay in the hut until I say otherwise, do you understand?'

'That's boring.'

'Come along.' Ellen watched as Mr Thwaite rode away from the yard, leading another horse. He passed Colm who paused and gazed at him.

Colm turned and glanced over his shoulder at Ellen, grinning. He knew what she had done.

'Mama, I don't want to draw,' Bridget whined.

'You'll do it and no arguments.' Ellen walked back to the hut as Riona joined her with Lily.

'She needs feeding, so she does.' Riona passed the baby to Ellen. 'Has Colm gone?'

Ellen kissed Lily's plump cheeks, her hands still shaking. 'For now. But I feel it'll not be the last we see of him.' Ellen lowered her voice. 'He threatened to take the boys back to Ireland.'

Shocked Riona reared back. 'Mother Mary!'

'He wants them to join the fight for Irish freedom.'

'That's insensible. He can't do that. The man has lost his mind. They are *your* sons.'

'He believes he has a say in what happens to his nephews.'

'The man is an eejit.'

'I've sent Mr Thwaite to Alistair.' Ellen moved so Bridget couldn't hear them talking where she sat drawing at the table. 'I've told Alistair to take the boys to Melbourne.'

'Melbourne? Holy Virgin! Why so far away?'

'Alistair's cousin Robin lives in Melbourne. Colm won't go there.'

'No one knows what Colm will do. Sure, and we never thought he'd come to Australia.'

'It's the only place I could think of. If Colm heads back to Sydney, he'll soon learn of the boys' school. It's the principal school where society sends their boys if they don't send them back to England for their education.'

'Well, if going to Melbourne means the boys are safe that's all that matters, so it does. But how long will Alistair keep them there?'

'I don't have that answer.' Ellen rubbed her forehead as she sat down and unbuttoned her bodice to feed Lily.

As the baby sucked contentedly, Ellen tried to think of a solution. 'It might be some months. Until Colm returns to Ireland.'

'How will we know when he does that?'

'Alistair knows every ship that comes and goes from the harbour because of his import and export business. He could easily check the passenger lists through his contacts in Sydney.'

'But if Alistair is in Melbourne, he'll not know if Colm has departed or not, will he?'

Ellen groaned, startling the baby. 'Sweet Jesus and His Saints! I've messed it all up, haven't I? I panicked and sent that note without thinking it all through.'

'Whist now. It'll be fine. Alistair is a sensible man, so he is.

He'll work something out to keep the boys safe. As you say he has contacts.'

Suddenly, Ellen stood and dumped Lily in Riona's arms. 'I'll go and bring Colm back. While he is here, then he is no threat to the boys.' She buttoned up her bodice.

Over Lily's grizzling, Riona frowned. 'Is that wise? Do we want him here?'

'Not at all and I doubt he'll come back with me for he'll realise I'm up to something trying to detain him. But all I can do is buy more time for Alistair to make a plan.'

Ellen rushed out of the hut, her mind whirling. Mr Watkins signalled to her that he wanted a word, but she waved him away and hurried along the cart track that served as their driveway. She couldn't see Colm in sight.

Pausing, she searched the surrounding fields, assuming he may have cut across them to reach the track leading to the village, but nothing moved except the cattle in the tall grass. She'd lost him.

CHAPTER 2

*E*llen spent a restless week waiting for any sign of Colm. She knew Mr Thwaite would have taken three days to reach Sydney and if he changed horses after speaking to Alistair and set off for Berrima the same day as arriving in Sydney, he'd be due back today.

She paced the building site, not able to concentrate on anything. Mr Watkins had stopped asking for her approval on certain things, sensing her disquiet and instead set the men to working hard on finishing the flooring.

Absentmindedly, Ellen watched the workmen take down the canvas coverings over the window gaps as new sheets of glass were placed into the rooms. The sight should have given her such pleasure, but she couldn't concentrate on anything else except her boys being safe.

Worried that Colm might take Bridget out of spite, Ellen had kept her daughter within sight all week, driving them both a little crazy in the process. Bridget was used to her freedom of roaming the property, and Ellen was used to not having her under her feet.

Riona did her best to help, but with Lily teething and the

demands of the property, Ellen was at her wits end by that afternoon.

'Damn and blast!' Ellen banged her hands together.

'What is it?' Riona asked where she sat on a blanket under the shade of a large eucalyptus tree. Lily was learning to crawl with Bridget's encouragement.

'I'm meant to be at the Dawsons' tea party.'

'Then go.'

'How can I?'

Riona frowned at her. 'Do you not trust me to look after the girls? I'd protect them with my life, so I would.'

'Of course, I trust you. But I can't leave until Mr Thwaite is back from Sydney and hear what message Alistair has sent.'

A gunshot startled them.

Shading her eyes from the midday sun, Ellen stared into the valley. 'A hunting party. Mr Jones did say they needed to shoot some kangaroo for the men. They've had salted pork and beef all week and asked permission to hunt for some fresh meat.'

'I wonder if Mr Jones will give me the hide, if I ask?' said Riona. 'We could do with some more rugs on the hut floor now this little one is shuffling about.'

'I'll ask him.' Ellen took a moment to squat down beside Lily and give her a kiss as the baby rolled over. 'Such a clever girl.'

'Mama, riders!' Bridget announced, sitting up and pointing to the track.

Ellen lifted her skirts and rushed through the debris of the building work to the drive. Alistair rode with Mr Thwaite behind. 'Alistair!' She couldn't believe her eyes. What was he doing here?

Their horses, blowing hard skidded to a halt in front of her.

'My dearest.' Alistair bounded down from the saddle and hugged her to him. 'I came as quickly as I could.' He took his hat off and kissed her.

'The boys! You're meant to be with the boys.'

'They are safe,' Alistair panted, his blond hair damp with sweat.

'How? Where? You should be with them!' Her heart seemed to stop beating in her fright.

Mr Thwaite dismounted and taking Pepper, Alistair's horse, led the horses away.

Alistair sucked in a breath. 'It was a hard ride.'

'Where are the boys!' She wanted to scream at him.

'On a ship.'

'What? Why aren't you with them?'

'They are on my and Rafe's ship, *Blue Maid*. It was in the harbour and ready to sail when Mr Thwaite found me. Captain Leonards is in command and Austin and Patrick are under his protection.'

'Captain Leonard?' She blinked rapidly in confusion.

'You remember the captain of the ship in which you came to Australia? A good and decent man of principle. They will be well cared for with him.'

'Yes, yes, but *why* are they with him and not you? I don't understand. Will he deliver them to Robin?' She held back her temper which wanted to rage at him for leaving the boys alone.

'When I read your note, I realised that this Kittrick fellow would soon find me wherever I went in the colony. My name is too well known. I asked around, and it seems Kittrick is in with a notorious Irish rebellion cause, which has a small society of members in Sydney. They are mostly ex-convicts, a rough lot indeed. However, they have sympathizers with some of the wealthy inhabitants of Sydney, who I am ashamed to say are helping with financing the situation in Dublin. They are intent on their actions of wrestling Ireland free from British rule.'

'Yes, I know this,' she snapped impatiently. 'Colm is in with them, the fool that he is. That's why I needed you to get the boys away before he found them and took them back to Ireland.'

'He won't get them now, my darling. I promise you. I acted

quickly and the boys have left Sydney without anyone being the wiser.'

'You should have gone with them. Are you certain Robin will look after them in Melbourne?'

'Melbourne?' He looked bewildered.

'You have sent them to Melbourne with Captain Leonards and he will see them safe to Robin?'

'No, my dear. The *Blue Maid* is sailing home for Liverpool, England. I've sent the boys to Rafe.'

'England? To Rafe?' The blood drained from her face. The breath left her lungs and her knees buckled. She felt herself falling and staggered.

'Dearest!' Alistair held her up by her elbows.

She reared away from him. 'Get away from me!' she cried, pushing him back.

'Ellen, my dear.'

She moaned; the anguish too deep to be kept inside.

Riona raced to her. 'Ellen! What is it?'

Sobbing, Ellen turned and buried her face into her sister's shoulder. 'They've gone!'

'Colm's taken them?' Riona wailed.

'No. No,' Alistair said quickly. 'I've sent them to England, to Rafe Hamilton. They will be safe there.'

'Safe?' Ellen swung to him, hating him. 'You've sent *my* sons to England without my permission! How could you do that?'

'I was acting for the best. I did not want Kittrick kidnapping them, and we would never see them again.'

'All I wanted you to do was keep them with you until Colm left again. He'll not stay here long. He's taking money and arms back to Ireland. He could be leaving within weeks.' Her face crumpled at the enormity of what Alistair had done. 'I fully expected you to take them to your cousin Robin in Melbourne. Holy Virgin Mother!' She couldn't take it in. 'I'd rather you'd brought them *here*, and *we* watched over them than to send them so far away.'

Her chest felt constricted with pain. She couldn't breathe. Ellen stumbled away, crying into her hands.

'I thought it was the best thing to do. Austin once told me that he would like to be educated in England like I was and the other boys in our circle are. I have asked Rafe to enrol them at Harrow, my old school. I have also written to my father. He will meet them, and Mother and Father will have them for holidays.'

'No!' Ellen screamed. 'You're to write to Rafe and tell him to bring them home to me! Send a letter on the next ship leaving for England. Hurry!'

'Dearest, please, this is the best option for them. The boys are away from Kittrick and will receive an excellent education befitting them as my sons. They will become gentlemen. They *should* be in school in England. It is what everyone does, you understand that.'

Ellen remembered Mrs Dawson and her mention of sailing to England in August so her boy can attend Eton. Still, even knowing it was the done thing, didn't stop the agony.

She glared at Alistair. 'I will *never* forgive you for this.'

'Ellen…'

'I can't bear to look at you.' She turned away from him before she could say anything else she may later regret.

Walking back to the blanket, she scooped up Lily. 'Come, Bridget.'

For once her wilful daughter did as she was told without argument and followed Ellen as she headed down the hill towards the river in the distance.

'Mama?' Bridget finally spoke after five minutes of walking.

'Yes.'

'What's happened to Austin and Patrick?'

Her arms growing tired, Ellen sat down on the edge of the

riverbank and placed a sleepy Lily on her lap. 'They have gone to England, away to school.'

'So, Uncle Colm doesn't take them to Ireland?'

Ellen looked at her sharply, realising not much got past her daughter. 'Yes.'

'I don't want to go back to Ireland.' Bridget tossed her head like a young queen. 'This is my home.'

'Then be thankful you are a girl and not a boy. Most boys go away to school.'

'So, I won't ever go away to school?'

'No. I promise you. We'll engage a governess for you and Lily.'

'Someone who can ride?'

'There's more to life than horses, child,' admonished Ellen gently. She hugged Bridget to her and cradled Lily closer. They were all she had left of her children to hold.

'One day I will have a big house and stables and ride all day every day and then dance at balls at night.' Bridget nodded with complete conviction.

'That sounds terribly busy,' Ellen's voice wavered. She swallowed back the lump in her throat.

'Can we have a ball when I'm older, Mama?'

'Of course, we can.' She let the tears fall as she stared out over the river. Black water hens glided serenely in the middle and on the other side, a kingfisher sat on a low branch of a tree, its eyes on the fish swimming below.

Bridget plucked a grass stem. 'I'll miss Patrick, and Austin, but mainly Patrick. He likes to ride like me.'

'He was becoming such an excellent rider.'

Rustle in the grass behind made them turn.

Riona sat down and tucked a stray tendril of ebony hair behind Bridget's ear. She stared at Ellen. 'Moira has made some tea. Will you come back up?'

'Not yet.' Ellen gazed down at Lily sleeping in her arms. She saw Rafe's features in the baby's face and her heart wept anew.

Rafe would soon have her sons in his keeping. For a mad moment she wished she was on the ship sailing to him as well. She ached to feel his arms around her, to see the love in his eyes for her.

Ellen touched Lily's soft cheek with a fingertip. She loved this child so much, hers and Rafe's baby. In Lily she had a piece of Rafe forever.

'I'm hungry,' Bridget piped up.

'Then go and have something to eat.'

Riona stood and held her arms out. 'Give me Lily. I'll put her to bed and Bridget and I will have tea.' She reached down and took the baby from Ellen. 'Bridget run ahead and tell Moira.'

As Bridget ran off through the grass kept short by the cattle, Riona stared down at Ellen. 'Alistair is beside himself, so he is. He imagined he was doing the right thing.'

Silent, Ellen watched the kingfisher.

'Colm will never find the boys now.' Riona sighed. 'Don't let this come between you and Alistair, Ellen. Don't let this one mistake ruin your marriage.'

'It's a rather large mistake.' She looked up at Riona. 'When will I ever see them again? I lost Thomas, and now I feel I've lost Austin and Patrick, too.' She still grieved over her son Thomas who died in a boating accident with her da before she left Ireland.

Steady tears ran down Riona's face. 'I can't bear to consider them gone either. It fair injures me, so it does. But I could easily blame you as much as Alistair.'

'Me? Why?'

'By marrying a wealthy protestant Englishman. You wanted to rise in society, so you did, and because of your insane need to have the boys become gentlemen, they are now going to be on the other side of the world.'

'I was happy for them to be educated in Sydney. This is Alistair's fault, and Colm's!'

'No, not really. It's yours, Ellen. If we'd stayed simple people, if we'd remained working for Alistair none of this would have happened.'

'Colm would still have come after them and I'd not been able to protect them from him as a simple housekeeper, would I?'

'We could have fled, gone in the night and never be found. Haven't we've done it once before? We could have done it again.'

'I didn't want to run again, having no money, no home, worrying myself to death where the next meal will come from. I had enough of that in Mayo! Is it so wrong that I want to build a good life for my children, somewhere they are safe and happy? That I want the best for my children?'

'No... and some would argue that you've achieved that now. The boys will be educated. They will be gentlemen. They just won't be with us for years...' Riona walked away with Lily.

Aching with a desperate longing to hold her sons tight, Ellen hugged her knees as the kingfisher swooped down into the water and came up with a fish wriggling in its beak.

* * *

It took days for Ellen to speak to Alistair or even to look at him and when on the morning of the third day he decided to return to Sydney she was pleased.

'I shall come back next month when the house is completed,' Alistair said, packing his saddlebags as the tent he'd been sleeping in was dismantled by some of the workmen.

Douglas led Pepper from the holding yard and began saddling him.

'Will you wish to host a dinner to celebrate the house's completion?' he asked Ellen.

'No.' Ellen held Lily while Bridget skipped over to Douglas. Riona and Moira stood near the hut waiting to say farewell.

'As you wish.' Alister buckled the second bag. 'There is money in the hut, in a leather wallet on the top shelf. It is for you to buy the land you wanted in Moss Vale.'

'Thank you.'

He sighed. 'I expect you will never forgive me, and I do not blame you. I acted rashly and without consideration to how you would feel. I have apologised several times. I shan't do so again for there is no point to it ... Ellen, please look at me if you can bear it.'

She raised her head from gazing at Lily to Alistair's face.

His handsome features were tortured in misery. 'I do not wish our marriage to be over. Perhaps time a part will heal the damage I have done.' His eyes fell to Lily's sweet face, and he kissed her plump cheek. 'Goodbye, little one. Be good for your mama.'

Ellen turned her cheek to him as he kissed her.

Without saying a word, he walked away.

She held Lily tighter as Alistair embraced Bridget and promised to bring her a new dress when he returned. As Douglas secured the saddlebags, Alistair mounted and pulled his hat brim low. He waved to them all and then reined Pepper about and trotted down the drive.

Ellen sighed deeply, feeling a great deal of relief as he rode further away.

Back in the hut, she placed Lily on the rug. She pulled out a box from under the bed and wiped off the dust. From inside she took out three books, *A Christmas Carol* by Charles Dickens, *Pride and Prejudice* by Jane Austen and *Wuthering Heights* by Emily Bronte. Three books given to her by Rafe when they had sailed from Liverpool. Whenever she held them, she felt closer to him.

The books were weathered, a little beaten by constant use, for they had been repeatedly read during the voyage over and since then Patrick had asked her to read *A Christmas Carol* again last Christmas.

Tears welled. She'd not be reading the book to him this Christmas.

Riona entered the hut in a state of excitement. 'Ellen, you'll never guess who has just arrived.'

'Who?' Ellen put the books back in the box, not really having the energy to be sociable. She'd sent a note to Mrs Dawson apologising for not attending the tea afternoon.

'The Duffy family.'

Ellen frowned. 'The Duffys from the ship? The ones we sailed out here with?'

'Sure, and it's the very same!'

'Why are they here?'

'Looking for work. Come out and see them.' Riona scooped up Lily and walked outside.

Finding some energy, Ellen tidied her hair and then stepped out to greet the family.

At first, Ellen could only stare at the ragged, unkempt family standing looking forlorn, then she remembered her manners and stepped forward to shake Seamus Duffy's hand. She had liked Seamus a lot. On the ship he'd been the first one to lend a hand to anyone, unlike his wife, Honor, who had an opinion about everything whether a person wanted to hear it or not. Their two girls, Caroline and Aisling, had played with the boys and Bridget and were sweet girls. Ellen hadn't seen the family since leaving the lodgings two days after disembarking from the ship in Sydney and going to work for Alistair. But the eighteen months since then had not been kind to the Duffy family if looks were to go by.

'It's good to see you, Seamus,' Ellen said warmly, noticing the holes in his boots and the buttons missing off his jacket. His black curly hair resembled a bird's nest.

'And yourself, Mrs Kitt... er... I mean, Mrs Emmerson.' He smiled over his mistake.

'On the ship you called me Ellen, and I called you Seamus. We have no need to return to formalities.' Ellen put him at his ease.

''Tis a grand place you've got yourself for sure.' He glanced around.

'Thank you. It'll look beautiful once the house is finished, and the gardens planted. It'll take years of work, but it'll be worth it.'

Ellen smiled at Honor Duffy. 'Welcome to Emmerson Park.'

'Thank you, Mrs Emmerson.' The other woman nodded, but her gaze didn't meet Ellen's. Honor Duffy had made it clear in the past that she didn't agree with Ellen rejecting the Catholic faith and no longer speaking their native Irish language.

'Moira is here, too,' Riona announced.

'Mrs O'Rourke?' Mrs Duffy spluttered. 'Is the entire ship's passenger list here?'

'Just Moira.' Riona jiggled Lily in her arms. 'And this is Lily, Ellen and Alistair's baby.'

Mrs Duffy peered at the baby. 'You didn't waste any time, did you?'

Ellen clenched her teeth and forced a smile.

'I'm looking for work, Mrs Emmerson, Ellen,' Seamus said, giving his wife a nudge with his elbow. 'We both are. I've been working around Sydney, trying my hand at most jobs. But we lost our home. It was getting pulled down and other places were expensive to rent, so we thought to try our luck in the country. Honor didn't like the city.'

'Dirty and noisy it is,' Mrs Duffy added with a sniff. 'I feared for the girls' lives every time they moved out the door. Inns and public houses on every street corner, men loitering around, rubbish piling in the gutters. A godforsaken place if ever I saw one.'

'Not all the streets are so ugly. George Street is a fine street and there are plenty more. I visited many grand houses along the harbour after my marriage and they impressed me and wouldn't look out of place in London or Dublin.'

'Do we have work for Seamus, Ellen?' Riona asked as Honor was about to argue.

'I'm sure we've something for you, if you're happy to do a bit of everything?' Ellen asked him.

'I am. Sure and I'll work hard for you, Mrs Emmerson.'

Mrs Duffy tutted ever so slightly under her breath, but Ellen heard it.

'Mrs Emmerson, are Austin and Patrick here?' Caroline asked quietly, always a quiet and shy girl.

Ellen swallowed. 'No… They are… They are on their way to England to go to school.'

'England?' Honor Duffy gasped. 'You've sent your sons to school in *England*?'

'My husband believed the boys would benefit from a gentleman's education,' Ellen defended. No matter what she felt privately, in public she'd support Alistair.

'But you've not been here very long and you're risking them on that hazardous journey again?'

'It's the only way to travel to England,' Ellen tried to make light of it, despite her own worry.

'The boys will be men before they return.' Mrs Duffy was incredulous. 'I couldn't imagine of anything that would be more soul destroying than not seeing my girls for years.'

Ellen stiffened at the insult. 'Rest assured, Mrs Duffy, the boys are well cared for and under the protection of Mr Hamilton, you remember him? The man who owned the ship we sailed in?'

'I do remember him. It makes sense now.'

'How so?'

'Well, Mr Hamilton was deeply interested in your affairs, wasn't he? More so than any of ours when we were in Liverpool.'

Riona swapped Lily to her other hip. 'I'm sure you're all in need of a drink? Moira would be pleased to see you, so she would. Come with me, girls, and we'll have a drink. Mrs Duffy?' Riona walked away, the girls following and after a small hesitation, Mrs Duffy went with them.

'Forgive my wife, Mrs Emmerson,' Seamus said softly. 'She hasn't had it easy since we arrived, and it's made her… well, let's just say she easily finds fault in all things, so she does.'

Ellen felt Honor Duffy had been doing that since the day she drew breath. 'I'm willing to give you work, Seamus, for I know you to be honest and decent, but I'll not be judged by your wife because I have done well for myself.'

'And I respect that, so I do. Honor will keep her opinions to herself, I promise you that.'

'Over there,' Ellen pointed to the other long hut on the east side of the property, 'that hut is the men's quarters. We have no families here as yet, just the men. We have carpenters, stonemasons, labourers, gardeners and fencers and for the beasts the stockmen and a groom. Mr Thwaite is the overseer and Mr Watkins the head builder. Where you fit into all that is up to you.'

'Sure, and I'm good with my hands. I'll make myself useful if given the chance.'

'Good. After a cup of tea, I'll take you to Mr Thwaite and introduce you.' Ellen glanced at their scant belongings all held in two dirty carpet bags. 'We'll have a tent erected for you. It'll be your lodgings for a while I'm afraid.'

'A tent will be grand. We've been sleeping in the open for the past week so a tent will be a luxury.'

She took him around to the back of her hut and to the outdoor kitchen where Moira was feeding the girls plates of currant flat cakes and cups of sweet milky tea, even Mrs Duffy was eating happily.

A cart rumbled down the drive filled with tall bare-limbed trees.

'Oh, that'll be the fruit trees from Camden Park that I ordered,' Ellen said as Mr Thwaite greeted the driver of the cart. 'Seamus, come and I'll introduce you to Mr Thwaite.'

'Perhaps I can give him a hand to dig the holes for the trees?' Seamus asked.

'Dig holes for fruit trees?' Mrs Duffy gave him a stern look. 'Holy Mother of God. You, Seamus Duffy, can lay bricks better than any man alive. Why would you be digging holes?'

'I'll do whatever Mrs Emmerson requires, wife, and that's an end to it.'

Ellen dared not look at the aggravating woman and instead led Seamus over to the cart and made the introductions, wondering if she could live with Honor Duffy on her property.

CHAPTER 3

*I*n the small mirror hanging on the wall, Ellen checked her wool dress for marks. The red and black check was lined at the hem with a black fringe, which was also on the sleeve cuffs. A row of black buttons lined the fitted bodice, and she wore black gloves and a small black hat tilted on her head at an angle to show off the red material flowers stitched under the rim.

For the last few weeks, rain had been intermittent with cold hard frosts and freezing nights, but at last today, the official day they were to move into the house, the weak August winter sun shone and the party they'd arranged was going ahead.

Ellen had relented to Alistair's request to hold a party to celebrate the house completion. Outside, guests, many local residents and Alistair's friends from Sydney who were keen to see 'Emmerson Park', were mingling, chatting and drink cups of tea, or sipping glasses of wine and eating a selection of delights Moira had been cooking for days.

Alistair having returned from Sydney two days ago was playing host, eagerly showing his friends around the estate, which in the winter sunshine was looking its very best so far.

Building debris had been removed and nearly all evidence of construction taken away or hidden.

Ornamental gardens had been dug and planted with roses and around it were camelias, which, in time would be trimmed and shaped into hedges to enclose the rose gardens. Intricately shaped beds that Ellen had filled with a mixture of native and imported plants from England gave the impression of what the future gardens would mature into. Alistair's mother, a keen gardener had sent many parcels of flowers seeds to her to grow, and this had given Ellen a hobby she never expected to enjoy.

Growing seedlings, drawing up the garden beds' designs and the planting took her mind off the pain of not having Austin and Patrick with her. She wanted to create a beautiful home for them to return to.

She planted wisteria along the verandah rails, intending for the vine to grow its way up the support posts and, in the years to come, provide a glorious display of hanging blue-purple blooms and shade greenery.

Beyond the formal gardens, Ellen had the workmen build a potting shed and a walled garden for the vegetables. In here, beds were cultivated and enriched with manure from the cattle, and rows of vegetables were planted to feed the entire estate. Ellen hired Mr Fenton, an old ex-convict who had worked in the government's botanical gardens in Sydney until he gained his ticket of freedom. Despite his age of at least seventy, Mr Fenton had settled in at the estate immediately, and although in charge of three other men, he never raised his voice, but spoke softly and with clear authority, which everyone listened to without question, even Ellen.

Under Mr Fenton's tutelage, she learned a great deal about botany. In Ireland she had worked in the fields, digging, sowing and planting potatoes until the blight wiped out their crops year after year. When she remembered those bleak black years, she never would have imagined that one day she'd be planting flowers for the sheer joy of it. None of her family had ever planted flowers before. Vegetables were a source of food and income; no one had time or energy to plant anything that didn't earn its keep.

'Are you ready?' Alistair stood at the door of the hut, dressed in a smart suit of chestnut brown. His blond hair was slicked down, and he was cleanshaven except for the moustache he now sported. Ellen couldn't deny he was a handsome man and since his return two days ago, he'd done everything in his power to try and make her happy. The boys were not mentioned, and the issue hung over them like a grey cloud.

'Yes, I'm ready.'

'You look beautiful.'

'Thank you.' She glanced at the mirror again, knowing she had to appear her best in front of the finest of local society and Alistair's Sydney friends.

'You are too thin though. Are you eating enough?' he asked, concerned.

'I've spent the last three weeks creating gardens and decorating the house like a mad woman. Eating wasn't high on my list of things to do.' She adjusted the froth of black lace at her throat, not dwelling on the real reason she'd lost her appetite was from worrying over the boys.

'Riona said you've been working all hours. Ellen, we employ men to do the work.'

'It's a hard habit to break. I'm used to being busy, you know that. I've worked all my life and to suddenly became a lady who does nothing but make calls… Well, it's not easy to accept. I'm doing the best I can.'

'I'm not complaining, my dear.' He glanced around. 'Your last day in this hut. From now on you will live in a house worthy of you.'

'That's kind of you to say, Alistair.' She knew he was trying his best to mend the relationship. Sucking in a deep breath, she turned and walked out of the hut.

Together, united for this one purpose, they smiled and spoke to their guests for several minutes before stepping onto the verandah in front of the double cedar doors.

Alistair raised a hand to quieten everyone. 'Ladies and gentlemen. My wife and I wish to thank you for coming here today to celebrate and share with us the wonderful occasion of our house being completed. For us it is a defining moment, for this house will be our family home, and we hope, for many future generations. The success of the build and the new gardens are the dedicated work of many skilled hands and all under the watchful eye of my wife, who has created this beautiful home for us.' Alistair took her hand and kissed it. 'Thank you all for coming near and far and let us toast to many more occasions where we come together at Emmerson Park.'

Everyone raised their glasses of wine, cheered and wished them well.

Alistair opened the double doors fully and Ellen walked in first, feeling a sense of accomplishment and pride. The wide entrance hall drew the guests' gaze to the central courtyard in the middle of the house, where Ellen had the stonemason build a pond and she had planted pansies in old barrels cut in half and had them placed in the four corners of the courtyard.

From the hallway, double doors opened into the formal drawing room and dining room, both which overlooked the slope down to the river.

Ellen and Riona, with Moira's and even Mrs Duffy's help, had hung the white lace curtains and heavy navy-blue drapes to frame each of the four tall sash windows. Fine wooden furniture in oak, walnut and rosewood showed an elegance of style. Light coloured fabrics of duck egg blue and cream were used in the upholstery of the occasional chairs, sofas and cushions. The polished cedar floor completed each room.

Ellen and Alistair led their guests from room to room. From the dining table with its polished rosewood table and twelve burgundy velvet chairs, to the morning room painted yellow and white, to Alistair's masculine study of dark timbers and country scenes on the walls.

Guests strolled along the verandahs encasing the entire house, peeping through French doors into the six bedrooms. Nods of approval and gushing compliments about the house brought Ellen a sense of happiness. She didn't have her boys here to share the day, but she had created a beautiful home for them.

Marrying Alistair had helped her achieve her goal to make her family secure and safe, and sipping her wine, Ellen relaxed the tightness from her shoulders and for the first time in weeks smiled with genuine feeling.

She strolled the verandah that overlooked the valley and the river. Here, she'd instructed for the tables of refreshments to be placed. She smiled at young Caroline who was helping replenish the pots of tea and platters of delicate cakes Moira produced in the new kitchen wing built to the side of the house, which was reached by a covered walkway from the dining room verandah.

Guests selected food from plates of sliced beef, cheese and cured ham that were joined by bowls of potatoes, salads and pickles. Another table held platters of soda bread, cakes and scones with pots of jam and cream.

To Ellen the spread signalled more than just food, it represented how far she'd come in only a couple of years. She could now eat all day every day whereas not too long ago, she'd been foraging in the hedges or on the beach or saving scraps of food from Wilton Manor's kitchen where she had worked to feed her children.

She glanced over the gardens to see Bridget playing with Aisling Duffy. Bridget wore a new dress of yellow and white stripe, her long black hair tied in white ribbons, and she wore shiny black boots. Her daughter looked as though she'd been born to wealth, instead of being birthed in a rundown cottage before a peat fire. As a baby she'd worn ragged clothes passed down from her brothers. Not one article of clothing had been new for Bridget until the day Ellen went shopping in Liverpool and spent the money Rafe Hamilton had given her. That had been two years ago...

'Ellen, is anything the matter?' Alistair came to her side.

'No. I was just remembering the past.' She kept her gaze on Bridget. 'I never supposed I would be in such a position. Oh, I wished for it, dreamed of it, but never thought I would rise so high.'

'Making good marriages has been doing that for people for centuries.' He grinned.

'As I have done. Without you none of this would have been possible for me. I had fully expected to gain my own land by myself without marrying. Maybe I would have done so, but never would I have achieved a home such as this.'

'You do not regret marrying me? No, don't answer that.' He smiled slightly and looked away. 'You have not told me if you bought the land in Moss Vale.'

She was pleased he changed the subject. 'I haven't done so yet, no. I've been too busy, but now the house is complete, I wish to expand our holdings.'

'Emmerson Park isn't enough for you?' He seemed a little disturbed.

'Not for four children, no. The more land we have the more secure the children will be.'

'Ah, Emmerson,' Mr Palmer one of Alistair's friends came towards them. 'What a splendid house.'

'Thank you.' Alistair took a glass of wine from the table and offered it to Palmer before taking one for Ellen, but she shook her head.

'And you, Mrs Emmerson, what is a house without the love and attention of a fine woman such as yourself? I've just been touring the gardens. Your fruit trees are well laid out. It'll be a fine orchard in years to come.'

'That's what we hope for, Mr Palmer.'

'You must visit my new abode in Campbelltown the next time you are on your way to Sydney. I would like your opinion of my garden layout.'

'Thank you, Mr Palmer, I would be delighted.' She glanced at Alistair and saw the sad expression on his face. He knew as she did that her going to Sydney would be not for some time. Sydney meant parties and balls, hosting and attending dinners and tea afternoons, all the things that didn't interest her.

'Emmerson was telling me that your terrace houses in Balmain are fully stocked with tenants. He told me the whole concept was your idea. Will you build more?'

'It's something I'm interested in doing again, yes, but Emmerson Park has taken all of my time recently.'

Alistair sipped his wine. 'My wife is a woman of many talents, Palmer. I fear the days are not long enough for her to achieve everything she sets her heart upon.'

'What a lucky man you are then, Emmerson.' Palmer chuckled. 'To have such a wife who prefers to make money rather than spend it! I need to have a gold mine to keep up with Mrs Palmer's spending.'

'Speaking of gold, did you read about the holdup by bushrangers of the gold escort leaving the McIvor Goldfield?' Alistair asked Palmer.

'I hope they hang them all. Those bushrangers are becoming too brazen, too powerful,' Palmer scoffed.

At the edge of the garden, Ellen spied Riona looking frazzled as she spoke to Bridget. 'If you'll excuse me, gentlemen,' Ellen murmured. 'I feel I am needed by my sister.'

Bypassing the guests, Ellen left the verandah and hurried through the rose gardens to the other side of the house where Riona had disappeared.

'Riona!' Ellen called as she rounded the corner to the drive that had been newly spread with pale crushed gravel. She stopped abruptly on seeing Colm arguing with Riona.

Furious, Ellen marched up to him. 'What are you doing here?'

He looked her up and down. 'Such a fine lady you are,' he slurred.

The stink of spirits flowed over Ellen. 'You're drunk.'

'And you're a witch!' He swayed, his eyes bloodshot. 'You think sending the boys away is enough? One day they will be men! Then they will want to come home. They will want to be true Irishmen.'

'Go away, Colm. My sons are no concern of yours,' Ellen snapped.

'They are my blood!'

'Will you look at yourself? You're a disgrace.'

'I'll tell you this for nothing, woman, you'll never know a contented day while ever I'm alive,' he sneered, 'that I promise you.'

A shiver trickled down her back, but she stared him down. 'You don't frighten me.'

'No, but the devil in hell will as that's where you'll end up, witch that you are. You cast a spell on me when we were kids. A spell that made me want you. You're like a fever in my blood, destroying my life, but you picked my brother, for what good it did him. He died breaking his back for you!'

'Malachy died in a fight from drinking and gambling and as for you,' she took a step closer to him, hating his black soul, 'I wish I was a witch, and I could curse you to hell for making my boys be sent away to stay out of your clutches and for the years of lust-filled looks I received from you. I hope *you* never see a happy day, Colm Kittrick, that is my *curse* on you.'

He staggered back and crossed himself. 'Holy Mother protect me!'

'Go back to Ireland, Colm, and if you ever come to my home again, I'll kill you myself!' She spun on her heel and strode away.

Later as the house grew quiet, the guests gone and the sun set, Ellen sat on a chair on the verandah holding Lily asleep in her arms. Shadows stretched across the valley and the bellow of the milking cow broke the bird calls.

Riona came out to her. 'All our things have been brought over now. The hut is empty of our belongings and ready for the Duffys to move in. Bridget is playing in her room, rearranging everything I've put in there.' She smiled and sat in another chair.

'Thank you for sorting it all out.' Ellen squeezed Riona's hand. 'You are the best sister anyone could wish for.'

'Well, I have to do my bit, don't I? After all, I'm living in this magnificent home at no cost to me.'

'You're my sister, not a servant. Where else would you be?'

Riona leaned back with a deep sigh. 'I wish Mammy could see us now. She'd be proud.'

'Would she?' Ellen was doubtful. 'Mammy would never have accepted me marrying a Protestant.'

'I did. Eventually, so would've Mammy.'

'I doubt it. It would have been another thing I'd done wrong, like leaving Mayo and taking us all to Liverpool, of making us all emigrate to the colony.'

'She'd have no choice. Without you, we'd have all ended up in the workhouse and she knew it.'

'Well, we will never know what Mammy would make of my marriage to Alistair, will we?' Ellen tried not to think of her mammy's demise on the ship coming over to Australia. One night she had fallen overboard, or jumped, as Ellen believed the truth to be, and had never been seen again.

'Will you forgive Alistair, Ellen?' Riona whispered. 'He's a good man. In his mind, he was doing the right thing.'

Ellen shrugged. 'It's too soon.'

'But—'

'I don't want to talk about it, Riona.' She shifted the baby in her arms a little.

'Shall I take her and put her in her cot?'

'No, I enjoy holding her. She has another tooth and is unsettled.'

'Yes, I was going to mention it to you this morning but with everything going on getting ready for the party I clear forgot.'

'I noticed Mr Connelly was paying you particular attention this afternoon.' Ellen raised her eyebrows at her sister.

'Mr Connelly is a nice man, but don't get any ideas. I'm not wanting to marry.'

'Does he though?'

'Stop it.' Riona rolled her eyes. 'Besides, we spoke mostly of you.'

'Me?'

'Aye, all the men here were so in awe of you. They are jealous of Alistair having such a wife as you, one who is keen to get things done. One who has a brain in her head and wants to talk of other things aside from fashion and piano playing, the weather or lazy servants.' She laughed.

'That's not true. Men *want* those things in their wives. They don't want to talk business with ladies. They understand the rules. It's me who doesn't. I'm the one who is the oddity.'

'If that's the truth then why do they flock around you, eager to hear your every word? Mr Connelly proclaimed you to be the best of women, pretty and clever, and he's not alone in thinking that way. I saw Mr Riddle asking you many questions, and Mr Palmer. Mr Stuart and Mr Amos would have never let you go if Alistair hadn't rescued you from their constant inquires.'

'It was a successful afternoon, that's all that matters.' Ellen stretched out the tension in her neck. 'I'm just pleased Alistair didn't see Colm.'

'Kittrick was here?' Alistair came out of the French doors. 'He was here today?'

'Yes.' Ellen sighed.

'He was drunk, but didn't stay,' Riona added. 'I watched him until he was out of sight.'

'I assumed he'd be on a ship to Ireland by now.'

'So did I.' Ellen gazed down at Lily, not wanting to think of Colm.

'What did he say? What did he want?'

'He knows the boys are gone.' Ellen looked at Alistair and his shoulders slumped. 'I told Colm to go away and never come back. There is nothing for him here.'

'Hopefully, he will now,' Riona said. 'He'll meet with his fellow rebellion members and go home. I pray it will be so.'

Alistair took out his fob watch from his waistcoat pocket. 'The guests who are returning for dinner will be here in an hour.'

Ellen rose. 'I shall put this one to bed then and dress. Caroline is going to sit with Bridget and watch Lily while our guests are here.'

'She's a helpful girl is Caroline. Mature for her age of nearly twelve,' Riona said. 'She's a wonderful influence on Bridget, too. Calms her a little.'

Ellen looked at Alistair. 'That reminds me, I wish to advertise for a governess for Bridget, but since there isn't a proper school in the village, a governess could also teach Caroline and Aisling, and then Lily as she gets older.'

'A sensible plan, I agree.'

Under an hour later, Ellen had washed and dressed in a pale green dress printed with silver flowers and edged with silver lace.

Alistair entered their bedroom. 'You look beautiful.'

'Thank you.'

'I wanted to talk to you privately before we go to dinner.'

Ellen turned away and pretended to pack her brush and combs into their case. 'Oh?'

'Tonight, we all sleep in the house for the first time. We have a shared room, Ellen...'

Her hand stilled on a pearl brooch Alistair had bought her for her last birthday.

He took a step forward. 'I will, if you wish it, move my things into the dressing room after our guests have gone.'

She had her back to him and felt unable to move. To deny him her bed would mean their marriage was over. Yet to agree to sleeping together would mean she'd forgiven him for sending the boys to England, and she still felt unable to do that.

'Ellen, I know you will not forgive me for my decision to send Austin and Patrick away, and I understand that. I also know that you do not love me and never have…'

Her heart thumped in her chest and her corset suddenly felt too tight.

'But I have admired you from the first moment I met you and from that I have grown to love you more than I believed possible. I do not expect you to feel the same, and I know you do not. However, I simply wanted to remind you how very much I care for you, and I would never willingly hurt you or cause you pain and that I have done so is the biggest regret of my life.'

She spun to him, tears on her lashes. 'I never got the chance to say goodbye to them. I never got to hold them and tell them how much I love them before they left. You stole that from me and no matter how many letters I write to them none of those words will have the same feeling as holding them in my arms.'

'I am utterly sorry for that.'

'It'll be years before I see them again. Years of them growing into young men that I'll not witness. I can't be there to protect them from harm. I feel as though I have failed as a mother yet again, as I did with Thomas.'

He hung his head. 'I realise that now. At the time I thought I was taking the correct course of action. For some time, I have sensed that the boys needed a proper education in England, but you would never agree to it. With the threat of Kittrick I took the opportunity to do as I wished. I was wrong. Selfish. Yet, I truly was acting in the boys' best interests, I assure you of that. At Harrow they will become fine gentlemen. With such an education they will be able to hold their heads up in any room and be accepted.'

Ellen looked at him and something inside her died. 'You are ashamed of them? They are your stepsons and are nothing but Irish peasants.'

He looked horrified. 'No! No. Good God is that what you suppose?'

'I'm not sure, Alistair. You say they will be accepted now they will be educated as English gentlemen, so obviously they were lacking before. I assumed my marriage to you would be acceptance enough, I see now I was fooling myself.'

'Ellen, please you must never think I do not adore the boys and Bridget. I will do everything in my power to make them happy, but there will always be people who will see their background, and yours, you know that. You had experience of it in Sydney.'

'So, if our marriage doesn't wipe out the stain of *my* past, then how do you expect schooling at Harrow to wipe out the stain of the boys' past?'

'I promise you, I'll make sure the boys' and the girls' futures will be secured in society. People will forget. We'll work together to give them the absolute best chances to be valuable members of society.'

'And what if the boys decide to attend Oxford or Cambridge? More years away…' Tears burned hot behind her eyes. 'They could be gone ten years.' Her chin trembled.

'Then I shall take you and the girls to England. We'll go to my parents and spend every other summer with the boys.' He crossed the floor and took her hands; the first time he'd touched her in over a month. 'I will do whatever it takes to make you happy. Look at what we have created, this beautiful house. We are so fortunate, Ellen. My business grows and we have such a good life.

I love you, and the children are healthy. You will miss the boys, as I will, but it is for their future.'

She nodded and turned away. 'We shall be late for dinner.'

'And later?'

'We will share the same bed, but there'll be no intimacy, Alistair. I'm not ready for that just yet.'

'I understand.' He held out his elbow, and she slipped her hand onto his arm.

She gave him a small smile and relaxed a little. For them to continue, she had to forgive him.

The evening passed with plenty of food and wine, and their ten guests enjoyed the occasion. It was after midnight before the last carriage pulled away into the night.

While Ellen checked on the girls sleeping in their new room, and said goodnight to Riona, Alistair turned down the lamps as the moon washed the gardens and house in a silver glow.

Once in bed, Ellen yawned. It had been a long and emotional day.

'Goodnight, my dearest one.' Alistair kissed her cheek.

'Goodnight.' Ellen turned down the lamp beside the bed and snuggled into her pillow. Last night she had slept in a hut and now she was living in a large and magnificent house. Although she didn't have the boys with her, she was grateful and thankful for the abundance of good fortune she had. Marrying Alistair had given her a great deal, but she had worked hard to achieve it, too.

How different would her life have been if Malachy still lived, or if she had gone to Colm when Malachy died? She'd still be in Ireland, living in a cottage, barely getting by and in constant fear of her children not having enough to eat.

Instead, she'd taken risky chances such as leaving Ireland and moving across to the other side of the world. Then working for Alistair and becoming his friend changed her life once more.

Alistair murmured in his sleep and rolled over towards her. His blond hair fell over his forehead making him look like a much younger man, though he was not old. In the moonlight spearing through a gap in the curtains, she studied his features. He was a handsome man and the stubble on his jaw added to his attractiveness. She felt a stirring of desire for him. It had been so long since she'd made love. Alistair hadn't slept with her since Lily was born for when he was here the hut wasn't large enough for the entire family and he stayed in a tent.

But now, Ellen felt the need of a man's touch. She wanted to be held and kissed.

Slipping a hand under the sheets, she traced her fingertips over his arms. She edged closer and kissed his lips, tasting the brandy he'd drunk with the gentlemen.

Slowly, she eased off her nightgown and then pulled up his nightshirt to run her hands down his chest. Alistair moaned, his mouth seeking hers and she gave it to him.

He kissed her sleepily and then moved down her neck and to her breasts. She felt him harden against her leg and her desire heightened.

'Ellen...' he whispered, his hands sliding down between her legs.

She arched into him, needing him. 'Yes...'

He kissed her deeply, his body covering hers and in moments he thrust into her.

'Ellen.' He murmured against her ear, holding her to him tightly, thrusting deeper and quicker.

She closed her eyes, ignoring her thoughts and just concentrated on her body's fulfilment and when it came, she sighed contentedly.

Alistair finished shortly afterwards. He held her to him and kissed her. 'I didn't mean to.'

'It's all right. I started it.'

'You did? I thought I was dreaming.'

She smiled in the moonlight. 'Go back to sleep.'

Once he'd rolled off her, he was soon asleep.

Ellen lay awake and then climbed from the bed and donned her nightgown. She stood by the French doors, watching the shadows playing over the trees and garden. A wave of guilt plagued her. She felt as though she'd committed adultery on Rafe and that by sleeping with Alistair she'd been disloyal to him. It was madness. Alistair was her husband, not Rafe. She was being unfaithful to Alistair for longing after a man she couldn't have.

Tears dripped over her lashes. She missed Rafe so much it was like a constant ache in her chest. Yet he'd only been hers for one brief evening. An evening when they had not only made love but come together as one soul, blending into each other to make a whole. Without him, she felt only half alive, which was nonsense and ridiculous. She had never been one for fanciful thoughts and dreams, but in this instance, she felt a part of her was missing since he'd returned to England and nothing and no one could make her complete.

A dull thud sounded, and she listened, thinking Lily might have woken. A muffled sound came from somewhere in the house.

Ellen grabbed her dressing gown and flung it on. Perhaps Bridget had woken and become disorientated in her new room. She was so used to sleeping with Riona, she might be looking for her.

Heading along the hallway, Ellen knew her way without a lamp. The girls' room was next to her own. Quietly she opened the door but found Lily fast asleep in her cot and Bridget curled up in a ball in her bed.

The noise came again.

Frowning, Ellen left the bedroom. Had Riona woken? Was Moira still in the kitchen? She walked around the central court-yard to the other side of the house where Riona slept.

A muffled cry checked Ellen's step in fright. It came from Riona's room.

Quickly she ran down the hallway and burst open the door. Two figures struggled on the bed.

'Get off her!' Ellen screamed, running at the man and pulling him off Riona.

Colm knocked Ellen away and slapped her hard on the side of her head.

She stumbled, shocked at being hit.

'Come on!' Colm yanked Riona off the bed and onto her knees. She cried out as he pulled her by her hair.

Ellen sprang onto Colm, hitting him with both hands.

'You bitch!' Like a crazed bull he swayed to dislodge her weight off his back. 'I'll kill you, woman. I'm sick to death of you.'

Ellen fought with a strength she didn't know she had as rage took over.

Colm's fist thumped her in the stomach, and she gasped, the breath knocked from her lungs. She fell to her knees.

Riona screamed as Colm pulled her up and over his shoulder. The French doors were open, and he staggered as Riona hit and kicked him.

'What the bloody hell!' Alistair stood in the doorway in his nightshirt and bare feet, holding a pistol.

'Christ!' Colm dropped Riona and ran across the verandah.

Alistair fired a shot over Ellen's head. She cried out at the blast. She scrambled over to Riona and hugged her tight.

'He's gone,' she soothed her sobbing sister.

'Was that Kittrick?' Alistair lit the lamp on the dresser, flooding the room with light.

Ellen heard Bridget crying. 'Bridget! Lily!'

'I will go.' Alistair hurried out of the room.

Ellen pushed away Riona's hair from her face. 'Did he hurt you?'

Riona shook her head. 'Not really. I'll have bruises on my arms.'

'He didn't force himself on you?'

'No. He wanted me to go with him. He said he was taking me to Ireland to teach you a lesson.'

'Holy Mother of God.' Ellen tightened her embrace. 'How did he think he could do such a thing and get away with it?'

'He said if I put up a fuss, he'd kill me.' Riona sobbed, her whole body shaking. 'I tried to fight him off, but he was too strong.'

'You fought well and saved yourself. Colm's no match for us sisters.' Ellen gave her a kiss on the cheek. 'He's gone now and won't be coming back. You're safe.' Ellen helped Riona to her feet as they heard voices outside. 'That gunshot will have woken everyone. We'll have some tea.'

They held each other as they walked to the kitchen. Ellen quickly raked the fire and put the kettle on the range.

Moira hurried in, wearing a nightgown and an old coat. 'I heard a shot.'

Ellen told her what had happened.

'Jesus, Mary and Joseph!' Moira crossed herself.

'He's the very devil, so he is,' Riona murmured, hugging herself.

'Aye, he is, and he's gone too far this time.' Ellen added tea leaves to the pot. 'I'll have the mounted police after him, you see if I don't.' She looked at Moira. 'Go back to bed and tell the others as well. I can hear them outside.'

Moira opened the back door where some of the estate men gathered. 'Back to your beds, you lot. Mr Emmerson will speak to you in the morning so he will.' She smiled over her shoulder to Riona. 'I'll see you in the morning, lass.'

While Ellen set out the cups, she kept an eye on Riona who was still shaking.

'Is there something wrong with me?' Riona asked. 'Twice now I've been attacked by men.'

'Whist, don't talk nonsense. There's nothing wrong with you. It's the two evil men who attacked you who are at fault not you.'

Ellen had made the cups of tea as Alistair entered the kitchen.

He sat at the table. 'Bridget has gone back to sleep, and Lily did not even wake up. I told Bridget she had a night terror. I stayed with her until she fell back to sleep.'

'Did you check the verandah door to their room is locked?' Ellen passed him a cup of tea.

'I did. The key is in my pocket. The doors will remain locked until Kittrick is in chains. I took a walk around outside but there is no sign of him. I have spoken to Mr Thwaite. He will organise a search party at dawn to hunt Kittrick down.'

'We must tell the police.'

'Indeed. I shall ride into the village as soon as it is light.' Angry, Alistair tapped his fingers on the table. 'How dare he come into my house and threaten my family? I shall see the man hanged.'

'Do you think you shot him?' Riona asked.

Alistair shook his head. 'I do not think so. I saw him running away, but hopefully, if the man has any sense whatsoever, he will stay away from here.'

Ellen gently rubbed Riona's back. 'He'd better find a ship back to Ireland quick, so he had, for if I ever see him again, I won't be responsible for my actions.'

CHAPTER 4

*D*escending the coach, Ellen breathed in the fresh crisp air of spring. The scent of eucalyptus was stronger in the country than in the city. She shook out her skirts and stretched a little after the cramped journey up the mountains. 'It's good to be home.'

She reached back for Lily. 'We're home, little one.'

Riona helped Bridget down from the coach, before stepping aside to allow Miss Lewis to step down.

'Welcome to Berrima, Miss Lewis,' Ellen said to Bridget's new governess as they stood on the verandah of the White Horse Inn.

They'd just spent the last four weeks in Sydney. The trip had been to secure a governess for Bridget and to acquire new clothes for the spring and summer. Ellen had fulfilled her duties as a wife and played hostess to dinners and afternoon tea parties, as well as returning calls and attending the theatre and soirees on Alistair's arm. It was her way of strengthening the marriage for Alistair enjoyed having her in Sydney with him. But after four weeks, she'd had enough and was eager to return to Berrima and Emmerson Park.

'Mr Thwaite should be here soon.' Ellen glanced up the street.

'I sent him a note last week of our return.' She looked at Miss Lewis who seemed all eyes as she stared around the small village.

'Hopefully, you will like it here, Miss Lewis,' Ellen said, trying to put her at ease. She felt sorry for the young woman who was now amongst strangers in a strange district. Miss Amelia Lewis was a young woman of twenty-one, originally from Lincolnshire, England, but who was now alone in the colony after her parents died of fever a year ago. She'd taken up a position of a teacher at a girl's school in Parramatta but had put an advertisement in the newspapers for a governess role. Ellen had interviewed her with Riona and Alistair and decided the quiet Miss Lewis would be a suitable match to rein in Bridget's wilfulness. On the journey from Sydney, the woman had been most helpful in looking after Lily and devoted her time to Bridget, giving Ellen and Riona some well-required rest.

'Will my piano have arrived?' Bridget asked, bending down to stroke a little white dog that was tied to the verandah post.

'I'm not sure, you'll have to ask Mr Thwaite when he gets here.'

Riona went inside the inn to ask for any of their mail. In a short time, she came out again with a bundle of letters. 'They're mostly bills,' she said, sorting through them. 'We have several invitation cards. Miss Augusta Ashford is inside, too. I do like her. She never looks down on me.'

'Nor should anyone,' Ellen muttered.

Riona passed the mail to Ellen. 'Well, that's not how life is, is it? Look at those women in Sydney's society. There are those few who accept me as your sister and invite me along and then there are those who ignore I exist and invite only you.'

'I know and I'm sorry for it.' Ellen watched the street, Lily heavy in her arms. She noticed that there seemed more traffic than usual. 'We're home now, and we don't need to think of those in Sydney and just concentrate on the friends we have in this area. They are far friendlier.'

'Mrs Emmerson.' Miss Ashford joined them on the verandah.

Turning, Ellen smiled at Miss Ashford, a resident of Sutton Forest, and also the daughter of one of the area's wealthiest families. Ellen knew the lady had recently returned from Melbourne. 'It's lovely to see you, Miss Ashford. How are you?'

'I am well, thank you, Mrs Emmerson. You have just come home from Sydney?' Miss Ashford untied her little dog and gave the lead to Bridget for her to hold.

'Yes. After a month there, I'm ready to leave. But we have engaged Miss Lewis for Bridget, so the trip had its advantages.' Ellen made the introductions.

'This district is such an improvement on Sydney, especially with the warmer weather coming.' Miss Ashford smiled, and although only having met her occasionally at parties, Ellen knew her to be a nice woman. Miss Ashford watched Bridget walk the little dog away a short distance.

'How is your family?' Ellen asked, switching Lily over to her other arm.

'All very well, thank you.'

'And Melbourne?'

'Terribly crowded.' She laughed. 'If one doesn't talk of gold, then there is nothing else to discuss.' Miss Ashford frowned at the sudden noise of several horsemen cantering through the middle of the village. 'Good heavens. What has them in such a hurry?'

'I noticed that the village is active today,' Ellen said as another carriage came trundling past. 'Gold hasn't been found nearby, has it?'

'I hope not. My brother, Gil, wouldn't be too happy about it. We struggle to keep labourers as it is. He moans dreadfully about the higher wages the men are demanding. If we don't pay, they leave for the diggings.'

'I'm fortunate that we have kept some of ours.' Ellen spotted

Mr Thwaite driving the buggy down the road with Douglas driving the farm cart for their luggage. 'Oh, here is Mr Thwaite.'

'I'll bid you a good day, Mrs Emmerson. Will I see you at the Throsby's ball next week?'

'I'm afraid not, my husband is still in Sydney. He knows the Throsbys more than me.'

'Then you and your sister,' she nodded kindly to Riona, 'must come and have afternoon tea with me and my mother. Say, a week on Friday?'

'We'd like that. Thank you.'

Miss Ashford took the dog's lead from Bridget. 'Good. I'll see you at three. Goodbye.'

Mr Thwaite pulled the buggy to a halt in front of the inn. 'Welcome home, Mrs Emmerson, ladies.' He nodded to them all with a special grin for Bridget.

'Did my piano arrive, Mr Thwaite?' Bridget asked.

'It did, Miss Bridget. It's in the drawing room.' He helped Douglas secure the luggage on the cart.

'No incidents, Mr Thwaite?' Ellen asked. 'No unwanted visitors?' She knew he'd understand her meaning for he'd been instructed to keep an eye out for Colm Kittrick.

'None, Mrs Emmerson,' he replied quietly.

Relieved, Ellen introduced Miss Lewis to Thwaite and Douglas and the governess climbed aboard the cart while Ellen took the seat in the buggy and gave Lily to Riona as she squeezed in beside her.

'Can I sit up in the cart with Douglas and Miss Lewis, Mama?' Bridget asked.

'Yes. That will give me and your aunt more room.' Ellen slapped the reins gently on Betsy's back and at last they headed home.

The drive to the house was fraught with overtaking carts and wagons. Ellen noticed a crowd in front of the courthouse and a good many of the inns held gatherings of men standing around by the road.

'What is going on?' Riona murmured as Ellen struggled to get the buggy past a large wagon.

They then saw a line of prisoners in chains being brought out of the courthouse and marched down to the jail. The crowd jeered but Ellen watched in silence before quickly urging Betsy to walk on. Sights of chained criminals reminded her too much of living poor and destitute in Ireland and of the numerous times people in her village were sent away in chains never to be seen again.

'Poor blighted souls. I'll pray for them at Mass tomorrow,' Riona said, crossing herself.

Ellen flicked the reins eager to be home safe in her own house. She thought briefly of Colm, but they'd not seen nor heard of him since the night he tried to abduct Riona. She hoped he'd sailed back to Ireland.

Guiding Betsy onto the track to the house, Ellen waved to the workmen building the impressive stone and iron gates at the entrance to the drive.

'They are looking so grand,' Ellen told them as she passed, pleased with their efforts.

Driving along closer to the house, she noticed that more trees had been planted and a brick pathway laid from the vegetable gardens to the service side of the house. Ellen halted Betsy in front of the house and stared at the bright new growth on the wisteria growing over the verandah.

'Look the roses are in bud,' Riona said in awe. 'So much has changed since we left.'

Four weeks of warmer weather and the winter behind them had seen the gardens burst into flowers. Daffodils and tulips added dashes of colour to the garden beds. Over in the orchard the fruit trees were in full bud, ready to show off their display of spring blossom.

'Look, Miss Lewis,' Bridget called out as she leapt from the cart. 'I planted this rose bush for my brother Thomas. He died. It has buds on it.'

'It is a beautiful tribute to your brother, Bridget,' Miss Lewis answered. She addressed Ellen. 'Mrs Emmerson you have a wonderful home.'

'Thank you. I hope you will be happy here.'

'I shall.'

Ellen took Lily from Riona and led them all inside. Bridget soon took Miss Lewis by her hand to show her the house and where she was to sleep.

'Do you want me to change Lily?' Riona asked. 'I know you're keen to find out what's been happening while we've been in Sydney.'

Moira came through from the kitchen. 'You're back, so you are. I've missed you all.'

'How are you, Moira? Did you and Mr Thwaite keep everything going for me?'

'Of course. No tighter run establishment could be found in this district, I'm telling you.' She grinned, chucking Lily under the chin. 'I've set up the spare room for Miss Lewis.'

'Thank you.' Ellen kissed Lily's cheek. 'Go to your aunt, my sweet, while I go and do the rounds.'

Ellen walked through to the kitchen with Moira. 'Nothing to report on at all?'

'Nothing, Ellen, I promise you.'

'No sign of Colm?'

'None.' Moira looked grave. 'Mr Thwaite kept the men on alert just in case, but we've not seen hide nor hair of the eejit.'

'Good.' Ellen yawned. She'd been awake since dawn and the three-day journey from Sydney was tiring.

'Why don't you go and rest for a bit?' Moira put the water on to boil. 'I'll bring you in a nice cup of tea, so I will.'

'I should speak to Mr Thwaite.'

'And surely that can wait an hour?'

'I suppose it can.' Ellen sat at the table. For the last few weeks, she'd been tired, and she had a sneaking suspicion she could be with child. She wasn't sure how to feel about it. It would be nice to give Alistair a child of his own, not that he knew Lily wasn't his, but Ellen did and after all he'd done for her, he deserved a child of his blood. However, the idea of being pregnant and giving birth again didn't make her clap with glee. She wanted to enjoy the house and build on their wealth. She had plans to buy more land in the district and to do that she wanted to be free to ride about the countryside and not be tied down to a baby needing her.

The door to the outside opened and Honor Duffy walked in carrying a basket of eggs. 'The chickens have started laying again, Moira. Only three, but it's a start… Oh, Mrs Emmerson, you're back.'

'Yes, Honor. How are you?'

'Well, thank you. Did you enjoy your stay in Sydney?'

'I did. Bridget has a new governess, Miss Amelia Lewis. She's very nice and well educated.'

'Grand.' Honor put the eggs into a straw-filled box on the shelf in the larder.

Ellen waited for her to come out. 'Alistair and I have been discussing the notion of whether you'd like Miss Lewis to teach your girls alongside Bridget.'

Honor's eyebrows rose. 'My girls?'

'Yes. They can be taught by Miss Lewis at no expense to you and it will save them from walking into the village in all weathers to attend the little school there, which more times than not is barely open. The teacher there is not reliable.'

'Because he's a Roman Catholic?' Honor defended.

'No, because he's always ill with one thing or another and not having a permanent schoolhouse reflects the state of schooling in the village.'

'Miss Lewis isn't Catholic, is she?'

'No, she isn't.' Ellen's anger began to simmer. 'You don't have to agree to have Miss Lewis teach Caroline and Aisling. However, it might be an advantage for the girls to have her in their lives. She is a decent and talented woman, and the girls can learn a lot from her, but if you'd prefer for them to walk into the village and go to school there, then that is fine by me.'

Emotions flittered across Honor's face. 'I'm not saying no…'

'Listen, Honor,' Moira butted in. 'That village school will only teach the basics. Under Miss Lewis, your girls will learn to be proper educated women, which will put them in a grand position later when they want to marry, so it will.'

'My girls will still be the daughters of a servant and a labourer.'

Ellen sighed. 'So? By giving the girls an education, they might be able to marry higher than a labourer or a servant. Don't you want that for them?'

'Unlike you, Ellen Emmerson, I do not strive to mix in the elite circles you crave. My daughters won't be made fools of!' Honor stormed from the kitchen.

Moira swore under her breath. 'Stupid woman. Is she blind? Can she not see the advantage it would be for those poor girls?'

Ellen stood. 'She does, Moira, but she doesn't like to admit it. She believes that her girls will never be more than what she is, a poor Irish peasant. The past never leaves us.'

Ellen went in search of Riona, needing to chat with her sister. No matter how wealthy she became, Ellen at times just needed Riona's sensible conversation. Her sister knew her better than anyone and could offer comfort with a single glance.

She found Riona sitting with Miss Lewis in the drawing room. Ellen stood at the doorway watching them talking. Bridget played with the keys on the piano while Lily crawled over the rug.

Suddenly Riona laughed at something Miss Lewis said and

Ellen faced the fact that her sister now had another woman to talk to, someone who would always be in the house with her, whereas Ellen was often out on various errands or calls or inspecting the property or investigating new ones. Riona would no longer be lonely during the day when Ellen was too busy to spend time with her.

Leaving them to it, Ellen entered the study. The bills and invoices were piled neatly on the desk, and she sat down to go through them. It pleased her that Alistair gave her full control over the estate, he was far too busy with his Sydney business to worry about extra paperwork. Most husbands wouldn't consider giving their wives access to their money, but Alistair knew Ellen could be trusted and what's more she had grown their wealth since he married her. The terraced houses in Balmain had doubled in value and were a source of income with continual rent from lodgers. She'd bought land in Moss Vale and in Mittagong, both parcels of land now held cattle.

While in Sydney she had persuaded Alistair to buy lots of land edging the foreshore along Elizabeth Bay, which she knew in time would be worth a lot more than what she bought them for. Sydney was growing faster than people expected. The gold rush in Melbourne had also brought money into Sydney as people bought and sold. Alistair had a head for business, and his imports and exports did exceptionally well, but she knew the value of land. Didn't she come from a country where land was valued more than people? The landlords in Ireland grew rich on the backs of the animals they grazed on their land. She'd read and seen how wealthy squatters were doing the same in this country and she intended to have a piece of the action.

Abruptly the sound of music drifted through the house. Miss Lewis was playing the piano and the sweet sound filled the air.

Ellen stopped sorting out the bills and listened. The music was haunting, beautiful and her chest tightened at the delicacy of the notes. She could barely believe that she sat in her own house while her daughter's governess played the piano. How had it happened to her? Only a few years ago she'd been digging in the dirt, her fingers squelching through the putrid mess of blighted potatoes and wondering how she'd feed her children.

Now she was a world away from those desperate times and there were moments when she thought she was dreaming, that none of it was real. Then she only had to think of Austin and Patrick and realise it was true. Her boys weren't with her in this grand house. They were gone from her, sent to be educated as gentlemen. They'd be arriving in England any day now. Did they miss her? Where they upset she had sent them away?

She bowed her head as the music gradually quietened. Had she done the right thing for them all? Had marrying Alistair given them what they needed, or had she made a mistake? Yes, they had plenty of food and clothes and wanted for nothing but the gain of that had split the family.

Oh, she didn't know what she thought. She simply missed the boys dreadfully. It wasn't the same as the grief of losing Thomas, which lay trapped in her heart, but it was close. And now she was likely carrying another child. She thought briefly of Rafe. What would he think to it all? He didn't know Lily was his. Would he feel betrayed? Unloved by her? Or had he met another and forgotten her?

She didn't ask after him when he wrote to Alistair, and her husband only mentioned him in passing, mainly to do with the business. Had Rafe fallen in love with another? She couldn't believe he would. He loved her as she did him. But was it fair for him to be alone when she had a family? She wanted him to be happy, naturally, but her heart broke at the thought of him loving a woman, someone who would receive his kisses, his desire.

A knock on the door brought her head up. 'Yes.'

Moira brought in a tea tray with a small pot of tea and a few currant cakes. 'I've taken a tray into the drawing room, but I thought you might like some peace for a bit longer.'

'Thank you.'

'That Miss Lewis seems nice.'

'She is.'

'Oh, and I let go the Barnes woman, useless she was, couldn't wash a garment if she tried. They came out of the tub dirtier than when they went in! Shameful. Now I know you gave me full control while you were in Sydney, so I did what I thought was right, so I did. I've asked in the village for anyone else to come and see me. Until then, Honor will do the washing for us all.' Stepping back, Moira took a breath.

'That's fine, Moira. I told you to do as you see fit. How's the girl getting on in the kitchen, Sally, isn't it?'

'Aye, Sally isn't too bad. I'll train her up, she's young yet. We could do with another maid though for the house. Sally has a sister in Mittagong who works at one of the inns, but she wants to come here.'

'I'll leave that all up to you and Riona.' Ellen sipped her tea, enjoying the refreshing taste. 'You know I don't like dealing with household staff. I used to be one, and it doesn't feel right to suddenly be making all the orders.'

'Aye, but you're the mistress, they expect you to be in charge.'

'Well, I am, but let's make you the housekeeper. With a formal title the indoor staff can be your responsibility.'

'No, I don't want to be responsible for the house. I have enough to do with all the cooking, so I have. Riona is the best one to be in charge.'

'Very well. I'll talk to her. Between you and Riona I won't need to worry about any of it. I have no time to see to maids. I've too much to do with the estate and my attention needs to be elsewhere. Will you be happy as the estate's cook?'

Moira beamed. 'Never happier, Ellen, and that's the truth, so it is.'

'If you have any concerns go to Riona.'

Behind Moira, standing in the doorway, Mr Thwaite waited to be seen.

'Come in, Mr Thwaite.' Ellen beckoned him.

Moira scowled. 'Did you wipe your feet, Mr Thwaite? Those floors have just been washed.'

'I did, Mrs O'Rourke.' He seemed a little frightened of the feisty Irishwoman.

Giving him a nod, Moira left them.

'She can frighten me, too, at times,' Ellen whispered to him, waving him to a chair.

He let out a breath. 'The woman is like a she-devil. Constantly on my back about something or nothing. Mad she is.'

Ellen chuckled. 'But has a soft heart, too. Now, shall you tell me all that's been happening for the last month?'

'Well, one thing. Yesterday, I visited Mittagong to call in at the blacksmith for the new hinges for the stable doors and I had to wait around as they weren't finished being made.' Mr Thwaite held his hat in both hands. 'Anyway, while I was waiting, I chatted to a shepherd who'd stopped to have his horse shod. He told me that there's a flock of sheep up for sale on a holding called, Smithdale, in Kangaroo Valley. I thought you might be interested.'

'The information is trustworthy?'

'Aye, the man seemed sound enough. He had nothing to lose or gain by telling me. He'd just been let go as his master can no longer afford to keep the property. The shepherd, Jim, was on his way to Sydney to catch a boat to Melbourne. He's off to search for gold, but his sister lives in Mittagong and he wanted to say goodbye to her first otherwise he'd have sailed from the coast.'

'We couldn't fit sheep on the Moss Vale property with the cattle, can we?'

'No, madam. You'd have to lease or buy some more land and stock the sheep on it.'

Ellen tapped her finger against her chin. Sheep were very

valuable, but so far, she and Alistair hadn't thought too much about having an enormous flock because they didn't have enough land to stock a large number of them or the workers to maintain them.

'If you leased some land, madam, we could hire a man to watch over them. Provide him with provisions and check on him once every few weeks. The Carter's farm at Tallong has land available for lease. You could try Mr Carter.'

'Shall we travel to Kangaroo Valley and inspect the flock first, Mr Thwaite?' Ellen asked, suddenly excited to think she could buy sheep.

'We can, Mrs Emmerson.'

'We should see their condition first before we find land.'

'I agree. When would you like to go, madam?'

'Tomorrow morning?'

'But you've just come back from Sydney. You must be exhausted from travelling?'

'I'll have a good night's sleep tonight and be fine by morning.' She knew that if she was pregnant then within a few months, the days of riding to far flung properties would be beyond her and then the birth and a new born baby would put her adventuring to a halt for some time.

'The road to Kangaroo Valley isn't good, madam. I suggest we ride on horseback and not by buggy. We have to travel down a very steep mountain.'

Ellen inwardly flinched. Riding wasn't something she was expert at. 'Very well, Mr Thwaite, if that's what you suggest.'

'We shall have to sleep one night in the valley. It's too far to go and come back in one day.'

'That'll be fine. We'll be away three days?'

'Yes. I'll take a packhorse with us to carry supplies.'

'Excellent. I'll pack light. We'll leave at dawn.' She felt a flicker of excitement build. She'd never been southwest before and was interested to see what the country was like down there.

The freedom of the open road was a draw after the weeks of being in Sydney, where every day she spent inside the house receiving visitors or going to make calls in other women's houses, women she didn't always like for that matter. Pretending to be a woman of society and talking nonsense for hours tried her patience, while shopping and walks in the parks soon became tiresome and repetitive. Whenever she was in the hectic, noisy city she yearned for the country.

Ellen went in search of Riona and found her outside showing the garden to Miss Lewis, with Bridget running about the rose beds.

'This will be a fine property in the years to come, Mrs Emmerson,' Miss Lewis said as Ellen caught up with them.

'We hope so.' Ellen smiled, liking the young woman, who was pretty in a delicate mousy way. Amelia Lewis would be an asset to the family. A gently reared and well-educated lady who would teach Bridget and Lily how to behave correctly in polite society, something which Ellen knew she couldn't do, at least not to the high standard that would be expected from the daughters of a wealthy man such as Alistair.

'Is Lily asleep?' Ellen slipped her arm through Riona's as they strolled towards the immature orchard.

'Yes. She fell asleep on the rug, so I've put her in the cot.'

'Thank you. I need you to be in charge for a few days. I'm riding to Kangaroo Valley tomorrow with Mr Thwaite. We leave in the morning at dawn.'

Riona stared at her. 'Tomorrow? We've only just returned home. Why must you go?'

'I wish to inspect a flock of sheep.'

'Send Mr Thwaite.' Riona brought her head close to Ellen's. 'What of Colm? He may return?'

'I doubt he will now. He'll be long gone. Alistair hasn't had any reports of him being in Sydney. You know he's sent out men to search the parts of Sydney where the Irish gather.'

'Just because he's not in Sydney doesn't mean he's sailed home.'

'He's nothing to stay for. The boys are gone. He'll conduct his business and leave. Mr Thwaite would have told me if he'd been heard of in the area. Colm has either gone back to Ireland or if he's still in Australia, he may well have gone to Melbourne to try his hand at gold digging.'

'I'd feel safer if you were here. We should have stayed in Sydney longer.'

'I was tired of Sydney.'

'It's not all about you, Ellen. You weren't the one he tried to abduct!'

'Keep your voice down. I don't want Miss Lewis leaving before she's even started!' Ellen fumed, glancing at the governess who was chatting with Bridget as they inspected a garden bed. 'Just keep calm. You have Miss Lewis here for company and I'll have men put on night watch. Mr Thwaite will see to it. If it makes you feel better sleep with Bridget and Lily while I'm gone.'

'And what of Lily? She'll not understand why you aren't here.'

'She has you.'

Riona raised her eyebrows. 'You know it's not the same. Lily is your special baby, and you are never far from her side.'

'Lily will be fine. She is weaned. Now I'm not feeding her, I have more freedom to do things I need to do.' Her special bond with Lily was because of Rafe. Their child was all she had of him. However, Lily and all her children needed her to secure their future. The days away were a small sacrifice to achieve that for them.

Ellen stopped to inspect the blossom on one of the apple trees. 'Shall I employ a nanny?'

'It might be a good idea, yes...'

'But?'

Riona sighed. 'Well, with Miss Lewis here, she will be with

Bridget constantly and I will have nothing to do. If you employ a nanny for Lily, I'll have even less to do.'

'I'd like you to be in charge of the house. I've formally made Moira the cook and in control of the kitchen and the staff in it, but the house needs someone to look after it and the maids we need to employ. You are excellent at seeing to the smooth running of the house. I don't have the time.'

'Be honest. You don't *want* to do it more like.' Riona gave her a superior look. 'We all know you don't enjoy the day-to-day arrangements of the house as much as I do.'

'No, I don't.' Ellen sighed. 'I adore this house, but...'

'Only it's not enough,' Riona finished for her. 'You're always striving for more, aren't you?'

'What's wrong with wanting to keep my family secure? Money keeps us safe.'

'Your lust for land will bring you undone, sister. Just be happy with what you have. I've said it often enough.'

'I will. Soon. But there's not enough property for the children after Alistair and I die. I need to build on what we have so there is enough to go around.'

'There is enough, Ellen. Your four children will have a fortune when the time comes.'

'There will soon be five.'

Riona grinned. 'Another one? Does Alistair know?'

'Not yet.' Ellen moved onto the next tree. 'We need more land and wealth to pass onto five children.'

'You have to stop thinking we'll be poor again as we were in Ireland. Alistair will never let that happen.'

Ellen glared at her. '*I* won't let that happen! I'm not solely relying on Alistair. I must do my bit as well. Alistair has given me money to spend as I see fit. He thinks it's for buying furnishings and clothes, but I care nothing about all of that. Land is what I'll buy.'

'You don't need to!'

'You don't understand how I feel. We lost everything in Ireland. That will never happen to us again. I need to know we will never be poor as we were before.'

Riona frowned. 'And we won't be. But you're not satisfied with that. You need more, always more. It's not good, Ellen, the way this greed, and yes, it is greed, is devouring you. Just be grateful for what you have.'

'Stop judging me. I'm doing this for the family, for the future,' Ellen defended.

'Are you? Or are you doing this to prove something to yourself?' Riona walked away to Miss Lewis and Bridget.

Ellen continued through the orchard, checking the stakes still held the young trees upright, but her movements were jerky with anger. Riona believed she knew it all. Her sister had never buried a son, never lost her husband or the home she'd created with her bare hands into something good and whole, only to see it all taken from her. Riona had relied on others to survive, their da and now Ellen.

Did Riona not think that Ellen would rather not be like this, forever worried, forever scared all this good fortune could go in an instant? All it took was a ship or two to sink and Alistair's business would suffer, they would suffer. He put too much investment into the business with Rafe. He thought her drive for land was simply whimsy. Yet, she would prove to him, and them all, that casting the net wide would prove a valuable judgement.

CHAPTER 5

*C*losing the drawer in his desk, Rafe Hamilton glanced up as Pollard, his clerk, knocked and entered his office.

'Sir, the *Blue Maid* has docked. A runner called a minute ago.' Pollard handed Rafe his coat and hat.

'Excellent news!' Rafe sagged a little in relief. Knowing his ship had safely made the journey from Australia across the world and home to Liverpool was an enormous weight off his shoulders.

'That's a nice birthday present for you, sir.'

'Indeed. I could not have asked for a better one.' Rafe pulled on his coat. 'I shan't be back this afternoon. I have a barber's appointment.'

A ship's horn sounded as Rafe left his office and walked along the crowded docks. Thick fog coated the River Mersey like a damp blanket obliterating the tall masts, cranes and buildings alike.

'Light your way, mister?' a ragged boy asked, running beside Rafe with a lit lantern.

Rafe tossed him a penny. 'I know the way, lad.'

He strode as fast as he could, dodging other folk doing the

same, hating the chill seeping under his collar. Horns sounded on the river, giving warnings. Groups of men loitered around the doors of inns, out of work and out of luck. Women with shawls covering their heads haggled for the best prices on fish stalls lining the wharfs.

In the cold October weather Rafe wanted nothing more than the sunshine on his back. Warm days of summer like those he experienced in Australia… No, he must not think of Australia for it reminded him of Ellen and that hurt too much. It was enough that she taunted his dreams at night and filled his mind during the day at odd times when he relaxed enough to let his thoughts wander. He missed Ellen's smile, her controlled energy, the way she held her head slightly to an angle when she was thinking, and so much more. Most of all, he missed the way she touched him, kissed him and her sighs with the pleasure he gave her. Their time together had been too brief, and he'd not been the same since.

At last, he saw her, the *Blue Maid*, his first ship, now joined by another and if his plans succeeded, soon he would have a third ship, one of those new steamers that were cutting sailing times down enormously.

He paused at the end of the gangway and gazed at the wooden hull, noting no damage on this side. Seamen were coming ashore carrying luggage, passengers mingled on deck and a crane was being winched up to begin the process of unloading the precious cargo which would be taken to his warehouse a few streets away and where he'd happily spend the next few days sorting and cataloguing with his manager, ready to sell it all.

Rafe hurried up the gangway to find and speak with Captain Leonards. He knew the ship well and strode straight to the saloon and knocked on the captain's private cabin.

'Mr Hamilton?' a voice called from behind him.

Rafe turned and stared at the two lads addressing him from across the saloon. It couldn't be? Ellen's boys? No. It wasn't possible. He felt a trifle stupid and blinked, his mind working rapidly to clear his confusion.

'Mr Hamilton, do you remember us?' Austin Kittrick asked, the taller of the two boys.

'Austin? Patrick?' He stared as though he was imagining them.

'Yes, sir.' Relief flooded Austin's handsome young face while beside him Patrick's face crumpled, and tears filled his eyes. He ran to Rafe and hugged him around the waist.

Taken aback, Rafe patted the boy's shoulder as Captain Leonards came out of his cabin.

'Ah, Rafe.' Leonards shook his head sadly.

'What... I mean why...?'

'Come in, come in.' Leonards beckoned Rafe into his cabin and the boys followed.

'I do not understand.' Rafe still held Patrick for the boy seemed uninclined to let him go.

'What a business.' Leonards shook his head again and handed Rafe a letter from his desk. 'It's from Alistair, explaining why the boys are on the ship.'

'What do you know?' Rafe took the letter, his heart thumping at the wild thoughts circling his head. Had something happened to Ellen? To Alistair? To the entire family?

'It was all incredibly quick. We were ready to sail down the harbour when a boat hailed us, and Emmerson climbed aboard with these two young men.' He smiled at the brothers. 'Emmerson said the boys' lives were in danger and I had to take them to you.'

'To me?' Rafe was dumbfounded. 'But their mother.' He turned to Austin. 'Your mother? Is she well?' He could hardly form the words.

'Aye, sir, last I knew.' Austin glanced at Patrick. 'We were at school at Parramatta. Alistair, I mean Papa, our stepfather, took us from there to this ship. We had to pack just a small bag. He said our uncle, Colm Kittrick, had planned to kidnap us and take us back to Ireland.'

Rafe's legs were a little shaky as the boy's words sunk in. Ellen was alive, thank God.

'It seemed Kittrick is an Irish rebel,' Leonards said. 'Emmerson was gravely concerned that the man would take the boys if they didn't get to safety. He thought you would keep them safe, or if not you, then they are to be sent to his father down south and to attend Harrow.'

Rafe thought fast, absorbing the news. 'So, you are to stay in England for school, for some time?'

Austin nodded, squaring his shoulders but Patrick knuckled his eyes, clearly distressed.

'As Emmerson's friend I assume you can attend to his wishes?' Leonards asked.

'Absolutely. I am his and their mother's closest friend.' Rafe squeezed Patrick's shoulder. 'They are my responsibility now.'

Leonards clapped Austin on the back. 'I told you all would be well, didn't I, lad?'

'Well...' Rafe sorted his thoughts. 'Let us get you two to my home, shall we? Go and collect your things.'

Rafe walked out with Leonards as the boys entered their cabin. 'This was the last thing I expected.'

'Aye, but what can you do when a friend is in need?'

'My plans for the day and the immediate future have changed that is for sure.' Rafe took a deep breath, the shock receding.

'They are good lads. It's been tough for them, especially the younger one. I kept them as busy as I could. They've read every book I own.'

'Thank you.' Rafe shook Leonards' hand. 'I had intended to discuss the voyage with you, but that shall have to wait until tomorrow. I think these boys need some reassuring that all is well.'

'Aye, I'll see you tomorrow. But rest assured the journey was a good one. I'll see that the cargo is unloaded and secured.' Leonards shook hands with Austin and Patrick as they joined them. 'It was a pleasure sailing with you, gentlemen.'

'Thank you, sir,' Austin said. 'My brother and me... and I are deeply grateful for everything.'

Rafe guided the boys towards the gangway, noticing that Austin had changed more than Patrick. Although both had grown taller, Austin was maturing, his speech becoming that of an educated young gentleman. The school he'd been attending in Parramatta had been altering him from the rough young Irish lad to an English young sir.

In the cab, heading home, Rafe struggled with his emotions. He was now responsible for two youths, the sons of the woman he loved. He could not fail her or them.

'How old are you now?' he asked Austin.

'I turned fourteen in September, sir.'

'And you, Patrick?'

'I'm twelve, sir.'

'And Alistair wishes for you to attend Harrow?' he asked Austin for Patrick was staring down at his hands clasped in his lap.

'Yes, sir.'

'What do you think about that?'

'I shall be glad to, sir.' Austin's tone was enthusiastic. 'It's a fine school from what I've heard.'

'I want to go home to Mammy,' Patrick murmured.

Austin nudged him. 'What have I told you a hundred times? You are to call her mama. We aren't in Ireland any longer.'

'I want to go home!' Patrick's defiant face was ravaged with tears.

'Now then, calm down.' Rafe soothed him as the cabbie halted the horse in front of Rafe's house. 'Here we are. Let us go inside and have a cup of tea and some of my cook's delicious cake. It's my birthday today, and she has made it especially for me.'

'Happy birthday, sir,' Austin and Patrick chorused as they alighted from the cab.

'I was going to attend a theatre show tonight. If you both are not too tired, perhaps you will join me?'

'Oh yes, that would be grand,' Austin said, smiling. 'I mean I would like that very much, sir.'

Rafe was suddenly excited that he would no longer be alone for his birthday. He had been invited to his sister and brother-in-law's house down south for the occasion, but he knew the *Blue Maid* was due into port so had declined. Happily, now he would have the two boys, who if he had been quicker to understand his feelings for Ellen, these two boys would be *his* stepsons and not Alistair's. Still, he could continue to be their friend as he had been when he was in Australia and what a wonderful thing that would be.

Rafe led them into the hall where they divested their coats with the help of Dilly, his housemaid, who came rushing out of the back part of the house. 'Dilly, will you make up two rooms for Austin and Patrick, please? They are going to live with me until they leave for school.'

'Yes, sir.'

'And will you tell Mrs Flannery?'

'I will, sir. Will you be wanting a tea tray brought in? The fire is lit in the parlour.'

'Yes, excellent. Thank you.'

Rafe ushered the boys into the front parlour where they both sat side by side on the sofa. Rafe poked at the fire, sending a shower of sparks up the chimney. 'So...' He didn't know where to start, but then remembered their hurried exit from their school. 'You both must have very little with you?'

'Yes, sir.' Austin frowned. 'We had to pack quickly and only have limited clothes with us.'

'Tomorrow we shall go and fit you out then.' Rafe took the letter from his pocket and gazed at it. 'I am still rather shocked by all this, but you both will be fine. I promise I will take care of you both.'

'Can we go home?' Patrick asked, his chin wobbling.

Rafe took a deep breath. 'Allow me to read Alistair's letter and then we shall discuss it.'

Dilly brought in a tray of tea with slices of cake, beef sandwiches and macaroons. 'Will I pour, sir?'

'Yes, thank you, Dilly. I think Austin and Patrick will be hungry.' He smiled, indicating for them to start eating.

While their attention was diverted, Rafe opened the letter.

MY DEAR FRIEND,

This letter will find you in a state of surprise I do not doubt. I am writing at speed so forgive my handwriting. The boys have been spirited away from school under the urgency of a planned kidnap by Ellen's former brother-in-law and the boys' uncle, Colm Kittrick. He has travelled to Australia for the purpose of taking them to Ireland and joining the rebel cause. Ellen has begged me to see them to safety and my thought was to send them to you on the Blue Maid, *which is leaving port today.*

Please forgive me for this unexpected but I hope not an unwelcome demand on our friendship. I know you hold Ellen in high esteem and consider us both as your valued friends. As such, I have tasked you with caring for the boys.

I have enclosed instructions regarding money and also my parents' address which is closer to Harrow than you are in Liverpool, and it is somewhere the boys can go on holidays if you are not able to accommodate them.

The boys are upset at the turn of events and were unable to say goodbye to their mother, such was the speed of the threat. I fear Ellen may not forgive me for my actions for I have placed them with you without her consent but be rest assured that I do so with the utmost respect for their safety. Colm Kittrick is a dangerous man and for him to secret them away to Ireland would be a worse fate for the boys and Ellen than for them to be educated at Harrow.

As my stepsons, they are to be gentlemen and as such need to be brought up in a style befitting that role. Harrow will achieve that goal and with you as their guardian I am assured that their future will be not only safe but successful.

I shall write again shortly. Please reply as soon as they boys are in your care.

With the deepest regards,
Your friend,
Alistair Emmerson.
July 1853 Sydney.

RAFE RAN a hand over his face and gazed at the boys munching on the food. Ellen did not know they were being sent to him. How devastated she must have felt when told. He ached to hold her, comfort her, reassure her that he would love her sons and see no harm comes to them.

'A cup of tea, sir?' Austin held up a cup and saucer towards him.

'Perfect.' Rafe took it from him and sat down opposite. 'I have read Alistair's letter, and he feels that an education is important to you both. An education in England.'

'I feel the same, sir.' Austin nodded with clear certainty in his eyes.

'Patrick?' Rafe prompted.

'I want to go home, sir.'

'Well, that is unachievable at the moment. Alistair wishes you both to attend Harrow. I believe your mother would want an education that is befitting your roles as stepsons of Alistair Emmerson. You are both to be gentlemen and gentlemen must have the best of schooling.'

Austin nodded. 'I told you, Patrick, you'll like it once we are settled just as you liked King's in Parramatta.'

'Yes, but there we could go home to Mammy... Mama. But we are stuck here on the other side of the world. She is not just a few days' ride away.'

'The time will go by quickly, Patrick,' Rafe tried to reassure the stricken boy. 'Your holidays will be spent either with me or with Alistair's mother and father, whichever you prefer.'

'Can you not take us home, sir?' Patrick asked.

Rafe thought quickly. 'As men sometimes we have to make decisions which are difficult. Therefore, I propose this. If you attend Harrow for one year and do not enjoy it and are still deeply unhappy, then I shall take you back to Australia.'

Austin glared at Patrick. 'We need to be educated. We've talked about this on the ship.'

'I can go to school in Parramatta. I don't want to stay in England!'

'Stop being a baby, Patrick!' Austin fumed.

'Enough, boys, please.' Rafe held his hand up when they looked to continue quarrelling. 'This will not do. Arguing and being at odds with each other will only cause resentment. You are brothers and must support each other. Austin, as the eldest, you need to lead the way for Patrick without fighting for that will not cure his homesickness.'

'Yes, sir.'

'And another thing. I feel you both should call me Rafe. I am your friend. I care about you both and want you to be happy. Calling me sir makes me feel as though I am your teacher or something equally insensible.' He grinned hoping to lighten the atmosphere. 'And as your friend I want us to enjoy our time together. Yes?'

'Yes.' Austin smiled.

'Patrick?'

'Yes.' The younger boy sighed miserably.

Rafe patted Patrick's knee. 'Finish your tea and then we shall unpack your belongings. Tonight, we shall go out for dinner and the theatre and celebrate my birthday. Now that is something to look forward to, is it not?'

While the boys ate, Rafe went into the study and began writing to Alistair and he would have to break his own promise to never to write to Ellen, but she would want a letter from him about the boys. The mail for the ship, *Ira Grey*, was open until three o'clock, for the ship was sailing for Sydney on the evening tide. He could write a short letter to them both and send it on the *Ira Grey*. In three months, Ellen would be reading his words and that gave him a deep sense of longing to be with her.

He paused. Should he take the boys back to Australia? Ellen would want them with her. Or would she? If he took them back was he putting them in danger again? Had Kittrick left Australia? Dare he risk the threat? After all, Alistair sent them to him for two valid reasons, to be safe and for an education.

Dear Ellen,

Be assured that Austin and Patrick have safely arrived in Liverpool and are with me. At present they are enjoying tea and cake in my parlour.

The boys have suffered no illness on board and seem to be in the best of health. Captain Leonards cared well for them. Patrick suffers from missing you and I know how he feels. Austin is keen to begin school.

Alistair requested me to see them educated at Harrow, though he mentions he has done this without your consent. I shall enrol them in Harrow should they pass the entrance test, which I am convinced they will do so, besides which a hefty donation to the school will secure their positions I do not doubt.

However, if on return of this letter, you advise me to bring them back to you, I shall do so with all speed.

Until I hear from you, I will do all that is in my power to make them happy and care for them as though they are my own sons.

I am and always will be,

Your devoted friend,

Rafe Hamilton.

RAFE READ the letter and paused. He sounded cold. Ellen would not want that from him, not now when she'd be missing the boys so much, and hopefully him as well. He screwed the paper up and threw it into the fire and started again.

MY ELLEN,

I cannot describe to you the utter surprise and joy at seeing the boys when they arrived in Liverpool today. Hearing their story, I suddenly knew you would be bereft. Please know and take comfort in the fact that they are in good health and in my care.

Please be reassured that I will care for them as though they are my own sons, and as they are yours, I will love them as such.

You will see that they have written to you, which no doubt will give you much joy.

I am in a hurry to post this letter with those the boys have written, so it reaches you as quickly as possible to put your mind and heart at rest. I understand you will feel pain at not being with them and they are so far away from you, but they will always be my first priority. I would never give you reason to believe they are not wanted by me.

Alistair wishes for them to be enrolled in his old school, and I will undertake that responsibility. However, they will be with me in the holidays, so please do not despair of them being without guidance and caring for I will treat them as my own.

I know I once promised to never write to you again, but this occasion was too important for such a promise to be upheld. I simply had to write to you and put your mind at ease. How I wish you had been on the ship with them. I still love you desperately.

With my fondest and most sincere love and devotion,

Rafe.

Liverpool. October 1853.

His heart aching, he sealed the letter.

He wrote a quick few lines to Alistair and addressed his letter to the office in Sydney whereas Ellen's letter was addressed to her at Emmerson Park, which he knew from Alistair was her preferred place of residence. It gave him a sense of stilted joy that they lived apart most of the time. The thought of Alistair sharing the same bed as Ellen tore at his guts.

A knock on the door saved him from his tormented thoughts. 'Yes?'

Austin entered, Patrick behind him. 'We thought to go up and unpack?'

'Good, yes, but first write a few lines to your mother. I can send out letters on the *Ira Grey*, which is departing for Sydney tonight. It's a steam ship as well as sails and is fast. She last made her last journey to Australia in eighty days. Imagine?'

'We have letters in our luggage that we have written on the voyage.' Patrick perked up for the first time. 'Can you send them for us, sir?'

'Call me Rafe, Patrick, and, yes, of course we shall post them. We will go and post them now, shall we?'

The smile brightened the boy's face and Rafe's heart softened with love for the boy. 'Here, write a note now and then we will go.'

As Patrick and Austin wrote a few lines each on the same piece of paper, Rafe donned his coat, then collected all the letters. 'How happy your mother will be to receive this bundle?' Rafe grinned, holding the large number of letters. The boys must have written twenty letters each on the voyage.

'Come along.' He led them from the house. 'The post office is only a few streets away. I remember when I returned from Australia after spending time with you all, I had a pile of letters waiting for me that your mother had written on the voyage out. Perhaps tomorrow you would like to read them and relive your voyage to Australia?'

'Yes, please.' Patrick beamed up at Rafe with utter trust and Rafe knew he could never let these boys down.

'Since I returned from Australia you have gained a little sister?' he inquired as they walked in the fog.

'Lily. She's very small, just a baby,' Patrick declared.

'What does she look like?' Rafe asked, wondering if the baby girl was his. Since Alistair wrote to him of the exciting news of Ellen being pregnant and then having a baby girl, he had worked out the dates and wondered if their one evening of passion had resulted in him having a daughter. Secretly he hoped it was so.

'She looks like Mama,' Austin said. 'Her eyes are blue, but Mama said all babies' eyes are blue at first.'

'Lily won't know us when we do get to go home.' Patrick's shoulders slumped.

'Your mother will remind her all the time that she has two big brothers.' Rafe tried to cheer him up and then, as they walked past a portrait studio, he had an idea.

CHAPTER 6

*S*trolling through the gardens, Ellen listened to her guests' chatter. After a week of rain, the sun shone in a clear blue sky, allowing the garden party to go ahead. The warmth of the November day gave thought to the summer ahead, of days going by so quickly. She was planning her next property purchase before Christmas and before the pregnancy halted her. Her wide skirts hid her condition somewhat but at four months along, she knew she'd soon be showing.

'Mrs Emmerson.' George Riddle and his wife sauntered towards her, each smiling widely. 'We are enchanted by your gardens,' he said. 'Aren't we, my dear?'

'We are, Mrs Emmerson, and I do adore your roses.'

'Then in the autumn you must have some cuttings, Mrs Riddle.'

'Really? You are too kind.' Mrs Riddle, her large bonnet obstructing most of her face, raised her gaze to her husband. 'Our home is in need of a better gardener than we have at present.'

'We shall rectify that, my dear.' Mr Riddle patted her hand on his arm. 'Mrs Emmerson have you heard that the Slater property in Mittagong is going to auction?'

'I did hear that, yes.'

'Will you bid on it?'

'I'm not sure. My husband isn't keen on the idea. He feels small farm holdings aren't worth the investment. He'd rather buy property in Sydney.'

'And what are your thoughts on the subject?'

'The Slater property is in good shape. My estate manager, Mr Thwaite, and I rode over there last week, but we already own a farm in Moss Vale, which I would like to extend if I could buy the land on either side of it. However, the owners are reluctant to sell at the moment.'

'You have gained a reputation of being a woman who knows how to invest,' Mr Riddle said as they walked along the rose garden. 'We were all astounded when you purchased five hundred acres in Marulan.'

'It was a sound investment.'

Mrs Riddle stared at Ellen. 'Am I correct in thinking that you bought the property in Marulan without your husband's knowledge?'

'Yes, you are correct, Mrs Riddle. Alistair is content for me to buy sensible purchases.'

'But five hundred acres isn't exactly a dress or a lamp for the house, is it?' She giggled. 'George would never allow me to do such a thing and nor would I want to.'

'That is because you have no head for business, my dear.' George's patronising tone was clear. 'Whereas Mrs Emmerson is clearly capable of dealing with men of business.'

Ellen wasn't sure if he was insulting her or praising her. 'Many women can manage businesses, Mrs Riddle. We mustn't let men have all the fun, must we?' Ellen forced a smile. 'Excuse me, I believe I am wanted.'

Marching away from the couple, Ellen expected to be the talk of the drawing rooms yet again. Well, she didn't care. Alistair said if she kept going the way she was doing, they'd have an empire and she thought that a marvellous thing even if he was jesting with her.

She noticed Miss Lewis was laughing with Bridget and another gentleman, Ellen had invited, a Mr Harold Tanner, who own a small farm nearby. Riona chatted to Augusta Ashford and her brother Gil, a handsome man that Ellen liked a lot. He was a true gentleman with a kind and intelligent manner. She wished his lovely wife, Pippa, was in attendance but she was heavily pregnant with their first child and made her excuses not to come today.

It pleased Ellen that she had a growing circle of acquaintances in the district, people who were more accepting of her background than those in Sydney. Still, her involvement in buying properties caused heads to turn, but the men of the area were becoming used to seeing her attend livestock auctions with Mr Thwaite.

'Mrs Emmerson, what a quaint little party. I am most entertained. Miss Lewis played the piano most prettily earlier.' Mrs Ratcliffe, a large older woman who, due to her husband's death, had become a very wealthy woman, sat on the verandah eating her way through the numerous cakes and tarts.

Ellen smiled in response to the woman she had met only a few times at other parties. 'I'm pleased.'

'Come and sit by me for a few minutes and tell me of your latest business dealings.'

Ellen took the vacant seat next to the woman. 'I doubt they will add to your entertainment, Mrs Ratcliffe.'

'Dear girl, business is the only thing that keeps me alive.' She guffawed, drawing attention to them. 'Are you bidding on the Slater property?'

'No, I don't think so.' Ellen wanted to grin at being called a girl at the age of thirty.

Mrs Ratcliffe raised an eyebrow. 'It has an excellent water source. The creek running through it is most advantageous for livestock.'

'True, but I feel it's not large enough.'

'I grant you it is not the five hundred acres you just purchased.' Mrs Ratcliffe's eyes narrowed quizzically in her round face. 'I like you enormously. I feel you are far more intelligent than people give you credit for.'

'Thank you.'

'They see a woman, not the brain.'

'Well, that's to their own detriment, Mrs Ratcliffe. Let them think that if it makes them happy.'

'Ha. They are not happy when you beat them at their own game. It is what I have been doing for years.'

'You have?' Ellen gave her all her attention.

'Tell me, what is your next purchase?' Mrs Ratcliffe bit into a lemon curd tart.

'Who says I'm purchasing anything?' Ellen edged.

The rotund woman laughed again. 'You don't fool me, Mrs Emmerson. I see the glint in your eyes. You are a kindred spirit, dear girl. I shall let you into a little secret. My husband only became as wealthy as he did because of me. I had money from my father, and I invested it wisely. Wilfred was a clever man, that's why I married him and between us we created a fortune. I see the same in you and your husband.'

'Not everyone has the same outlook as you do. My husband's friends in Sydney see me as a fortune hunter. A poor Irish widow who snatched the city's most eligible bachelor.'

'Tsk. Do not give those fools in Sydney the satisfaction of being brought low because of their gossip. Jealousy creates monsters.' Mrs Ratcliffe nodded sagely, finishing the tart.

'I simply want to provide for my children.' Comfortable in the other woman's presence, Ellen relaxed. 'I refuse to spend my time doing nothing when I can be doing something for our future.'

'You married a good man who will let you. Not many would allow such freedom with finances. I miss my husband every day, but in some ways, I am glad to have full control again.' She paused to take a bite from a piece of apple pie. 'I will buy the Slater property for it joins two other properties I own.'

'Someone might outbid you.' Ellen grinned.

Mrs Ratcliffe shook her head, a steely look in her eye even though she smiled. 'No, they will not.'

'I'll get you another cup of tea.'

'Thank you, dear. Oh, and Ellen, I may call you Ellen? I'm too old to be wasting time with formalities.'

'Of course.'

'If you ever need to discuss anything, just come to me.'

Grateful to have found a new friend, Ellen was touched by the offer. 'I will. Thank you.'

As Ellen was pouring a cup of tea, Honor Duffy brought out another jug of lemon cordial for the refreshments table. 'Thank you, Honor. The guests are thirsty.'

Honor stacked some of the empty plates. 'That's because they are stuffing their faces, so they are. Such food. Tables of it and yet not so long ago we were all starving.'

'They do not know of the hunger we experienced for sure, but we cannot judge them on that. Be thankful we are now in the land of plenty.'

Honor's lips became a thin line.

'You are happy here, aren't you?' Ellen asked.

'Do I have a choice?'

Taken aback, Ellen frowned. 'Of course you do. I'm not keeping you here against your will. If you want to leave, then do so.'

'And upset my husband and daughters? Unlike you, Ellen Emmerson, I put my family first.' Honor stormed off to the kitchen.

'What was all that about?' Alistair said from behind.

'Alistair!' Ellen embraced him. 'When did you arrive?'

'Just now.' He smiled and kissed her. 'I know I said I would not make it, but I have been missing you and needed to come and spend time with you all.'

'You stay in Sydney too much,' she chided gently.

'I must do so to keep the business successful, but no talk of business today. I am home and with you. What more can I ask for?'

'Come and greet everyone. I've spent the first hour explaining to people you were in Sydney. They will see me as a great liar now.'

Alistair's sunny disposition brought new life to the party. The chatting and laughter grew more animated, and the wine and ale flowed into the late afternoon.

When at last the final guest left as the sun was slipping behind the trees, Alistair took Ellen to one side in the study.

'Is something wrong?' Ellen asked, aching to sit down. Tiredness made her yawn.

'No, nothing at all. However, I have something to discuss with you.'

'Oh?'

'I heard reports of a large property for sale north of the Goulburn Plains. A sheep farm. Ten thousand acres, with a cottage, stables, woolshed and a creek.'

'I've heard nothing about it and between Mr Thwaite and I, we hear most things.'

'This is not common knowledge yet, dearest. Roger Maxwell, the jeweller in Castlereagh Street, told me about it when I stopped to have my watch repaired. He found out through the owner of the property himself, a Mr James Miller, who had gone to him to sell some of his late wife's jewels. She died in childbirth and he, Miller, is returning to England with the baby.'

'How tragic.'

'Indeed. But once I heard this news, I thought perhaps we should have a visit to the property.'

'Why are you so interested? You usually don't care for sheep farms.'

'That is true. Yet something tells me this is an excellent investment. Miller has thousands of Merino sheep. Merino wool is much prized and sought after in England. I should know, I have exported enough of it. It seems only sensible to have our own farm.'

'I did mention that to you before.' She gave him a stern look. 'You weren't interested then. When I bought the five hundred acres at Marulan, you were not keen. You said it was too much for us to control and that we knew nothing about sheep farming.'

'More fool me.' He grinned. 'But in truth, I have done more research since then and spoken to a few friends who have such concerns themselves in the country up north. They are making considerable wealth. Of course, there are droughts to worry about, but as long as there are water sources on the properties then they say sheep farming is a sensible investment.'

Excitement grew in Ellen. 'Can we afford it?'

Alistair walked behind the desk, scratching his head. 'Well, it will be a considerable expenditure. This concern is much larger than Marulan. We'll have to find a suitable manager for it. I believe the returns are there, but it might leave us a little lean in our finances until the next wool clip is sold or the next cargo shipment is advertised. Another ship isn't due for a month yet.'

'Then we mortgage a few of the properties. The terrace houses in Balmain?'

'My thoughts exactly. They will be of higher value than the Moss Vale farm, or the property in Kangaroo Valley.'

'Then let us do it.'

He smiled fondly. 'Dearest, we have to view the place first.'

'Then let us leave tomorrow.'

'I have only just arrived.'

'Yes, but if word gets out, we won't be the only ones in the bidding on the place.' She thought of Mrs Ratcliffe. 'Sometimes, we just have to make the first move and take the gamble.'

'What have you become?' He laughed, coming to her side to hug her to him.

'Your business partner!' She raised her eyebrows at him to dare to contradict her.

'What a wife I have! I have missed you, dearest.' Love shone from his eyes.

Her heart fluttered. She wanted to make him happy. And although she couldn't love him as deeply as he loved her, she could still give him something special. 'I have something to tell you.'

'Oh? You have not bought another property, have you? I am still in disbelief about the Marulan place.'

She shook her head and laughed. 'No, you'll prefer this piece of news a lot more.'

'I am intrigued.'

'I'm to have a baby.'

His green eyes widened. 'A baby!'

'Yes. Due around April sometime.' She smiled, despite the sinking feeling that soon she'd be trapped within the estate.

He crushed her into his chest. 'My darling. What joyous news! Perhaps it will be a boy?'

She grinned up at him. 'I'd like to give you a son for all you have done for me and my family.'

'Your family is *my* family, dearest. I do not need your thanks just your love.'

'I hope you will not be disappointed if it is a girl?'

He leaned back to stare down at her. 'No, indeed not. Though a boy would be nice.' Then he frowned. 'You are with child so the journey to Goulburn would be too much for you. I shall go with Thwaite.'

'Oh, no. I'm going, Alistair, and don't you try to stop me! I've travelled to Marulan and down the mountain to Kangaroo Valley while pregnant.'

He stepped away. 'How far along are you?'

'Four months.'

'Then why did you travel to those places and endanger yourself?'

She gave him a fierce look. 'There was no danger. Do not wrap me up and think of me as delicate! I've been pregnant five times and each time, except for Lily, I have worked the land right up until I had my first pains. I am not a fragile slip of a girl, Alistair, like your friends' wives are.'

'Still, I would prefer if you stayed at home.'

'No.' She faced him with a tilt of her chin. 'Do not constrain me. I won't allow it. You know it's not my nature.'

'Very well.' He sighed heavily. 'I will not argue with you over this, not when you've made me so happy. Though I shall worry the entire time.'

'Why should you? I've had five babies before with no problems. I'm sure this one will be no different. I'll go and tell Riona of our plans to leave in the morning.' She left the study to find her sister, wishing she hadn't told Alistair about the baby until they returned.

* * *

SEATED UP IN THE BUGGY, Ellen gazed about her at the sloping plains and rugged hills in the distance. The sun shone between flat grey clouds as crows cried from high in the branches of eucalyptus trees.

'Look, an eagle.' Alistair, driving Betsy, pointed to the graceful bird riding the air currents high above them.

'It is beautiful country out here,' Ellen murmured. Low on the horizon a large flock of white cockatoos created a cloud of their own as they flew together.

They'd left the staging inn at Marulan at dawn after arriving there late last night. Before reaching Marulan they had stopped at the farm Ellen bought last month and restocked the hut with produce for the station hand who watched over the cattle herd.

'A little barren for my liking.' Alistair gazed about him. A small mob of kangaroos grazed at the base of a hill on their right.

'That is because you are a city gentleman,' Ellen teased. 'You wouldn't have admired my country in Mayo. Rock strewn fields and bare hills to the sea, not many trees at all.'

'It is true I much prefer the city to the country.'

'Which do you prefer, Mr Thwaite?' Ellen asked him as he rode alongside the buggy.

'Country every time, Mrs Emmerson. I can't breathe in the city... Too many people.'

'I agree.' She lifted her face to the sun. The sky seemed so vast out here on the flat plains.

'This is fine sheep country, Mr Emmerson,' Mr Thwaite mentioned, taking his hat off to run his fingers through his hair.

Alistair nodded. 'It looks it.'

'The road isn't too bad either. We'll be able to get the bullock wagons out here.' Mr Thwaite replaced his hand and sat back in the saddle, one hand on his thigh. 'Let's hope it has decent rainfall.'

They drove on for another few miles, leaving the flat plains and following the track through a wide valley lined with large high hills. In the distance, a tree-covered mountain range rose up on either side of the valley.

'The other side of the mountains is the start of Goulburn Plains, Mr Emmerson,' Thwaite told them.

'We need to get the map out, dearest,' Alistair instructed Ellen.

From a bag she pulled out the map and directed Alistair off the track and through open country north-west of the small township of Goulburn.

They forded a narrow creek and drove for another half an hour until they found a well-used track and turned north onto it.

Ellen noticed a band of mounted men riding towards them. As they neared, the lead rider, wearing a red handkerchief, stared straight at her. He checked his horse for a moment, slowing it enough to peer at Ellen, then kicked it on into a canter.

Ellen's heart thumped in her chest. Could it be? Surely not... The red handkerchief! Instinctively, she knew it was the Irish bushranger who'd held them up two years ago. She twisted in her seat to watch them ride off, hoping they wouldn't turn back.

'I see a cabin ahead.' Alistair frowned. 'Did those men come from there? I hope it was not Miller and we have just missed the opportunity to talk to him. Or those men were buying the place before we have a chance to offer for it.'

'We'll soon find out.' Shaken, Ellen climbed down from the buggy without waiting for Alistair to help her.

A man came out onto the hut's verandah. 'Welcome. Are you lost?'

'Good day to you. Mr Miller, I take it?' Alistair went to shake his hand.

'It is.'

'I am Alistair Emmerson, my wife, Ellen and my manager Mr Thwaite.'

'How can I be of help?'

'We heard you were selling, Mr Miller,' Alistair said.

'Did you?' Miller, a man in his forties with a deeply tanned face and a long moustache invited them in. His clothes were filthy as was the cabin. Clothes were hung on hooks in the walls and thrown over stools. Dirty plates and pans filled buckets, which attracted the flies.

Ellen's eyes took a second or two to adjust to the dimness then she immediately saw the cot in the corner. A baby grizzled within. 'May I?' she asked Mr Miller.

'Yes. A woman's touch might satisfy the mite, for he does nothing but scream for me.'

Ellen swooped up the baby, which she guessed was about two months old. His napkin was wet and so she laid him on the bed and changed him.

'I am looking to sell, yes,' Miller said, coming to stand beside Ellen. 'I need to get this fellow to England to my sister. My wife died having him and I can't be a farmer and a mother at the same time.'

'May we have a look around?' Alistair asked. 'We are interested. For the right price.'

'Certainly. I'll show you about the place.'

Ellen followed them out carrying the baby, who was thin and appeared weak. 'We passed some men just now. Are they offering for the farm too?' Though she knew they weren't.

'No, they are just a group of men wanting work.' Miller didn't meet her gaze and pulled his hat brim down low. 'Come this way.'

Ellen knew he was lying, but maybe he was protecting himself. She remained quiet while Alistair and Thwaite asked him questions about the stock and grazing and water supply.

Holding the baby as he fell asleep, Ellen couldn't help but think that soon she'd be doing the same with her own baby. It seemed no time at all since she had Lily and now another baby would soon be in the family.

Alistair stopped walking and turned to Ellen. 'What are your thoughts?'

'I like what I've seen.' Ellen gazed about the surrounding fields that Miller had ploughed with wheat and vegetables. A small stable and yard held Miller's horse and a milk cow and calf, beyond that the fields lay flat until they reached the bottom of a range of hills. No trees were close by, and the bareness touched Ellen.

Suddenly she saw the cross in a fenced off area some way from the hut. Miller had buried his wife there. Ellen stared at the cross for some moments and thought of Thomas, her son buried in Ireland.

'The creek is at the bottom of the field behind the hut.' Miller pointed to their left, breaking into Ellen's thoughts. 'My wife grew a good number of vegetables for our table. We've been here five years and never run short of water. The creek has been extremely low during a couple of summers but never completely dry.'

'And further out?' Thwaite asked. 'The sheep are healthy?'

'We can go and inspect them if you like?'

Ellen noticed the ashes of a campfire near the stable field. Empty bottles lay beside logs used as seating. On closer inspection she noticed a broken clay pipe and carcass bones. She stared southwards in the direction of where the gang of men had ridden. She believed they had stayed here. 'Those men, Mr Miller. Did they stay here?' She indicated the campfire.

'Aye, Mrs Emmerson, they did.'

'Do you know who they are?' She hitched the baby in her arms more comfortably.

He sighed and rubbed his bristled chin. 'Do you?'

'I do.'

'Ellen?' Alistair was suddenly interested. 'What is wrong?'

'Mr Miller had bushrangers here. The same ones who held us up a couple of years ago. Eddie Patterson and his gang.'

Alarmed, Alistair turned to Miller. 'Is that true?'

'Aye. They arrived yesterday. I didn't know who they were at first. I have nothing of value here, except my horse and cow. They don't have the skills to round up my sheep. Anyway, being friendly might have saved not only my stock but my life. They only wanted food. The baby was crying, and Patterson said I had enough to deal with. I expected them to take my horse this morning, but they didn't.'

'You should have reported them!' Alistair said incredulously.

'They did no harm to me. In fact, Patterson held my boy for

an hour or so to give me a rest and we ate kangaroo together. Patterson even fed him some milk. To be honest with you, they seemed rather exhausted.'

'They are *wanted* men!' Alistair snorted.

'Are they coming back?' Ellen asked, not knowing how to feel about Eddie Patterson. He was a criminal and yet, there was something about him that intrigued her.

'I shouldn't think so,' Miller replied, his face tired, his shoulders sagging. 'In truth it was pleasant to have some company. No one has been here for months, not since my wife died. I've been to Sydney once in that time which was difficult with a newborn.'

'I can imagine.' Ellen felt sorry for him. What fascinated her more was that Eddie Patterson hadn't done this man any harm when he could have easily for Miller was vulnerable with a new baby and no other person here. Patterson had every opportunity to rob Miller of everything he possessed and didn't. Was Patterson as bad as people thought him to be?

Miller stared over at the wooden cross at the end of the grave. 'It will be hard to leave her... She was a good wife, and I loved her. We had such plans for this farm. Mariah wanted to give me strong sons... I don't want to leave her... But I have to do what's right for Thomas.'

Ellen jerked. 'Thomas?'

'Aye.' Miller touched the baby's cheek. 'Thomas is all I have now. I can't take care of him here alone.'

Staring down at the puny baby in her arms, a baby called Thomas like her own dear lost boy, made Ellen want to weep. 'What is your price for this property?' she asked Miller.

He told her and she held out her hand. 'Done.'

'*Ellen*, I have not decided,' Alistair snapped.

'*I* have decided for both of us.' Ellen gave him a stubborn glare. 'Mr Miller needs to get back to England for his son.'

'Ellen, we have not yet seen the sheep!' Alistair's voice rose in irritation.

'I don't need to see the sheep. I trust Mr Miller.'

'Are you mad?' Alistair was furious.

'I trust my instincts, Alistair. That's what you do in business.' She smiled at Miller. 'We will take care of your wife's grave.' With a nod to Miller, she returned to the hut with Thomas, tears slipping over her lashes.

Perhaps she was being irrational because of the pregnancy, but something told her this place was special. Her Thomas had been robbed of a life, but this Thomas would be given the chance to live and be happy. If she could have a hand in that then, in some small way, she could feel a little easier in losing her own boy.

Alistair followed her into the hut. 'Are you sure about this?'

'Completely.'

He looked at the baby in her arms. 'I would never have expected you to make a business decision with emotion.'

She paused in putting the baby in the cradle as he began to whimper. 'Sometimes I just know when to do something. I don't understand it. I simply know when it's right, and this is right.'

'Because his son is called Thomas as yours was?'

'No, it's more than that.' She placed the baby in the cradle and walked out of the hut with Alistair. She stopped and looked around the wide expanse of dry grassy plains. 'This place is what I imagined when I journeyed to this country. Fields of grass and distant hills.'

'Are you saying Emmerson Park falls short of that?' he asked in amazement.

'No…' She sighed. 'You don't understand.'

'No, I do not. You have a magnificent house and gardens that many would kill for.'

'Emmerson Park is beautiful, and I love it, of course I do, but all that is left to do is to watch the trees and gardens grow.'

'And what is wrong with that?'

'It's not enough, Alistair. I am not like other women. I don't want to spend my days receiving callers and making return calls, of sorting out the dinner menus for the week or attend meetings on how to raise money for the church roof.'

'You are a wife and a mother. Your main concern is raising our children.'

'And I'm also me, Ellen O'Mara, then Ellen Kittrick, the girl from Mayo who has worked all her life. That's who I am, Alistair. I need to keep myself occupied. My brain needs to keep working.'

'I give you free rein to do exactly what you want.' He sounded jaded. 'My friends laugh at me. I am a joke in Sydney. The man whose beautiful wife prefers to live in the country and not be by my side.'

'And having me living in the country has made you even richer.'

'It is not always about more money, Ellen. I am wealthy enough.'

'You can never be wealthy enough,' she scoffed.

'You're not in Ireland anymore. There is no danger here of you being poor and without a home or food. This is not Ireland. You have to let the past go.'

'I have.'

'Really? I do not believe you.' He rubbed his hands over his face. 'I cannot compete with your ghosts.'

Her heart melted at his distress. 'I'm sorry, Alistair. I don't mean to be so difficult.'

'It is true I do not fully understand you.' He gave her a wry smile. 'I suppose that is why I love you so deeply. You are unlike anyone I have ever known.'

She hung her head, wishing she could love him as much as he did her.

Alistair glanced over to where Thwaite and Miller stood talking by the stable. 'We shall go into Goulburn with Miller and complete the sale. We will have to spend the night there for I do not know how long the transaction will take. We need witnesses to oversee the deal.'

'I will stay here with Thomas. You and Mr Miller can go into Goulburn.'

'No. You cannot stay here alone at night.'

'Mr Miller wouldn't want to take the baby into Goulburn.' Ellen linked her arm through Alistair's. He tensed a little before he let out a deep breath and patted her arm.

She tilted her head at him. 'Buy him a meal, Alistair, the man looks ready to drop. I'll be fine. Mr Thwaite will stay with me.'

'I want Thwaite to go up into the hills and inspect the sheep.' Alistair waved for Thwaite to join them.

'He can do that and then return to the hut tonight.' Ellen smiled at Mr Miller and told him their plans. 'Do you agree, Mr Miller? It is your choice, of course.'

'You'll stay and take care of my son while I'm in Goulburn?'

'I will.'

'Thank you.' Relief flooded his face. 'I will get a full night's sleep for the first time in months.'

Within a short time, Ellen watched Alistair and Miller drive off in the buggy and Mr Thwaite rode off in the direction of the sheep flock.

Ellen stood surveying her land. A heady feeling overcame her. She had finally found a place she felt at home. This dry wide land was nothing like the lush greenness of Ireland, but it had a wildness that reminded her of home. She could walk this land and not see a soul for days.

Checking the baby was asleep, she headed off behind the hut towards the grave. The sun shone from a clear sky and crows called from somewhere in the hills where eucalyptus and acacia tress grew. The white-painted wooden cross was roughly carved.

Here lies
Mariah Miller

1828 - 1853
Beloved wife & mother

ELLEN KNELT and pulled out the weeds growing at the base of the cross. 'Your husband and son will be just fine, Mariah. Rest in peace.'

Leaving the grave, she walked down to the creek. The water ran well, clear and a foot deep in places. Further down the creek flowed around an outcrop of rock, and what looked like an old tree stump. Here the water pooled, and she noticed it was the place where Miller must fetch his water from as a rope was tied to the tree stump to stop the bucket from floating away.

Returning to the hut, Ellen fetched a jug before going to milk the cow, which bellowed suddenly, breaking the quietness of the land. Wanting enough to feed the baby and perhaps add some to a cup of tea, Ellen bent beneath the cow and started milking, a chore she'd not done since leaving Ireland years ago. The simple pleasure of doing something useful gave her great satisfaction.

However, feeding baby Thomas proved another matter. The little mouth fussed over the nipple of the glass bottle. More milk spilt over his chin than dribbled into his mouth.

'Dear heaven, little one, you are starving yourself.' Ellen shifted to a better position on the bed and tried again. After stops and starts for ten minutes, a couple of ounces of milk was finally in his belly. Propping the baby over her shoulder, she added wood to the little oven in the corner and put a pan of water on to boil.

'You need a bath, young man. You don't smell too sweet.' It didn't go unnoticed by her that she was tending to a stranger's child when at home she had two daughters missing her, but it would be worth it.

She would make this hut a proper home for Bridget and Lily.

This farm would be somewhere they could come sometimes and be free of the constraints of growing up as ladies. Patrick would like it here, too. He'd ride his horse for miles. Abruptly, the familiar pain of missing her boys hit her in the chest. She stiffened, fighting the ache. When she had quiet times, her mind would think of them, which was why she needed to keep busy.

This property would become her new project. There was a lot to do, and she'd do it for her boys. One day this would be theirs.

With the baby washed and dressed and once more asleep, Ellen made a cup of tea with tea leaves that look overused. Again, she was reminded of the weak tasteless tea they drank in Ireland when the famine hit. She remembered those back in the home country, the people she once lived amongst and would never see again. How were they coping? Was Kathleen, the maid at Wilton Manor, married now? She'd not written to the staff at the manor, or even Mr Wilton himself for a year. She should rectify that once she was back in Berrima.

Using the last of the sunlight, Ellen swept the hut's floor and tidied Miller's belongings into some sense of order. She fetched two buckets of water and washed the plates and pots. A meat safe held a half loaf of campfire cooked damper bread and she cut a slice and spread it with a smear of strawberry jam.

At the door she stood and watched the sunset over the ranges and half an hour later, Mr Thwaite came riding back and dismounted in front of the hut.

'Are they in good condition?' she asked him.

'Not bad. A good number of lambs that I could see. The flock is spread far and wide, right up into the hills. We'll need men to round them up and count them.'

'A good investment then?'

'Aye, Mrs Emmerson. A sound investment. Excellent grazing land and a nice flock of sheep.' He gazed around. 'Some more buildings are needed. If you're looking to increase the flock, you'll need a bigger shearing shed and some proper yards. Not sure how Mr Miller managed it without yards unless he had makeshift ones.'

'We'll turn this place into a grand sheep station, Mr Thwaite. I'm giving you managership of the place.'

His eyes widened in shock. 'What about Emmerson Park and the other properties?'

'You are needed here more.'

'Aye, well, if that's what you want, Mrs Emmerson.' He looked down at his boots, subdued.

'We worked well together at Emmerson Park did we not?' she prompted, trying to grasp his sudden turn of mood.

'Aye, madam.'

'We can do so again here.'

'Aye.'

'You are not happy with the idea of being a manager here?'

'Not really, madam. Not on my own. I enjoy being with the family at Emmerson Park. Before you came, I spent years alone watching the animals. I like the company.'

'Oh, I see. Right well, we shan't hurry into any decision yet then. Perhaps we can talk about it more later.'

'Very good, madam. I'd best pitch the tent before all light goes.'

'I'll make us some supper, though with what I cannot imagine.'

'Roast lamb?' Thwaite grinned.

CHAPTER 7

'It is good to be home,' Alistair said as they drove through the gates of Emmerson Park three days later.

Ellen squinted into the sunlight that speared through the trees as the sun lowered on the horizon. 'It'll be nice to sleep in our own bed.'

She ached from sitting in the buggy since dawn. They'd left the inn at Marulan before sunrise, wanting to make it home today. Mr Miller's farm was now theirs and Ellen had helped Miller pack up his belongings and seen him and baby Thomas onto a coach in Goulburn for the long journey home to England.

'Has Riona invited guests?' Alistair asked, indicating to a selection of carriages near the house and women standing around.

'Not that I'm aware of.' Inwardly, Ellen groaned. She didn't want to entertain. The jaunt had exhausted her.

Closer to the house, people broke apart and started hurrying towards them. Betsy shied at the fuss.

Ellen's stomach swooped. Riona stood sobbing with Miss Lewis comforting her. Climbing down from the buggy, Ellen's heart twisted in anguish. 'What's happened?'

Riona ran to Ellen. 'Bridget's missing!'

'Missing?' Ellen clenched her hands together. A shiver of fear ran through her. 'Tell me everything.'

'She was out riding with Douglas early this morning. Douglas came back as Pepper had thrown a shoe. Bridget said she was going to ride to the river and straight home, but she's not returned yet.'

'How long has she been gone?' Alistair demanded to know.

'Since eight o'clock this morning.' Riona wiped her eyes.

Alistair took out his fob watch. 'It is ten past five. That is nine hours.'

Moira, standing behind Riona, stepped forward. 'I sent all the men out looking for her, so I have.'

Riona gripped Ellen's hands. 'When she didn't return after an hour, Douglas searched all along the river, but couldn't find a trace of her. He then rode into Berrima and spoke to the mounted police. They've sent two men out who are searching, along with our estate men. Douglas has also ridden to all the neighbours asking for help.'

'If she'd fallen in the river, Princess would have returned home by now,' Alistair said, his words heavy in the air.

Ellen stared towards the valley and the ribbon of water that wound through it. A cold realisation swept over her. 'Colm's taken Bridget.'

'No!' Riona's eyes widened. 'It can't be him. He's been gone for months, so he has. He's likely gone home to Ireland.'

'He has her.' Ellen knew with a mother's instinct. She turned to Alistair. 'Ride for Sydney. He'll be taking her back to Ireland to punish me. Check the shipping lists.'

Riona let out a wail.

'We do not know that for sure,' Alistair said, but a wounded look entered his eyes. 'She could be lost in the forests having ridden too far and not know her way back.'

'She knows to follow the river. Mr Thwaite and Douglas have

taught her how to read the position of the sun, to follow animals tracks for they lead to water…'

Alistair ran a hand through his hair. 'She is only eight years old.'

'But smart. Mr Thwaite,' Ellen called to him where he stood with Moira. 'Did you not teach Bridget when we first came here that if she got lost to stay by the river, or follow it, as it would lead to people?'

'I did, madam. Miss Bridget is clever. She would know her way home.' He looked distraught. 'I'm going to join the men in searching for her.' He strode away.

'Colm has her,' Ellen spoke quietly, her tone resolute.

'I will go to Sydney now. We must waste no more time.' He kissed Ellen. 'We will find her.' He strode for the stables.

Ellen nodded, unable to feel anything. Several minutes later, she watched him trot down the drive as a buggy came towards them. Mrs Ratcliffe drove it.

For her large size she was quickly by Ellen's side. 'My dear, I just heard the news. The entire village is talking of it and word has spread to the other villages. Men are rallying to search through the night. I spoke to Mr Riddle just now, and he has five men with him, they are heading along the Sydney Road to Bargo Brush. I don't fancy those men in that area at night.'

Frowning, Ellen stared at her.

'Bushrangers, my dear.'

She instantly thought of Eddie Patterson. Could he help her? He'd know the local ruffians who would lie low. Maybe they'd heard of Colm? But where would he be and how could she get word to him? The last time she saw him he was riding towards Goulburn and that was a two-day ride away. Would he help her anyway?

She paced along the verandah as lamps were lit and pots of tea made. A simmering rage burned in her chest at Colm. She would kill him herself for doing this. How dare he frighten

Bridget this way? She shivered with fear for her daughter's safety.

Riona came with a woollen shawl and wrapped it around Ellen's shoulders. Together they stood and watched the drive for anyone coming along with news.

As the hours dragged on, all light faded. Ellen walked the gardens, a lamp held high. Moira joined her and at times Riona and Miss Lewis. On the night air they heard the men calling Bridget's name and in the distance the pinpricks of lamp lights could be seen near the river or through the trees around the property.

'They are wasting their time,' Ellen said to Mr Thwaite when the men returned at midnight for refreshments and a short rest.

'She could have fallen and hurt herself, madam. It's worth searching everywhere in case she can't walk back home.'

'Colm has her. They'll be miles from here by now.' She felt impotent. Her daughter was out there somewhere, and Ellen couldn't reach her. She didn't have a clue where she could be and the worry and dread that Colm would successfully take her to Ireland churned her stomach. She couldn't eat the food Moira offered.

The native birds' morning chorus and the cockerel's crowing sounded before the dawn broke.

Ellen left the chair she'd been sitting in all night and stretched her aching body. As the light turned from black to grey then to a soft pink, she walked along the drive to the gates. There she stood and waited with only the birds in the trees for company.

An hour later, Riona joined her. 'I'm sorry.'

'What for?' Ellen continued to stare down the tree-lined track that led to the village, willing for her daughter to come.

'Bridget was in my care.'

'Whist now. It's not your fault. She goes riding every morning with Douglas. Even if I'd been here, she still would have been allowed to go for a ride and Colm still would have taken her.'

'Douglas is beside himself, so he is.' Riona looked down the track as Ellen did.

'They are good friends. He's been her companion since we came here.'

'He blames himself, too.'

'He shouldn't. Colm would have been waiting for the opportunity. He was likely watching us all for weeks, ever since we came back from Sydney, waiting for the opportunity to strike in some way.'

'You are certain it's him?'

'Yes.' Ellen took a deep breath of crisp morning air. 'He has her.'

Riona slipped her arm around Ellen's waist. 'Come in and rest. You'll tire yourself out and we don't want anything to happen to the baby.'

Ellen checked her step and put a hand on her stomach. 'I had forgotten all about the baby.'

'Come away inside, please. Lily has missed you. She doesn't understand what's happening but can sense something is wrong.'

Back at the house, Moira poured Ellen some tea, but she couldn't face anything to eat. Instead, she held Lily on her lap and watched her darling daughter feed herself some eggs.

The day grew older. Noon came and went with only the men returning to eat before they resumed their searching.

Once more, Ellen walked the gardens, unable to sit still. Her gaze drifted from where Lily played on a blanket with Miss Lewis down to the river in the shallow valley. Living on a hill gave her a sweep of the wide valley and the river running through it. On clear days such as today she could see across to the distant hills on the other side where the wheat farms of Moss Vale stretch for miles.

How Colm had managed to slip Bridget away, she didn't understand. Bridget had been riding Princess, so he must have encouraged her to ride with him if he had a horse. Did Colm have a horse, or was he on foot? And, if he'd taken Bridget from Princess then why hadn't the pony been seen since or returned to its stable? Had he shot the horse or tied it to a tree somewhere deep in the bush?

The thoughts whirled around in her mind until her head throbbed.

The afternoon wore on, the heat building. Ellen grew tired but couldn't sit and rest as Riona implored her to do.

Mrs Ratcliffe kept a quiet vigil with Riona, while Miss Lewis cared for Lily and Ellen paced.

At three o'clock a lone mounted policeman came riding down the drive.

Ellen rushed out to him. 'Any news?'

'None, Mrs Emmerson. I'm sorry. The entire district has been alerted. We have many men and women out searching, some children, too, who know of good hiding spots in the forests. The men at the FitzRoy Iron Works are searching the bushland around the works and we have sent word to outlying farms in all directions.'

'Thank you.'

He stroked his long dark beard, eyes kind in a weather-beaten face. 'We all pray your daughter will be found alive and well.'

'Would you care for some refreshment?'

'Thank you, but no. I'll be on my way. I'm heading for Sutton Forest to see if anything has been seen.'

'Thank you coming.' Ellen stepped back as he mounted his horse and rode away.

Riona stood behind her. 'Someone will find her.'

'Will they?' Ellen wasn't convinced. 'If Colm had fresh horses staged along the way, he'd be close to arriving in Sydney now.'

'It takes three days to get there, so it does.'

'Not on fresh horses and not stopping to sleep it doesn't.'

'He couldn't do that with Bridget. She'd not last the ride. Besides, the roads are too bad to travel fast.'

'Will he care if he damages horses? He's not coming back, is he?' Ellen returned inside. The anger at being so useless fought to consume her. She rubbed her aching neck. Her eyes were itchy with exhaustion.

'Here.' Mrs Ratcliffe joined her in the drawing room and gave her a glass of something.

'What is it?'

'Brandy. Drink it down.'

'I've not eaten.'

'What does that matter? Drink it.'

Doing as she was told. The fiery liquid burned down her throat and into her stomach. Ellen coughed.

'Now sit,' Mrs Ratcliff instructed. 'I shall have a bath prepared for you.'

'A bath?'

'Indeed. I bet it has been a week since you've had one. They do wonders for your muscles. It will relax you.'

'I don't want to relax.'

'Do you want to be useless when Bridget returns, or so weak you can't comfort her? No, you do not. A bath will revive your senses.' Mrs Ratcliffe sailed out of the room.

Within a short time, Ellen was in her bedroom, sitting in a tin bath of warm water. She drew her knees up and lent back against the bath. Her head felt heavy, and she closed her eyes.

Riona brought in another jug of hot water. 'Come now. I'll wash your hair.'

'I don't have the energy.'

'You don't need to do anything but sit there.'

In silence, Ellen sat as Riona washed the Goulburn dust from her hair. It felt wonderful to be so indulged.

A knock preceded Moira who carried a tray of food. 'Mutton stew and damper and a cup of tea, and a raspberry tartlet if you can manage it. Honor is driving me mad, I tell you. The Holy Mother wouldn't have the patience to deal with that one.'

'Thank you. What has Honor done now?' Though Ellen didn't really care.

'She believes they will take her girls next. She won't let them out of her sight and Aisling is doing nothing but crying in fright, poor lamb. I have Caroline helping me to keep her busy, but Honor won't let her out of the door to go to the vegetable garden!'

'I'll talk to Honor.' Ellen sighed, reaching for the towel.

'No, you won't,' Moira declared, walking out the door. 'I'll see to her, so I will.'

'Eat all of that food,' Riona demanded as she stood in front of the wardrobe and pulled out clean clothes for Ellen. 'Does this fit you?' She held up a green and white striped dress.

'Yes, I wore it when pregnant with Lily,' she replied, drying herself.

'I thought you did.' Riona laid it out on the bed. 'I'll leave you to dress and check on Lily. Miss Lewis is rather scared, too.'

'I suppose she never expected one of her charges to be kidnapped.' Wrapped in a dressing gown. Ellen forced herself to eat, knowing she'd need the energy.

The day seemed to drag on. The not knowing drove Ellen mad. She walked the gardens again until the men returned, fatigued and hungry.

The men sat on the grass behind the kitchen, smoking and accepting tankards of beer that Ellen insisted Mr Thwaite pour from a keg. She thanked them for their efforts and helped Moira and Honor to serve them food.

'Bridget will be all right,' Caroline said, walking beside Ellen as they returned to the kitchen for more food. 'Me or Aisling would be scared and very frightened, but Bridget won't be. She is fearless.'

Ellen stopped and looked at the pretty girl who was wise beyond her twelve years. 'I hope you are right.'

'Bridget has always been braver than me. She rides better than any girl I know and faces jumps on Princess that scare me. My da says she might be only eight years old, but she's quick and clever and feisty.' Caroline smiled sweetly. 'I wish I could be more like her.'

For the first time, the tears welled hot behind Ellen's eyes, but she blinked them away. Crying would break her. It would mean admitting defeat. She had to be strong and not crumble. 'Thank you, Caroline. You are a good girl.'

Ellen walked away, around the side of the house to the front. She took some deep breaths and then saw the rider coming down the drive.

Douglas reined in and dismounted. 'Any news, Mrs Emmerson?'

'None.'

The light died in his eyes and his shoulders slumped. 'I'm so sorry.'

'It's not your fault, Douglas.'

'I shouldn't have left her. My job was to escort her around the estate.' He took his hat off and wiped a hand over his eyes. He looked like he'd not slept either.

Ellen wanted to reassure him. 'I know my daughter, and she would have convinced you to go home.'

'She said she was just going to our beach and then she'd be right behind me.'

'Your beach?' Ellen quizzed.

'It's not a beach. It's simply a spot along the river bend where, when the water is low, a wide flat area is exposed. We call it our beach. She likes to dance along it.' His voice broke on the last sentence.

Ellen watched the emotions flit across his face. Douglas was about eighteen, a decent and hard-working lad. Yet she realised he and Bridget spent a great deal of time together. In a few years, Bridget would be growing up into a young lady. Ellen would have to curb her daughter's friendship with the groom.

'I'll go back out and search.' He gathered up the reins, his tone dejected.

'Have something to eat first. Rest the horse.'

He nodded, eyes downcast. 'I feel so helpless. Miss Bridget is like a little sister to me.'

'She'll come home, Douglas.' Ellen turned away as another rider came galloping down the drive.

The stranger jumped off his lathered horse. 'Mrs Emmerson?'

'Yes?'

He gave Ellen a note.

DARLING, *no sign of Bridget or Colm yet. I inquired of her at Bargo Brush and Myrtle Creek. Changed horses at Picton and wrote this note. Making all haste to Campbelltown. Much love, Alistair.*

ELLEN CLOSED HER EYES.

'Mrs Emmerson?' Douglas asked in hope.

'No news.' She scrunched up the piece of paper. 'Take this young man to the kitchen, Douglas. You both need a rest.'

* * *

BY THE EVENING of the third day, Ellen could no longer stay in the house. She had Douglas harness Betsy to the buggy.

'Where are you going?' Riona asked, holding Lily in her arms as she entered Ellen's bedroom.

Ellen pinned on her straw hat. 'I can't stay here another minute. I need to get out and do something.'

'You can't leave. What if we hear word, or she comes back?'

'I won't be gone long. Just an hour or so. I'll drive into the village or go into Mittagong.' Ellen kissed Lily's soft cheek. 'I need a change. I'm trapped in the house.'

'I'd rather you stayed. You've not been sleeping hardly at all. It's not safe for you to drive a buggy when you're exhausted.'

'I'll be fine.' In the hall, Ellen glanced at the platter full of calling cards and notes from neighbours and friends who sent their best wishes or offered to help search.

'Take Douglas with you then,' Riona said.

'Where's Mr Thwaite?'

'He's still out with the morning group. They'll be back soon.'

'I doubt he's slept in days,' Ellen murmured, slipping on her gloves.

'Nor have you!'

'Riona I can't sit around for another day.' She strode outside into the warm sunshine. 'I shan't be long.'

As she lifted her skirts to climb up into the seat, her head swam. Her vision blurred, everything became fuzzy. She felt herself falling.

'Ellen!'

When she woke, she was on the drive, the gravel biting into her cheek. She blinked to clear her mind. Voices filled her ears, and she raised her head as a dozen shoes came into her vision.

'Help her up. Carefully.' Riona was kneeling beside her, Lily sitting on the drive behind her.

Douglas and Mr Thwaite took an arm each and eased her up to her feet. Slowly they walked her back inside into the drawing room. Miss Lewis picked up Lily and ran for Moira.

'I'm fine.' Ellen gratefully sat on the sofa.

'Fine!' Riona barked. 'You fainted. Are you hurt?'

'No.' She didn't feel any pain, just a soreness on her cheek.

'Shall I fetch the doctor?' Mr Thwaite asked.

'No.' Ellen held her hand up. 'I don't need a doctor.'

'But it's bed you're going to and no arguments.' Riona turned and whispered something to Mr Thwaite, and next Ellen knew she was gathered up in his strong arms and carried to bed.

Flushing slightly at the intimacy, Mr Thwaite hurried out of the bedroom.

Riona pulled off Ellen's shoes, gloves and unpinned her hat. 'If you leave this bed, I'll not be responsible for my actions, so I won't. I can't have you to worry about as well. Promise me you'll have a nap.'

Ellen nodded and settled into the pillows. Weariness overwhelmed her, and she closed her eyes. She'd have a short nap and then go into the village. Just a small nap...

Something woke her, dragging her from a deep sleep. Sluggish, Ellen moved her head, slowly opening her eyes. The bedroom was in darkness, the curtains drawn, and a blanket thrown over her.

She needed the pot desperately. Drowsy, she relieved herself, then climbed into bed, curling up on her side. She could sleep for a week.

A small sound snapped her eyes wide. She listened for it. Was it a door opening? Lily crying?

The curtains moved, broke apart. A shadow stood framed in the French doors.

Ellen jerked up. The man flung himself onto the bed, grabbing her.

His hand over her mouth, he dragged her towards him. 'Don't scream. I'll not hurt you.'

In the darkness she couldn't see his face, but his accent was Irish. Colm?

Shaking, Ellen nodded.

He gradually lifted his hand from her mouth. Fumbling, he lit the lamp beside the bed, flooding the room in a weak golden light.

Ellen stared. Not Colm.

Eddie Patterson yanked down his red handkerchief from his face. 'You know who I am?'

'Yes,' she whispered, staring into a face she often wondered about, not that she could see much with his long beard covering most of it.

His gaze held hers. 'I want you to come with me,' he murmured.

She scuttled backwards on the bed. 'No!'

'Quiet!' he whispered harshly. 'Holy Virgin Mother. I'm not abducting you, woman.' He crept to the French doors. 'Hurry now.' He slipped outside without waiting for her.

After a moment's hesitation, Ellen left the bed. Grabbing her shawl, and wrapping it about her shoulders, she pulled on her boots and followed him out onto the verandah.

He held a finger to his lips and then pulled the handkerchief up over his face.

In the pale moonlight, Ellen followed him across the gardens and into the fields beyond. Clouds covered the moon, and he slowed his pace so she could keep up with him.

A thin boundary of trees separated the property from the neighbouring one. Here, Patterson had tied up his horse.

He mounted in a swift movement then put out his hand for Ellen. 'Be quick now.'

She hesitated.

'God in heaven, woman, hurry! Put your foot in the stirrup.'

Impulsively, she gripped his hand, and he pulled her up into the saddle with him. His horse protested for a moment, skipping sideways and Ellen thought she'd fall, but Patterson held her tight about the waist and clicked his tongue for the horse to walk on.

They rode around the edge of the village, heading southwards. After crossing the bridge over the Wingecarribee River, he spurred the horse on, and they cleared the surrounding farms and merged into thick scrub and bushland.

Ellen held onto the saddle. The rocking of the ride jarred her teeth and bones. She had lost her mind. She must have done to be riding in the middle of the night with a wanted bushranger.

When Patterson slowed the horse, Ellen focused a little more.

The moon broke free from the clouds, lighting the way a little. They crossed a shallow creek and eased into a thick strand of trees.

The smell of smoke reached her before she saw the red glow of a campfire. Logs had been rolled close to the fire and the roasted remnants of a small kangaroo lay about while nearby saddles and other equipment littered the ground. A horse snorted from the shadows. They were not alone.

Dismounting, Patterson helped her down and led her to the fire and waved for her to sit. 'Wait here.'

The enormity of what she'd done began to sink in and her hands shook. What a fool she was. What had possessed her to do this? She was in the bush with wanted men. Yet, something, some instinct, told her she'd be all right. That coming here was the correct thing to do.

Scuffling from behind her made her spin around on the log. In utter amazement, she stared as Bridget ran to her, thumping into her arms nearly knocking them both onto their backs.

'Bridget! Darling.' Ellen kissed her head, holding her tight. 'Sweet girl, Mammy's got you.' She leaned back to peer at her daughter's face. 'Are you hurt?'

Bridget, tears running down her dirty cheeks shook her head and then cuddled up onto Ellen's lap, her face buried in Ellen's shoulder.

Over her head, Ellen watched Patterson drag Colm from the trees, his hands tied in front of him. A hatred so fierce constricted Ellen's chest. She stood, pushing Bridget behind her. 'You! I knew it was you! You evil *swine!*'

Gagged, Colm gabbled a sound. In the flickering shadows, Ellen noticed the bruises on his face and was glad.

'He's your girl's uncle?' Patterson asked, pulling down his handkerchief.

'Yes. He came to steal my boys away back to Ireland but when he couldn't get to them, he took my daughter instead.'

'Filth.' Patterson spat.

Ellen glared at Colm. 'I'll see you hang for this. Prison will be too good for you. Do you know what you've put me through?'

Colm gabbled and raised his hands as though begging.

She glanced at Patterson. 'How did you know Bridget was my daughter?'

'Holy Mother, I didn't, not at first. We'd heard a little girl was lost when we stopped north of Marulan. We have friends there who had been into town and heard the report from a mounted policeman. We felt it was time to move on if there were people out searching. We didn't want to be found, too. Anyway, not long after we were on the road, we met *him*, so we did. I saw him resting his horses with the girl near a creek. When we got talking, he seemed a little vague. He told us he was heading to the goldfields. But I thought it a long way to travel by road with a youngster in tow. Most go by boat, so they do. Journeying across country to the goldfields would take him weeks, that's if he survived and didn't get lost. Then I remembered the report of a missing girl. I asked the wee one her name and when she said Bridget Kittrick-Emmerson, he,' Patterson jabbed Colm in the shoulder, 'jumped in and said she was his niece, Bridget Kittrick. He acted shifty. I suspected something was wrong.'

Ellen marched up to Colm and ripped the gag down his chin. 'Goldfields? Really? You were going back to Ireland via Melbourne? You were risking my daughter's life for your revenge!'

'I wanted you to pay for all you've done to me.'

'I've done *nothing* to you!'

'You've been a thorn in my backside for years. Malachy died because of you. Then you take my family away. Sure, and didn't your bloody husband shoot me in the arm. I nearly died!'

'I wished you had! You are insane. Malachy died by his own reckless actions, and I took my children away from hunger and death. Stop blaming me for your own pathetic life.'

'Bitch!' Colm spat in Ellen's face.

She recoiled, shocked.

Patterson punched Colm in the side of the head, and he fell sideways, wriggling like a worm on a hook.

Patterson stood over him, his expression one of hate. 'Touch her again and I swear by all that's holy I'll shoot you dead.'

'Bastard,' Colm mumbled.

Patterson rubbed his knuckles and came to Ellen's side. 'Are you all right?'

She nodded, aware of Bridget watching the scene. 'Thank you. Though the words seem pitiful after you have saved my daughter. We've been searching for days. I thought he'd take her on the first ship out of Sydney.'

'He was counting on that. You would have all believed him long gone by then and given up searching and he'd been able to move around in Melbourne freely, that's if he'd made it there. Stupid fool doesn't understand how far away it is.' Patterson stared down at Colm. 'What do you want me to do with him?'

Before she could answer, Bridget came to her and placed her hand in hers. 'He won't come and take me again, will he, Mammy?'

Bridget's frightened words jolted Ellen. Her daughter had always been full of spirit, hardly ever frightened and acted older than her age. But those words said in such a small voice twisted Ellen's heart in agony. Colm would always be a shadow, wanting to tear apart her family.

In an instant, she turned her back on Colm, and looked up at Patterson. 'Do whatever you want with him.'

Eddie Patterson's gaze didn't waver. 'He's seen my face… You know what that means?'

A chill ran through her, but she nodded.

Patterson whistled and from the darkness of the trees, two men emerged and dragged Colm away into the blackness.

Colm fought like a demented animal. 'Ellen! Ellen! Stop them! Holy Mother of Christ. Ellen!' he yelled until he was muffled.

'Come, I'll take you both home.' Patterson let out a deep breath.

'No, you'll be putting yourself in danger.' Ellen glanced down at Bridget. 'Where's Princess?'

'Tied up with our horses,' Patterson replied for her.

'We'll take Princess and leave you.'

'Let me walk you out of the bush to the road.'

Patterson soon had Bridget on the back of Princess, and he led them out of the trees and through the scrubland to the dirt road. 'Head north. It'll take you to Berrima.'

'How do I thank you?'

'You don't tell the police about me.' His direct stare unnerved her but not in an intimidating way. He captivated her, this man of the bush.

'I'll not tell a soul,' she promised. 'I'll explain that strangers found Bridget. Colm was gone. He'd left her…'

'And will your daughter say the same?'

'I'll tell no one, mister,' Bridget declared, sounding more like her old self. She peered at Patterson. 'You saved me, but I don't know your name.'

Patterson grinned in the moonlight. 'Your mammy will tell you when you're older.'

Ellen took a few steps with Patterson away from her daughter's hearing. 'I will never betray you. That is my solemn promise.'

'Thank you, Ellen.'

'Tell me, did you know it was me when we passed on the road near Goulburn a week ago?'

'Aye. How could I not? You've a face not many a man would forget. It's the beautiful face I've dreamed about a few times now, so I have.'

She was glad the semi darkness hid her blushing. 'That property north of Goulburn, Miller's Farm. I own it now. It's called Louisburgh, after the village where I grew up. You'll always be welcome there to rest.'

In the silver moon shadow, he smiled and took her hand. 'As a wanted man I doubt I'll be long on this earth, sweet Ellen, but I thank you.'

He walked back into the trees and disappeared.

Ellen dragged in a deep breath, then turned and took Princess's reins. She kissed Bridget's cheek. 'Let's go home, darling.'

CHAPTER 8

$\mathcal{I}$n the stifling January heat of summer, Ellen placed a damp handkerchief on the back of her neck to cool herself. No breeze could be felt in the valley, but earlier she had paddled in the shallows of the river and enjoyed the freshness of the water.

Tiredness, not only from the heat, but the party last night celebrating the new year of eighteen fifty-four made her lethargic. She was grateful that Alistair was up at the house dealing with estate concerns with Mr Thwaite for she didn't have the energy today to deal with ledgers and bills.

Resting in the afternoon sunshine, she watched Bridget splashing in the shallows with Caroline and Aisling with Miss Lewis supervising, while Riona, skirts tucked up, dangled Lily's feet in the water making the baby squeal.

'Can I pour you another drink, Ellen?' Mrs Ratcliffe asked, sitting on a chair beside Ellen under a large tarpaulin that Mr Thwaite and Seamus Duffy had erected for them. On the blanket in front, Honor Duffy and Moira set out a picnic.

'If I have any more to drink, Mrs Ratcliffe, I'll never make it back up the hill to the house. This baby is pressing on my bladder enough as it is.'

'Oh yes, you're in a delicate state. I keep forgetting as you are not showing hardly any signs of the impending offspring. When is it due again?'

'April. Three months to go.'

'You're not at all big. Some women are the size of cows, huge.'

'I feel enormous!' She grinned, but in truth she was carrying this baby differently than the others. Lily had been small, but Ellen feared this baby had hardly grown such was her tiny stomach.

'She's not very big because she's never still.' Moira tutted. 'Up and down the road to Goulburn she is.'

Mrs Ratcliffe, who'd been away for a few months in Sydney, gave Ellen a frown. 'You've been spending a lot of money I hear on the Goulburn property.'

Ellen grinned. 'Nothing gets past you, does it? Even when you've not been in the district for months.'

'I have eyes and ears everywhere, my dear.' The chair creaked with Mrs Ratcliffe's weight as she moved to pour another cup of tea from the small table by her side.

'Louisburgh needs a lot of work to fully capitalise on its potential.'

'Hark at you!' Mrs Ratcliffe laughed. 'You sound like a businessman.'

'I'm a *businesswoman*.'

'Indeed.' Mrs Ratcliffe took a sip of tea. 'I'm considering journeying to London.'

Ellen's eyes widened at the sudden declaration. 'London? Why?'

'I have a cousin there. Percy. A dull fellow, to be certain. His letters bore me and only deserve reading just the once. However, I have recently learned he is dying. Poor man. And for reasons I have yet to understand, he is asking me to travel to London to help him put his affairs in order. He has no one else, you see, and doesn't trust friends to do it.'

'What a sad task for you.'

'Indeed.' Mrs Ratcliffe sniffed. 'I am, of course, going to do it. Though the idea of three months at sea and then living in London for several months and then the journey back here is rather tedious.' She sighed heavily. 'I was hoping that perhaps you would come with me, but I realise that it isn't possible with the baby. I'd take Bridget and Miss Lewis, but I fear that would make you pine for her, especially after what her uncle did.'

Ellen pondered on the concept of going to England. To go to London would mean seeing the boys and how her heart ached to do that, but she was just three months from having a baby. 'If I wasn't with child, I would take you up on that, but I can't risk giving birth at sea. Alistair has promised to take us all once the baby is over a year old and less vulnerable.'

'There's no select age to fall ill, Ellen.'

'No but travelling with a tiny infant is a challenge and one I don't wish to embark on, despite my longing to see my boys.' How she would enjoy spending time with Austin and Patrick, but it would also mean seeing Rafe and she didn't believe her heart could take seeing him again only to say goodbye once more.

'Well, I thought as such. Never mind. I will call on your boys at their school and see them in person if you wish?'

'You would?' Ellen grasped Mrs Ratcliffe's hand. 'What a true friend you are.'

'I do have a favour to ask, however.'

'Oh?'

'I wish for you to oversee my properties while I'm gone. It's nothing too strenuous, mainly I need you to make sure the man, Sampson, I have put in charge has someone to answer to. He's trustworthy, but it is wise to have him realise that he has you watching over him. He can send his reports to you each month and you can correspond with him on any concerns.'

'I'm honoured that you've asked me. I will help in any way I can.'

'Thank you.' Mrs Ratcliffe dabbed her hot face with a handkerchief.

'When do you leave?'

'Next week on the eighth. I managed to get a cabin on a ship at short notice.'

'That is soon. Even if I wanted to go, I'd never be ready in time.'

'Completely understand. I'm rushing the preparations myself. I anticipate my cousin wishes me with him as soon as possible.'

'It's my birthday tomorrow. Will you come for dinner?' Ellen waved a fan in front of her face to cool herself.

'No, my dear, thank you all the same. I need to pack and sort out my affairs both here and in Sydney. I leave for Sydney in two days' time, and I'll call to say goodbye then.'

'Mama, watch me!' Bridget called from the middle of the river, where she began swimming back towards the bank.

Ellen waved to cheer her on, knowing the current was weak in the summer and the middle not so deep.

'She seems to have overcome her traumatic experience?' Mrs Ratcliffe asked, accepting a plate of sandwiches from Honor.

'Yes. Rather quickly she behaved as though nothing had happened. For a week she stayed by my side or Riona's and didn't want to go riding or play with Caroline and Aisling, but gradually she realised that there was nothing to be worried about and became her normal self again, which was a relief to us all.' Ellen watched Bridget swim confidently in the water.

Her daughter had promised not to mention Patterson, and she hadn't said a word about him, even when the police asked her numerous questions. She'd told them Colm had left her on the side of the road and she'd rode back to Berrima in the night. Ellen had told everyone that she'd been walking in the garden at night unable to sleep, and found Bridget on the driveway.

Everyone believed their story and praised Bridget for being so brave. Alistair had sent newspaper reporters off the property when they wanted to interview Bridget and thankfully the excitement calmed down as Christmas approached.

Looking at her now, Ellen wondered what went through her eldest daughter's mind about the episode. Bridget had returned to acting older than she was and under Miss Lewis's guidance was learning and studying well, despite her temper remaining the one thing no one could control. Once again, Bridget called Ellen Mama and not Mammy as she had done when frightened in the bush. Ellen knew her eldest daughter was always going to be a person who surprised her.

'Children adapt more quickly than adults,' Mrs Ratcliffe murmured. 'She'll be a beauty when she's older, Ellen. You'll have to watch out for her. Gentlemen will never be off your doorstep.'

They all clapped as Bridget successfully swam to the bank and climbed out and challenged Caroline and Aisling to a swimming race, which they both hurriedly declined.

'I think it'll be the men who will have to watch out for her, not me. She'll terrorise them!' Ellen chuckled.

Mrs Ratcliffe laughed as Alistair joined them for the picnic.

While Alistair chatted to Mrs Ratcliffe, Honor called to Caroline and Aisling and ushered them back up the hill to the house, ignoring their protests that they wanted to stay with Bridget and enjoy the picnic.

'What's wrong with Honor?' Ellen asked Moira.

'What's ever right with the woman?' Moira sighed, waving flies away from the food. 'She's as sour as three-day-old milk that one.'

'Well, she's always off with me, but lately Riona tells me she's barely talking to anyone. For the last week she's kept Caroline and Aisling from taking their lessons with Miss Lewis as well.'

'Who can understand that woman's mind? She's a torment to

134

herself, so she is. How Seamus puts up with her I don't know, poor eejit that he is.'

'I'll talk to her later.'

Moira gave her a side-glance as she poured out lemon cordial into glasses for everyone. 'She'll not tell you anything. As closed as a clam she is.'

Later, after Mrs Ratcliffe had left and Mis Lewis and Riona were giving the girls their supper, Ellen walked to the Duffys' hut and knocked on the door.

Honor came out to her, wiping her hands on a cloth. 'Am I needed in the house?'

'No, not at all. I simply wanted to talk to you.'

'Have I done something wrong?' Honor was instantly defensive.

'No.' Ellen's shoulders sagged, knowing how prickly this woman was she doubted their talk would be enjoyable. 'I've come to ask why you aren't letting your girls have their lessons with Miss Lewis.'

'My girls are from simple folk. They don't need to be educated by a governess.'

'Why? It is for their own benefit.' Ellen strove for patience. This same old argument was taxing.

Honor's dull grey eyes narrowed. 'How can it be?' She swept her arm backwards encasing the hut. 'This is where they live. Not over there.' She pointed to the house. 'My girls aren't the same as yours and to teach them otherwise will only cause problems when they are older.'

'I don't believe so.'

Folding her arms, Honor's expression twisted. 'You don't think it'll harm my girls when they see Bridget and Lily marrying some posh gents, the same gents who will look down their noses at my girls? Bridget and Lily will have the Emmerson name and money. They will be raised as ladies to fit into a society that shuns my girls.'

Ellen sighed. 'I understand, I do. I've faced the same hostility myself by not being good enough to join the elite society of Sydney.'

'Then I don't have to explain myself, do I?' Honor defended.

'No, but the girls could still be educated. Caroline talks of being a governess like Miss Lewis. Do you want her to achieve a grand position such as that or to work as a skivvy all her life?'

'Aye, course I want her to find a grand position.'

'Then she needs an excellent education. Miss Lewis can give her that.'

Honor rubbed her hands over her face. 'You don't understand. Seeing them with Miss Lewis as she teaches them to be ladies fills me with dread, because within an hour of them having piano and dancing lessons, they are helping me and Moira in the kitchen scrubbing pots. I don't want them feeling worthless or second best to your girls, so I don't.'

'No one wants that,' Ellen agreed. 'It can be difficult for your girls seeing Bridget and Lily have the things you and Seamus can't give them, but at least let them have an education so they can gain positions which will give them a better life than we had growing up. This is a different country, a new start for us all, Honor. You came here so that your girls would have a future, let them have it by allowing them to be educated to a standard that will give them a good chance for being happy. That's all we want, don't we?'

'Oh aye, sure and I want my girls to grow up and be so clever that they are ashamed of their mammy who can barely read or write!'

'They would never be ashamed of you. They love you, but they might not thank you if you stop them from learning, especially if it helps them find decent positions when they are older. Do you want them to be scrubbing pots all their lives? Or is it more important that they aren't smarter than you?'

'This isn't about me!'

'Isn't it?'

The silence stretched between them for several moments.

Wringing the cloth between her hands, Honor finally spoke. 'Very well. They can have lessons with Miss Lewis.'

'You've made the right decision.' For Caroline and Aisling's sake Ellen was relieved.

'Have I? I suppose that'll remain to be seen in the years to come.' Honor walked back inside and slammed the door.

* * *

'HAPPY BIRTHDAY, MAMA,' Bridget crowed, coming into Ellen's bedroom to wake her up. She carried Lily who smiled showing her little teeth.

'Thank you, my darling.' Ellen sat up and kissed them both.

'Moira is making you a special breakfast.' Bridget dumped Lily on Ellen's lap. 'I have to go and help. Papa is out picking flowers for you.' She slapped a hand over her mouth. 'That was meant to be a surprise.'

'I'll act surprised.' Ellen grinned, kissing Lily's cheeks and tickling her stomach.

Left alone, Ellen rose and dressed as Lily stumbled around the bedroom learning to walk with the aid of the furniture.

She chose a pink and cream striped dress with cream lace at the throat and cuffs. She brushed out her hair and rolled it, holding it in place with combs.

'You're up!' Alistair came into the bedroom. He gathered Lily into his arms. 'Happy birthday, my dearest.'

'Thank you.' She accepted his kiss. 'I'm hungry!'

'Breakfast awaits. How does it feel to be thirty-one?'

'The same as thirty, thankfully!'

In the dining room, flowers adorned every surface in various vases and jugs. It looked like a flower garden brought inside.

'Oh, it looks incredible.' Ellen gasped, the scent of roses and other flowers filled the room.

'I don't think you have any flowers left in the gardens though. Riona and I went a bit mad,' Alistair confessed. 'Mr Fenton says it'll be fine and encourage new buds so do not worry.'

'Thank you.' Her smile encompassed Riona and Bridget as well.

'What shall we do today? Your choice naturally.' Alistair filled her plate with bacon and eggs and then his own.

'I'm not sure. It's already hot,' Ellen replied, spooning boiled eggs into Lily's mouth.

'A swim!' Bridget suggested from the sideboard where she filled her plate.

'You swam yesterday,' Riona reminded her, pouring a cup of tea. 'It's not your choice.'

Ellen greeted Miss Lewis who was last at the table.

'Many happy returns of the day, Mrs Emmerson,' Miss Lewis said, taking a seat next to Lily's highchair.

'Well,' Alistair prompted, 'what do you wish to do?'

Before Ellen could answer, Moira sailed in with a bunch of wildflowers. 'This is from Mr Thwaite, Ellen.'

'Oh, that is lovely of him.'

'He respects you greatly,' Alistair said.

'He's gone into the village to collect any mail from the morning coach when it arrives,' Moira told them as she tidied the sideboard of empty plates.

Ellen ate some of her breakfast. 'Perhaps we could walk along the river this morning and later.' She glanced at Alistair. 'I'd like to go Louisburgh.'

'Pardon? Louisburgh?' He frowned. 'You are becoming obsessed with that property.'

'I want to see the improvements on it. I've not visited for a month.' The Goulburn property had soon become her favourite place to be despite lacking the refinements of Emmerson Park. It was raw and unsophisticated, missing the basic comforts, and yet she adored being there.

Perhaps it was the lack of any society nearby. The Goulburn settlement was an hour's ride away from Louisburgh. She knew no one in Goulburn and didn't plan to. She liked the space and the freedom of the wide-open plains. Louisburgh was hers. Alistair hadn't been too impressed with it and since the purchase, he'd left everything to her to oversee. He thought the sheep station would always be run by managers and only be somewhere they visited once a year or so. Ellen didn't agree. In her mind, she would eventually live there permanently. One day, Emmerson Park would be handed over to Austin, or one of the children, and she would go to Louisburgh and live out her days in peace and tranquillity.

'Can I go to, Mama?' Bridget asked, chewing on her toast. 'I can ride Princess.'

Ellen smiled. 'We shall all go. The entire family. Lily and Miss Lewis, Riona, Moira, too, if she wishes.'

'Me?' Riona asked her cup midway to her lips. 'Why?'

'I want you to see it. I want you all to see it.'

'We'd have to sleep in tents, Ellen.' Alistair looked none too pleased. 'The hut there is too small. It's nothing but a stockman's hut.'

'Then we'll take a wagon of tents and bedding and supplies. We'll stay for a couple of weeks.'

Bridget clapped excitedly. 'When can we leave?'

'Tomorrow,' Ellen decided, just as thrilled as her daughter. 'We'll spend today packing and organising what we need. I'll ride over to Mrs Ratcliffe and say goodbye to her.'

'I hadn't expected this, Ellen.' Alistair's scowl annoyed her.

'A family adventure will be fun.' Ellen finished her breakfast and made to rise. 'I'll go and see if Mr Thwaite has come back from the village. He'll know what we need.'

'Do you not want your present from me?' Alistair asked, pushing away his plate, halting her.

'That would be lovely.' Ellen regained her seat, forcing herself to smile when knowing she had irritated Alistair.

From a drawer in a small table at the end of the room, he took out a little box and brought it back to Ellen. 'I hope you like it.'

Ellen opened the black box and inside, laid on a purple velvet cushion, sat a gold and diamond bracelet. 'It's beautiful.'

'I was informed that jewellery is not only a way to a woman's heart but a very good investment.' Alistair laughed.

The statement made Ellen cringe. An investment? Her birthday present was an investment. Was he planning to sell it one day when its value increased? Was it only on loan to her?

'Put it on, Mama.' Bridget gently touched the bracelet.

'No, not yet. I can't wear it during the day as I might lose it. It's to be worn at special dinner parties or the theatre.'

'Lord above, do not lose it.' Alistair thought it a joke, but Ellen closed the lid and rose. 'I shall put it away.'

'No, give it to me, dearest.' Alistair held out his hand. 'I shall lock it in the cash vault.'

Ellen gave him the box happily. As beautiful as the bracelet was, she knew she'd barely wear it. It was a showpiece. Something to be worn at the theatre or a ball. Neither of which she attended, unless in Sydney.

'Shall we walk down by the river until Mr Thwaite returns?' Ellen asked. 'Then we'll pack.'

Riona nodded, her gaze wary as she glanced at Ellen.

'Shall I stay with Lily, Mrs Emmerson?' Miss Lewis offered. 'She'll only want to get down all the time and try to walk and it's too rough for the perambulator.'

'Thank you, Miss Lewis. She does want to try and walk everywhere now.'

'I'll sit with her under the tree on the other side of the orchard.'

For a time, Ellen and Riona strolled in silence as Bridget ran along the riverbank, collecting wildflowers and inspecting butterflies and dragonflies.

'Alistair wanted to go to Sydney in a few days' time,' Riona said, bending down to snap a tall blade of grass. She twirled it in her fingers. 'You know he doesn't like to be away for too long.'

'Then I'll suggest he not come to Louisburgh but go to Sydney.'

'I fail to see what the draw is to that farm when you have the most comfortable home here.'

Ellen paused as a small flock of red and blue rosellas swooped down from the sky and landed in the grass on the other side of the river. 'Those birds are so beautiful.'

'They are. Bridget wants one in a cage, but I told her they are wild birds, and would she want to be free one day and then caged forever the next?' Riona smiled softly. 'You can imagine her answer.'

'She'll not be tamed that one.'

'No.' Riona looked at her. 'You haven't answered my question.'

Ellen hooked her arm through Riona's. 'In many ways, Louisburgh is more my home than here. Louisburgh is mine to do with as I wish.'

'I thought you felt that here?'

'I do, of course I do, but it was always Alistair's property. This place is paradise after Ireland and even Sydney. Yet, Louisburgh feels... as though it is mine. It's the land I always dreamed about on the ship coming here. The land is what I wanted for us all.'

'Look around you, Ellen. You live on five hundred acres. You have land.'

'This is Alistair's property. It was granted to *him*. *He* designed the house to build on it.'

'And you're his wife.'

'You don't understand. I wanted my own land.'

'No, you're right. I don't understand you at all.'

'Louisburgh is mine. It was my decision to buy it and Alistair doesn't care for it.'

'One day you have to stop with this obsession about land.' Riona glanced back up the hill. 'Moira is waving the red scarf.'

'Let's go back. Bridget,' Ellen called, pointing to the red scarf, which was the signal that you were wanted at the house.

Once at the top of the hill and walking through the gardens towards the house, Moira excitedly ran to them. 'The post. Mr Thwaite has returned with the post. I've made tea.'

'Why are you so thrilled about the mail arriving?' Riona laughed at Moira.

'You'll see!'

Ellen's heart flipped, and she gripped Moira's arm. 'Letters from the boys?'

Moira nodded, nearly hopping from foot to foot such was her happiness. 'Go, quickly. I want to hear all their news.'

Ellen gathered up her skirts and dashed into the house with Riona and Bridget behind her. She hurried into the study where Alistair sat at the desk, sorting through a large pile of letters.

He looked up. 'Well, your birthday has suddenly become brighter for you, hasn't it?' He handed her a thick pile of letters.

Ellen wondered if her heart would simply burst. She clutched the letters to her chest as Alistair gave Riona several letters as well.

'Don't I get any letters?' Bridget whined.

'I'm sure the boys mention you in their letters, poppet.' Alistair smiled. 'I've received a letter from Rafe,' he told Ellen. 'My father writes as well. I shall share the contents with you once I have read them.'

Ellen nodded and spun away, wanting somewhere private to read in peace. She walked outside and sat on the verandah, the letters in her lap. She flipped through them and then saw an envelope she knew to be from Rafe. A shiver of longing rippled through her. She couldn't sit here and read his words. She didn't want to be disturbed and she could hear Bridget through the open windows asking Riona to read the letters out loud.

The baby kicked as Ellen strode across the lawn and back down the hill towards the river. Once on the bank, she sat on the grass and opened the envelope. Three pieces of paper fell out. Scanning them, she saw one each from Rafe, Austin and Patrick. She read Rafe's first.

MY ELLEN,

I cannot describe to you the utter surprise and joy at seeing the boys when they arrived in Liverpool today. Hearing their story, I suddenly knew you would be bereft. Please take comfort in the fact that they are in good health and in my care.

A sob broke from her. Until she had proof, she'd been suspended in a heartbroken state that her boys would come to some harm on the journey. It was a fear she couldn't share with anyone but to know they were safe with Rafe gave her some relief.

You will see that they have written to you, which no doubt will give you much joy.

Please be reassured that I will care for them as though they are my own sons, and as they are yours, I will love them as such.

I am in a hurry to post this letter with those the boys have written, so it reaches you as quickly as possible to put your mind and heart at rest. I understand you will feel pain at not being with them and they are so far away from you, but they will always be my first priority. I would never give you reason to believe they are not wanted by me.

Alistair wishes for them to be enrolled in his old school, and I will undertake that responsibility. However, they will be with me in the holidays, so please do not despair of them being without guidance and caring for I will treat them as my own.

I once promised to never write to you again, but this occasion was too important for such a promise to be upheld. I simply had to write to you and put your mind at ease.

How I wish you had been on the ship with them. I still love you desperately.

With my fondest and most sincere love and devotion,

Rafe.

Liverpool.

October 1853.

Ellen closed her eyes and kissed the letter as tears dropped over her lashes. Her heart ached with love for a man she would never meet again. How was she to bear it?

Focusing, pushing that pain aside, she picked up Austin's letter.

DEAR MAMA,

We have safely arrived in Liverpool and are with Mr Hamilton at his house. We are soon walking to the post office to post all our letters we wrote on board the ship.

I am very sorry not to have been able to say goodbye to you, but I am not unhappy to be going to Harrow as I will learn a lot there and make you proud of me. Mr Hamilton says we will be with him every holiday and also we shall visit Papa's parents, too. I am excited to be attending an English school and be educated as a gentleman like Papa and Mr Hamilton.

I have taken care of Patrick for the entire voyage as he was very sad and I will look after him at school, too.

Give my love to all,

Your son,

Austin Emmerson.

P.S. Before we sailed Papa told me to go by the name of Emmerson, which I will do so. I would rather take that name than my own father's who I am not proud of.

. . .

THE LAST LINE made her jerk. Austin felt that way about his father? Austin had never told her that. He'd rather be an Emmerson? She felt hurt on behalf of Malachy. True, at the end, through the struggle of the blight and crop failures for several years, Malachy had been a changed man. In the last few years of his life, he'd not done enough to care for his family through the famine and devastation. Yet, for all that, Malachy had loved his children and no man could have been prouder when Austin was born. It saddened her that his eldest son drew no comfort from being a Kittrick. In fact, the name shamed him, and Colm had done more damage.

She unfolded Patrick's letter.

Dear Mammy.

I want to come home. I miss you and everyone. Can you send for me please?

Your son, Patrick Kittrick. I do not want to be called Emmerson but Austin says I must.

Her heart broke anew for her second son. Tears flowed freely as she stared at his simple note. He was missing home, and she couldn't hug him and keep him with her as she so desperately wanted to. Patrick was so different to Austin. Patrick was softer, gentler than his older brother. He enjoyed a simpler way of life. Patrick didn't want the attention like Bridget, and he wasn't a high achiever like Austin. She prayed he'd be all right at boarding school. She had a feeling he would hate it whereas Austin would excel.

She spent the next hour reading their letters from when they were on the ship. Smiling at the antics Austin described and swallowing back her sorrow at the pain of Patrick's homesick letters. Austin thrived under the supervision of Captain Leonards, filling the pages with details of what Captain Leonards did and why, and that the captain gave Austin lessons on navigation and the running of a ship. Patrick did a few drawings of the seamen and parts of the ship and Ellen noticed he had a raw talent with sketches. She hoped he could develop that while at school for it seemed to be something he enjoyed doing.

Eventually, once she'd read all the letters, she strolled back up to the house and gave the bundle to Alistair, Riona and Bridget to read, keeping Rafe's note tucked into the inside of her bodice.

Then she went to find Lily. Miss Lewis was in the girl's bedroom, changing Lily's napkin.

'I hear you have received happy news, Mrs Emmerson?' Miss Lewis said, passing Lily over to Ellen.

'Yes, my dear boys are safe in England.' Ellen held Lily close. The sweet feel of Lily's baby arms encircling her neck brought fresh tears to burn behind her eyes. 'I shall take over for a while before I visit Mrs Ratcliffe,' she told Miss Lewis, and sat in the rocking chair by the window.

Left alone, Ellen hummed the Irish tunes her own mammy once hummed as Lily snuggled into her. Crying softly, Ellen rocked Lily to sleep, wishing Rafe could hold his daughter that looked so much like him and wishing her beloved sons were home.

CHAPTER 9

*E*llen flicked the reins to slow Betsy down as they turned into the track that would lead them a mile to the hut. 'We're on Louisburgh land now.' She beamed at Riona and Miss Lewis, who held Lily.

Beside them rode Bridget, Alistair and Mr Thwaite and Douglas. They'd travelled that morning from Marulan after staying the night at an inn.

'It's very barren. The only trees are those lining the range of hills in the distance.' Riona seemed unimpressed as they drove through dry brown grassy fields.

'The hills on either side of us are pretty,' Miss Lewis said.

'I like it, Mama.' Bridget steered Princess alongside Ellen. 'I can ride for miles.'

'You can, darling, but you must always have someone with you as you don't know the area and could easily get lost.'

'That's fine. Douglas is here. He'll ride with me.'

'That girl is never off her horse,' Riona muttered. 'She gives Miss Lewis ultimatums over her lessons, you know. She'll only listen to Miss Lewis if she's promised a ride each afternoon.'

'Is that true, Miss Lewis?' Ellen asked as they neared the hut.

'I'm afraid it is, Mrs Emmerson.'

'I'll talk to her.' Ellen halted Betsy and Alistair dismounted beside the buggy to help the ladies down.

Ellen gazed around, feeling a sense of homecoming. In the few times she'd been to the property since the purchase, she'd felt a weight lift off her shoulders. Here she was simply Ellen, not Mrs Emmerson, mistress of Emmerson Park, wife of a prominent Sydney businessman, the woman who had to act a certain way, be a member of society that makes calls, receives visitors, be on charity committees, discusses menus with Moira and all the rest that was expected of her.

Louisburgh was a haven away from being social. She never wanted to invite people here.

'We'll pitch the tents,' Alistair said. 'Then Mr Thwaite and I will go find the shepherd and check the flock.'

'I wanted to check the flock, too,' Ellen told him, lifting a bag from the buggy.

'Why?'

'I want to see how well the lambs are doing and because you've made it plain that this place is of no interest to you.' She gave the bag to Riona. 'So, I'll learn how to make it profitable, and it'll not be a nuisance for you.' She stared at the hut. 'I have a great many plans, we'll have to design a house, build better stables and—'

'May I have a word in private please, dearest?' Alistair took her elbow and led her away from the others.

'What is it?'

His expression was stiff and cold. 'There will be no house here.'

She stepped back in surprise. 'What do you mean? We need a house.'

'No, we do not. This place is a sheep farm, to be run by a manager who will live in the hut and need no more than that.'

'No, Alistair. I want this to be my home.'

His lips thinned in irritation. 'You have a home. Emmerson Park is your home, the children's home, our home! Not this backwater!'

'You know I like it here,' she argued, anger building.

'What is more there is no spare money for this place until the sheep start making a profit. The sale of the wool clip paid off some of the mortgage and the sale of the lambs will pay off a little more, but there are the running costs and taxes. It was never in my plans to make this into a comfortable place. It was only ever to be somewhere to breed sheep.'

'Are you telling me we can't build a house?'

'Correct. We have no spare money for it.'

'Are we financially in trouble?'

'No...' He glanced away.

It shocked her that Alistair might be keeping something from her regarding their financial status. 'What aren't you telling me?'

'Nothing. Simply I will not spend money I can ill afford on this property.' He waved his arm around to encompass the small timber hut, the single stable, the lean-to beside it and the bareness of a non-existent garden. 'Look at it, Ellen. No one wants to live here.'

'I do. Me. I want to come here and be—'

'What? Free of your responsibilities? You have dragged us all out here for what?'

'To have some change. To be free of the commitments that rule our days. Here we can just relax and not socialise. We can ride and have picnics, read and not have to dress for dinner...'

'Everything you do now?' He was awfully still. 'You want to turn your back on your life?'

'Don't be silly, Alistair,' she fumed. 'I want somewhere to go to be myself.'

'Because being my *wife* is distasteful to you?'

'Why are you saying such things? This is not about you, Alistair. It's me. I want to be here to do as I please.'

'And you cannot do that at Emmerson Park?'

'I can, but only to a certain extent. Berrima is becoming more like Sydney where I am receiving callers every day, or I have to return calls. I'm not made for any of that.'

'But you wanted it for your children. You married me to give them a position in a society you do not care for. That's the price you have to pay,' he sneered.

'I understand that, and I will willingly play my role for the children, for you, but I would also like somewhere to go when I need to.'

'Most women would envy your position. You have homes in the city and the country, the best of everything, yet it isn't enough for you.' He sighed. 'I will never understand you.'

'I'm sorry you feel that way.'

'Tomorrow I shall ride back and head on to Sydney. Will you join me there in a week or two? I have tickets to the theatre for the beginning of February, the fifth, I think. I would like you to accompany me if possible. Afterwards, we are invited to a supper at the Gardner-Hills' house.'

Ellen flinched. She and Mrs Gardner-Hill did not get along. 'Very well. If you wish it, but I'll not stay long. A couple of weeks only. I don't want to give birth in Sydney.'

'No, God forbid it would mean you staying with me.' He turned to walk away.

'Oh, and Alistair?'

He glanced over his shoulder at her, his eyes dull and showing no interest in what she had to say. 'Yes?'

'I will find a way to make Louisburgh worthy. It might take me some years, but I will make it not only profitable, but also comfortable.'

'No doubt you will, Ellen. When you have a passion for something, you give it your all.' He spoke as though it was an insult, not praise, and Ellen bristled at him.

Alistair joined the others, but too fraught to be civil, Ellen walked the other way towards the grave of Mariah Miller.

She bent and tied the weeds growing around the base of the cross.

'Who is this?' Bridget asked, coming up behind her.

'Mrs Mariah Miller. She was the wife of the man who owned the property and who sold it to us.'

'Mariah is a pretty name.'

'It is. She had a little baby called Thomas.'

'Did he die, too?'

'No. Mr Miller has taken him to England.' Ellen stood and smiled at her daughter. 'We have to take care of Mariah's grave for him.'

'That's nice. I can help. We can plant a rose for her. We can bring one from Emmerson Park.'

'What a wonderful idea, darling. We will.'

'Is the creek deep enough to swim in like our river back home?' Bridget skipped towards the creek bank.

Ellen followed her. 'No. It's too shallow, but on hot days we can paddle.'

'I like it here, Mama.' Bridget pulled a grass stem. 'Patrick would like to ride the hills with me, I know he would.'

'And one day he will.'

'Papa says we are to go to Sydney next week. I don't want to. I will miss Princess.'

'It'll not be for long. We'll be back at Emmerson Park for your birthday.'

'Miss Lewis says Sydney is too hot in the summer.'

'That's true, but we must be with Papa when he requires us.' Ellen fought back a sigh.

'Mr Thwaite says I'm to rest Princess tomorrow, as she's been ridden a long way. What shall we do instead?'

'Your lessons with Miss Lewis?' Ellen suggested with a grin.

'That's so boring!'

'Explore on foot then?' Ellen winked.

'Can we?'

'We can. We shall go for a long walk and see all the land that we own.'

The next morning, before the sun had risen over the ranges, Alistair mounted Pepper. He'd given his farewells the previous night, but Ellen rose with him at dawn.

They'd not spoken much since their argument yesterday. In the afternoon they had gone to inspect the flock and admire the healthy lambs, praising Mr Jollis who was the shepherd.

In the evening they had sat around a campfire and chatted of many things. Riona had sung them a few Irish songs and Miss Lewis had also serenaded them with a ballad before shyness overcame her.

Alistair had slept in a tent while Ellen shared the bed in the hut with Riona and Lily. As she lay listening to the sounds of the night, Ellen had made plans in her head of the improvements she'd do to Louisburgh.

'Ride safely,' she said to Alistair, standing with her hands on her belly in the pale pink light of dawn. Native birds called their morning chorus from the trees in the hills creating a symphony of noise.

'You will be in Sydney soon?' Alistair asked, adjusting his position in the saddle.

'I will.'

He bent down to kiss her again. 'Be careful on your walks. Always take Mr Thwaite with you. And do not overdo it. Think of the baby.'

She nodded, irritated that he should have to remind her as though she was a child.

Watching him ride away, Ellen felt relief. She cared for Alistair a great deal, but there were times when they didn't see eye to eye, and she knew she failed him. He wanted a subservient wife, one to do his bidding without question, as his friends' wives did.

He'd been attracted to her independence, her intelligence and how different she was to women of his circle, but that attraction was waning. He wanted her to conform, to be like the other wives who were happy to sit and take tea, and sew or read, to attend dress fittings, make calls, go on carriage drives in the city parks. All the things that bored her senseless.

How were they to overcome it? Would the years stretch ahead of them spent apart, arguing over theatre dates and dinner invitations?

Ellen didn't think she could bear it.

'Mama, I'm hungry.' Bridget came out of the hut, rubbing sleep from her eyes.

'Well, we can't have that, can we?' Ellen hugged her to her side. 'Shall we start making breakfast for everyone?'

'Then we can go exploring?'

'We'll take a picnic up into the hills, shall we? Mr Thwaite might be able to shoot a kangaroo for our dinner.'

* * *

ELLEN FELT uncomfortable and fat in her dress of cream and blush pink. All through the evening's entertainments at the Sydney Theatre, she'd squirmed at the tightness of the bodice. The gown had become too restricting as her pregnancy advanced, but she'd arrived in Sydney later than planned, much to Alistair's annoyance, and hadn't the time to make arrangements to be fitted for a new dress at Mrs Haggerty's Salon.

Now, as she sat on a chair near the refreshment table in the Gardner-Hills' mansion after the show had finished, she was deeply aware of the straining material and of the glances given to her from the women in the room. She'd heard one mention that Ellen's skin was nearly native in colour from being outside too much, while another mentioned she'd been living rough with the stockmen and actually drove herself around the wild country.

She hid a yawn behind her hand. She was exhausted from the late night and from the dreary women's chatter.

Several of Alistair's friends had commandeered her attention the minute they arrived at the supper, wanting to know about the land near Goulburn and asked her opinion of farming there. She'd happily told them what she'd learned after spending the last few weeks at Louisburgh. She and Bridget had walked miles, exploring every part of the property. Mr Thwaite had taught Ellen to shoot a rifle, and Mr Jollis, enjoying the company, had offered to teach Ellen a great many things about sheep, lambing, shearing and breeding. The two weeks at Louisburgh had turned into three, and it had been a rush for Ellen to make it to Sydney in time for the theatre as she promised Alistair.

'Good evening, Mrs Emmerson.' Mrs Percival, one of the wives whose husband did business with Alistair, came and sat beside her. 'You must be depleted.'

'I am a little.' Ellen glanced at the Longcase clock and noticed it was gone one in the morning.

'I hear you have only just arrived in Sydney from somewhere out in the wilds of the country?'

'That's correct.' Ellen tried to be friendly even though this woman had been rude to her in the past.

'How very daunting.' The other woman's gaze roamed the ballroom as though looking for someone.

'Not really. I enjoy the open spaces of the country. The city is too confining.'

'You think so? I am the opposite, I'm afraid. The country, the little I have seen of it, frightens me to death. The dangerous beasts, the untamed and wild forests, the bushrangers... The list is endless. I refuse to leave the city.'

'How very boring for you to never leave town.'

'I begged Mr Percival to buy us a little place on the water down the coast as a place to escape the heat of summer in the city, but well, I confess I do not like the coast either and rarely go there. Mr Percival does enjoy it, however, and often travels there to do some sailing and fishing on the rivers.'

'It must be peaceful for him.' Ellen couldn't help adding the little dig.

'Indeed. Oh, there is Mrs Hinch talking to Helen Swan. Do you know her?'

'Who?'

'Mrs Helen Swan.'

'No.'

'She is recently from New York would you believe. She is on her honeymoon. Her husband is enormously wealthy and is touring the colony. Word is that he is heavily invested in Melbourne, in the gold diggings, and she once graced the *stage*. Can you believe it?' Mrs Percival's voice dropped to a whisper. 'An *actress*, here, amongst us. No one knows what to say to her.'

'Perhaps saying good evening would be a start?' Ellen was thoroughly bored and wished to leave.

'They are only staying in Sydney a few weeks, which is a blessing for the embarrassment to socialise with an actress is too much.'

Ellen raised her eyebrows at Mrs Percival. 'Really? Is that what you think?'

Mrs Percival stared, not comprehending.

In a huff, Ellen heaved herself out of the chair and walked directly to Mrs Swan, a beautiful tall woman with an angelic face and thick blonde hair. She was simply stunning to look at.

'Mrs Swan?' Ellen held out her hand.

'Yes?' The graceful woman smiled kindly and shook Ellen's hand.

'I'm Ellen Emmerson, pleased to meet you.'

'You are Mr Emmerson's wife? I met him at a dinner last week. I am pleased to have met you now, too. I've been told you are beautiful and Irish.'

'Well, I'm definitely Irish.' Ellen laughed, drawing glances from others nearby.

'My grandparents were Irish, from Cork.'

'So, the true blood runs through you, too.' Ellen grinned.

'It does.' Mrs Swan's eyes were warm and kind. 'When I hear Irish singing, something happens to me.'

'It's your ancestors voices, calling to you,' Ellen said softly.

'That's a lovely way to put it. I'll remember that from now on, thank you.'

'I hear you are an actress from New York?'

The tall woman stiffened, which made her appear even taller. 'I am.'

Ellen could sense this woman was used to people gossiping about her. 'I think that is marvellous. How brave you are to perform in front of so many people. I couldn't do it at all. My mind would go blank, I know it would. How many hours of practise do you do?'

'I practise for several hours each day when I'm performing.'

'I would like to see you perform one day. I hear you are on your honeymoon?'

'We are, yes. After leaving Sydney, we'll start making our way back to New York, for I have a play beginning in October.'

'Are you missing home?'

Sensing that Ellen was being nice and genuine, Mrs Swan's shoulders dropped and she relaxed. 'There are days when I wish we were home, but then there are days when I find I don't want our honeymoon to end. Once we arrive back in New York, my husband will be busy with work and so will I.'

Ellen fought another yawn, tiredness creeping up on her. 'Forgive me, Mrs Swan. I assure you it isn't your company.'

The woman's gaze dropped to Ellen's stomach. 'You must be sapped of all energy at this time of night.'

'I am.' She glanced around for Alistair, wanting to go home.

'I long for a baby.'

Ellen saw the raw emotion on Mrs Swan's face. 'They are a blessing.'

'And one I shall never have...' As though realising what she'd said out loud, Mrs Swan stirred herself and pasted on a smile. 'I should go and find my husband.'

'Me, too. It's been lovely meeting you.'

They gave each other an understanding nod and went their separate ways.

In the carriage on the way home to the house in Lower Fort Street, Ellen dozed.

'How did you find, Mrs Swan?' Alistair asked her.

'Extremely nice,' she replied, coming awake.

'Her husband, Wilf, is an intelligent man. I've spoken to him a few times concerning business. I was thinking of inviting them to Emmerson Park next week.'

'Next week? I've only just arrived, Alistair.' Ellen glared at him. 'You wanted me to come to Sydney so here I am. I really don't want to turn around and trail all the way back to Berrima again. I need a few days' rest and there's shopping to do for Bridget's birthday.'

He held his hands up. 'All right. Steady on. We shan't invite them to Berrima and will entertain them here.'

Ellen wearily closed her eyes. 'I'm about eight weeks from giving birth, Alistair. I don't want to be spending every evening entertaining.'

'No, but you can spend time in the middle of nowhere playing farmer!' he snapped. 'My wife should be by my side, helping me and that involves entertaining business associates to build on our prospects.'

'I'm sorry that I fail you, Alistair.'

'You *do* fail me, Ellen.'

She bit her lip from speaking out for it would do no good and only cause more resentment.

He sighed heavily and, in the dark, reached for her hand. 'Forgive me for my outburst. I've not been sleeping very well lately.'

'Why?'

He shrugged and took a long time to answer her. 'I shall be fine. It is nothing for you to worry about.'

Sullen that he'd shut her out, Ellen stared out the carriage window at the darkened streets, wishing she was back at Louisburgh.

CHAPTER 10

*C*atching her breath, Ellen rested her head on her arms on the writing desk in the front room of the house on Lower Fort Street overlooking the harbour. Labour pains had been growing in intensity for the last three hours, but she kept the agony at bay by walking around the house.

This morning she'd pretended she was fine, and Alistair had gone into the city none the wiser. She'd encouraged Riona and Miss Lewis to take Bridget and Lily for a walk after their midday meal, leaving her at home with Mrs Lawson, the cook and Dilly the maid, who were busy doing their own work.

Ellen tried to concentrate on the letters she was writing to the boys in response to their last letters, which arrived only yesterday. Knowing she'd receive word from them every three months gave Ellen something to look forward to.

Outside, April winds blew the leaves from the trees, showering the streets in autumn gold and reds. From the kitchen she heard Mrs Lawson humming as Dilly came in with a tea tray.

'Mrs Lawson thought you might like a cup of tea, Mrs Emmerson?'

Ellen smiled and stood, only a pain sharper than before knifed through her stomach, sending her to her knees.

'Oh, Mrs Emmerson!' Dilly nearly dropped the tray and quickly put it on a side table before coming to assist.

'Run for the midwife, Dilly,' Ellen said through clenched teeth. 'Hurry.'

'Mrs Lawson!' Dilly ran from the room crying for the cook.

A moment later, the older woman came in, wiping her hands on her apron. 'Now then, Mrs Emmerson, shall we get you upstairs and into bed?'

'I think that would be wise, Mrs Lawson,' Ellen panted.

An hour later, Ellen lay exhausted, her body aching from delivering her baby.

'There, Mrs Emmerson, are you all comfy now you're washed and wearing a clean nightgown?' asked the midwife, a woman who thankfully only lived a few streets away.

'I am, thank you. Send your bill to us. My husband will pay it promptly.'

The midwife chuckled and handed the bundled baby into Ellen's arms. 'He may not when he sees it's another girl.'

Ellen stared down at the tiny red face. All her previous babies had been born with black downy hair, but this little one was so fair she looked bald at first glance.

'She takes after Mr Emmerson,' Mrs Lawson said, collecting the soiled canvas sheet that had protected the bedsheets and mattress during the birth.

'Aye, she'll be fair all her life will that one,' the midwife added. 'I can tell, and I've seen enough to know.'

Left alone with her baby, Ellen removed the coverings around her and inspected the tiny body for any imperfections. Her new daughter was perfect in every detail. Ellen's heart flowed with love for the precious child. 'What shall we call you?' Ellen whispered, then hearing the strident tones of Bridget she knew her peace was shattered.

Moments later, Bridget burst through the door with Riona close behind.

'Mama, you've had the baby, Dilly just told us. What is it?' Bridget bounded onto the bed before getting a tap on the hand from Riona.

'Whist, child. Behave. Your mammy has just given birth and will be tired now.' Riona peeped at the little face. 'Oh, Ellen.'

'It's a girl,' Ellen told them.

'Another sister?' Bridget sounded disappointed, but Riona scooped the baby from Ellen and held it close.

'She's beautiful, Ellen, and so fair. She's taken after her da, so she has.'

Yawning, Ellen nestled into the pillows. 'She has indeed.'

'I'd have liked a brother. Maybe next time?' Bridget said, climbing off the bed.

'I'm in no rush to repeat the event, thank you,' Ellen said drowsily.

'Shall we take her downstairs and give you a rest?' Riona asked.

'Aye. You take her. I would like to sleep.'

When Ellen woke hours later, dusk threw shadows across the room. She felt a little fuzzy, waking from a deep sleep, but when she moved her body, it all came back to her. Her limbs were stiff, and she was sore everywhere else. She looked for the baby, but the cradle was empty.

'Riona!' she called, summoning the energy to get out of bed.

Within seconds the door opened and Riona rushed in with the baby. 'You've been asleep for four hours, pray. She needs feeding, so she does.'

'Has she been crying?'

'No, not a peep. She's slept the same as you.'

Ellen put the baby to her breast and felt the familiar pull on the nipple. 'It's so tiresome to be back feeding again. I'm restricted once more.'

'The time will soon go by. Though I do think you need to hire a nursemaid. Miss Lewis and I can't do it all and you know you'll be wanting to be out and about as soon as possible.'

'I agree. Put an advertisement in the paper, will you? We'll hire two nursemaids.'

'I'll go into town first thing.'

They heard a male voice downstairs.

'Oh, Alistair is home,' Riona said. 'I'll send him up.'

Ellen waited for him to enter the bedroom and smiled tiredly at him.

'Why did you not send word? I would have come straight home,' he said, sitting on the bed. He peered at the little face feeding contentedly. 'Riona would not tell me the sex and clamped a hand over Bridget's mouth to prevent her from telling me too. Is it a boy?' he asked hopefully.

'I'm sorry to fail you, but it's a little girl.' Ellen felt protective over the baby knowing how much Alistair wanted a boy.

'A girl...' A flash of dissatisfaction crossed his face for only a second, and when Ellen unlatched the baby and passed her to Alistair, his eyes lit up.

'Look how fair she is! So different to the other children, especially Lily.' He gazed in complete adoration at the small face. 'She looks just like me.'

'Then she'll be a beautiful child, especially if she has your dimple and your colour hair.' Ellen beamed, inwardly wincing at the mention of Lily's dark looks.

'No, she'll be fairer than me, more like my mother. We must call her Ava, after my mother. Does that please you?'

Having received many sweet letters from Alistair's mother, along with seeds and bulbs for the gardens, Ellen had no qualms about the name. 'Your mother is a dear woman. Ava will be proud to be called after such a kind-hearted woman.'

Alistair kissed the top of Ava's head and then kissed Ellen.

'Mother will be so delighted by her namesake. We shall have a sketch drawn of Ava and send it to them.'

Ellen nodded. She leaned back into the pillows. 'That's a grand idea.'

'I know we have been polite with each other these last months...' Alistair changed the way he held the baby and didn't look at Ellen. 'I am grateful you stayed in Sydney and didn't return to Berrima or Louisburgh despite wanting to. You did that for me.'

'Yes, I did. I have stayed in Sydney so we could work on our marriage, yet you've hardly been home. I should have gone to Berrima weeks ago, but I didn't want you to think I wasn't trying, Alistair. Then it became too late to travel with the birth so close.' Ellen searched his face for answers. She had changed her plans for him. She had wanted to have the baby in Berrima. Staying in Sydney for months had tried her patience, even more so when she'd remained to be with Alistair, and he'd spent so much time at the office or with his friends.

Had she wasted her time trying to repair their marriage, which was becoming more difficult each day? She was tired of striving to be what he wanted and failing.

Alistair touched a finger to the baby's cheek. 'I know it is my fault. Much has kept me busy at the office. But the last shipment is on its way to England and the recent cargo has been delivered to Melbourne. Robin's letter today tells me the cargo arrived safely, and he has managed to sell most of it all ready.'

'Does that mean you will be less concerned than you have been?'

'Yes...'

She didn't believe him. Something was wrong. 'I feel you are keeping something from me, Alistair. I'd like to know what it is.'

He handed the baby back to her and stood. 'It is nothing for you to worry about, my dear. Rest and regain your strength. Leave the business to me.'

His last comment angered her. Such a cutting remark when he knew she was good at business. How many more times would she have to prove it to him?

Long after he'd left the room, Ellen pondered on his distant demeanour. Of late he'd been staying longer hours at the office, and when at home he was distracted. For him and their marriage, she'd decided to stay in town and, right up until two days ago, she'd entertained the city wives and attended all the invitations sent to her. Had it all been for nought?

However, now the baby was safely delivered, she wanted to leave and head home first to Berrima for a while and then to Louisburgh. She had done her time in Sydney, not that Alistair seemed to appreciate it.

* * *

Leaving the hansom cab in the High Street, Rafe hurried up to the path to the main red-bricked building of Harrow, the prestigious school north-west of London. Within the panelled walls, he stopped a student. 'Headmaster's office or the sick room, hospital?'

'Down there is the sick room, sir.' The boy pointed to the right. 'Go through those doors and along the corridor and turn left.'

After negotiating several corridors, Rafe found a man carrying a stack of books. 'Sick room?'

'Sick room, sir?' The man looked down his nose at Rafe, which was difficult to do since he was inches shorter than Rafe. 'The infirmary is behind me, sir. May I ask who you are?'

'Are you in charge?'

'No, I'm senior clerk to the headmaster.'

'Rafe Hamilton. I was sent a letter about my ward, Patrick Kittrick. He is ill.'

'Ah, yes. Nasty business. Do follow me.'

After exiting that building and crossing open space to another building, Rafe finally entered an office.

The clerk knocked on another door, spoke to whomever was inside the room and then beckoned Rafe to enter.

A man wearing a black suit and a long black cape stood behind his desk and held out his hand to Rafe. 'Charles Vaughan, Mr Hamilton. Welcome to Harrow.'

'Thank you. My ward, Patrick?' He'd received the letter about Patrick yesterday morning and immediately caught the train to London from Liverpool.

'He has been extremely ill. I am glad you came as quickly as you could. Come with me. I shall take you to him.'

Rafe followed, the tiredness of a sleepless night catching up with him and also the anxious journey where he spent hours wondering if he was too late.

'Your ward is terribly ill, Mr Hamilton. The doctor has been in constant attendance.'

In a small, windowless room, bare of any comforts, Patrick lay on a bed, covered by a thin white sheet. The stale stench of body refuse wafted over Rafe. The boy looked like a skeleton, the weight stripped from him, his skin pale, black smudges under his sunken eyes. His head shaven.

Rafe gasped, believing for a moment that it wasn't Patrick at all. That it had been a mistake.

'Doctor Rutledge, Mr Hamilton.' Mr Vaughan made the introductions.

Wordlessly, Rafe shook the fat hand of a rotund gentleman.

'A fever, my good man. I do not hold out much hope, I'm afraid to say.' Doctor Rutledge blew loudly into a handkerchief, inspected the contents and then tucked it into his coat pocket. 'Dreadful waste of a young life.'

Stepping forward, Rafe gazed down on Patrick, the boy who he'd developed a close bond within the short time he and Austin had stayed with him in Liverpool before coming to London to board at the school last October.

Four months ago, Rafe had both Patrick and Austin with him for two weeks at Christmas and what a time of it they'd had. He'd treated them like his own sons as he promised Ellen he would, and it had been easy to do for the boys were likeable and engaging. The three of them had visited theatre shows, gone shopping, ice-skated on a pond, made mulled wine and eaten the feasts his cook had prepared for the holidays. They'd exchanged presents on Christmas Day and then gone for a long walk along the docks. In the evening they'd dined a sumptuous meal and then played cards for hours.

From that healthy boy landing in Liverpool last year to this wasted body seemed unbelievable.

A lump formed in his throat, and he had to swallow several times before he could speak. 'He must live.'

It was all he could think of. For Ellen he had to keep this boy alive, make him healthy again. He couldn't let Ellen down. He promised to take care of her boys.

'It is doubtful he'll last the night.' Doctor Rutledge checked his fob watch and coughed.

Rafe could smell alcohol on the large man's breath. Peering at him, Rafe recoiled at the sweat dripping down the man's brow. Snuff stained his waistcoat. The man looked barely able to take care of himself never mind his patient. 'What have you done to my ward to try and heal him?'

'He has a fever, probably some inner infection... I have bled him many times, and it makes no improvement. Fevers are tricky, of course, they lay within the body and either the patient has the strength to withstand the onslaught of an attack, or they die.'

Rafe clenched his teeth and glared at the man. He spun to the headmaster. 'Is he capable as a doctor? He reeks of spirits.'

'I say!' Doctor Rutledge protested at the insult.

Mr Vaughan shifted uncomfortably. 'Doctor Rutledge has

been very successful in the past attending to the illnesses of our boys, Mr Hamilton.'

'I want Patrick removed from his services. I will pay for my own doctor to see to Patrick.'

'Now, let us not be hasty.' Vaughan held up his hand.

Doctor Rutledge bristled. 'I want my fee!'

Rafe only just refrained from hitting the fat toad. 'Is there a hospital local to the school?'

Vaughan nodded. 'A mile or so away. It's only a small concern.'

'It is where old people go to die,' Rutledge spluttered. 'It hardly more than an alms' house.'

Rafe glanced at Patrick, who looked so ill. He had to do all he could. 'Have you a carriage I may loan?'

'Yes, indeed. It's at your disposal.' Vaughan stepped to the door as there was a knock. He opened it to reveal Austin.

'Rafe?' Austin's eyes widened. 'Is Patrick...?'

'He still breathes,' Vaughan said kindly, ushering him in.

Austin stood by the bed but spoke to Rafe. 'My house monitor told me I could visit Patrick after this morning's lessons.'

Rafe smiled slightly at Austin. 'I'm taking Patrick to my sister's house near Watford. Do you wish to come?'

'I have a history test this afternoon. I need to do well on it.'

'Perhaps Austin can come to you on Saturday?' Vaughan interrupted. 'He can stay a few days.'

Rafe laid his hand on Austin's shoulder. 'He will have better care away from this room.' He glanced at Rutledge to get across his meaning.

Austin nodded. 'I've been worried about Patrick all night.'

'If you take him from this room today,' declared Rutledge, 'I will not be held responsible for the outcome.'

'I shall take the chance,' Rafe sneered.

Within the hour, Rafe held Patrick across him on the seat of a carriage Vaughan hired for them and was trundling their way across mud-splattered roads. Rain pounded down in torrents, hindering their fast progress, yet Patrick did not move or murmur. The boy felt so lightweight in his arms that Rafe wondered if he'd survive the journey. Had he been wrong to take him?

At the gates of Cherrybank, his sister's husband's estate, Rafe waved to the gatekeeper, and they passed through, circling the open deer park and coming to a stop in front of the impressive Tudor mansion.

Babcock, the butler, opened the front doors and two footmen hurried down the steps to open the carriage door. They hid their shock on seeing Rafe inside.

'Mr Hamilton?' Babcock came down the steps holding an umbrella. 'We weren't expecting you, sir.'

'Babcock, my ward is very ill. I need a doctor. Fetch my sister, if you please.' Rafe spoke from within the carriage.

'Certainly, sir.'

Moments later, Iris was holding her skirts up and running down the stairs to the carriage. 'Rafe! What in Lord's name has happened?'

'Patrick is desperately sick with fever. We need somewhere to stay, but I shan't come into the house. Do you have a cottage on the grounds where we can stay?'

'A cottage? No, they are all tenanted. Come into the house, surely you wouldn't think I would have my brother and dear Patrick staying anywhere else?'

'But the risk to little Edmund?' He couldn't put his sister's baby at risk.

'He's in the west wing. I'll put you in the east wing away from Edmund's nursery.' She turned to Babcock. 'Have someone fetch Doctor Griggs and have the rooms prepared, please.'

Babcock issued orders to the footmen and Rafe descended the carriage steps and then turned to gather Patrick in his arms, praying he had done the right thing in bringing the boy here as Patrick remained limp and hot to touch.

Rafe carried Patrick up the steps and into the house.

'Darling?' Mama came out of the drawing room.

'Stay away, Mama,' Rafe grimaced and took the stairs up to the east wing.

'The first room,' Iris instructed, opening the door. She ran to the bed and flung back the blankets and sheet.

Once they had made Patrick comfortable, Iris instructed a maid to build a small fire in the fireplace. Iris asked Babcock to replace the fine Louis XIV chair in the corner of the room with a more comfortable winged-back chair from another bedroom, knowing Rafe would need a chair to rest in.

While all the preparations were being made, Rafe poured water from a jug into a bowl and using a cloth wiped Patrick's hot forehead, his cheeks and neck.

Iris came to stand beside him. 'We will make him better again, brother. Do not worry if you can help it.'

'He must regain his health, Iris. I cannot let his mother down.'

She rubbed his back. 'I think his mother would know you would do your best for her son.'

'You should not be in here. Think of Edmund.'

Iris smiled reassuringly. 'Edgar has our son out in all weathers. Edmund is as strong as a little bull. He has an appetite of a giant. Now he is walking, Edgar goes riding with Edmund sitting up on the saddle in front of him. Edgar refuses to have our son treated like a delicate piece of porcelain.' She paused, realising she'd been rambling. 'I shall go down to Mama and wait for Doctor Griggs. I shall have a tray sent up to you.'

'Thank you.'

She paused at the door. 'Have you written to Patrick's mother?'

'Not yet. I wanted to wait...'

'Until he is well, and you can send *good* news,' she finished for him. She clasped Rafe's hand. 'He will be well again.'

CHAPTER 11

$\mathcal{T}$he cool autumn winds of late May stripped the last remaining coloured leaves from the imported trees in the garden at Emmerson Park, but the native eucalyptus trees, edging the boundary of the property provided an ideal wind-break as the wind hurled up the hill to batter the house.

'If the weather is better tomorrow, can I go out for a ride?' Bridget asked Ellen as she came into the bedroom where Ellen had just finished feeding Ava.

'Yes, with Douglas, and as long as Miss Lewis tells me your lessons are finished for the day.'

'I'm doing extra lessons today because of the weather.' Bridget sat on the bed and watched Ellen pat Ava's little back.

'I have been listening to you practise the piano. You're getting very good.'

Bridget preened. 'I'm better than Caroline and Aisling, aren't I?'

'You are, but don't be smug about it. Remember Caroline can sing better than you, and Aisling is the better singer out of all three of you.'

Bridget shrugged. 'I don't care to sing, anyway. I am the better dancer. When does Papa arrive?'

'Next week.' Ellen tried to inject a positive note into her voice. Since leaving Sydney last week, six weeks after Ava's birth, Ellen had felt a great relief to be away from the city. The long spell of time spent not only in Sydney but with Alistair had grated on her nerves. Alistair was keeping something from her. She couldn't tell exactly what it was, but she believed it was something to do with the business.

A knock on the door brought her head up from gazing at Ava's sweet little face. 'Come in.'

Rachel, the nursemaid Ellen had hired in Sydney, entered the room. 'Are you ready for me to take the baby, madam?'

'Yes. She's wet.' Ellen handed Ava over after giving her a kiss. Having Rachel, and also Lettie as nursemaids was a new freedom Ellen rejoiced in. After each feed she was free to go about her day and Rachel cared for Ava, who was a good baby while Lettie attended to Lily.

Ellen marvelled how she had three daughters to three different men and the difference between them showed. Bridget had always been a strong baby, even during the famine when food was scarce, and Ellen had fed her such small amounts of food. Now though, as she looked at her, Ellen was amazed at the beauty of her raven-haired eldest daughter. Bridget's eyes were a mixture of blue and grey and she had a strength of character that made her stand out. Whereas Lily was dainty, her hair turning more the colour of deep chestnut, her eyes a dark blue. She had the elegant features of Rafe and a quiet manner, but she was always watching everyone around her. Then Ava, who at six weeks old, was showing signs of being so fair, her blonde hair was nearly white.

Ellen loved her daughters, especially the differences in them. If only she could have her sons with her, too. She thought briefly of dear Thomas. He would have turned twelve at the end of

April… How she missed his sweet dear face, the smiles… The look of his white body lying on the sand…

She shook herself out of her memories and held out her hand to Bridget. 'Shall we write to Austin and Patrick?'

'We only sent letters yesterday.' Bridget took her hand as they walked out of the bedroom.

'I know but that was all about our journey coming back from Sydney and having the axel break in the carriage.'

'And we had to walk to the next village.'

'Today why don't we write about going to Louisburgh in a few days?'

Bridget glanced up at Ellen. 'Papa said we weren't to go as Ava is too little for the journey.'

Ellen bristled at the commands Alistair had given her regarding Ava before she left Sydney. He was besotted with the baby, more so than with Lily, and insisted on Ellen treating the baby like she was a fragile angel. She'd told him how with Bridget, she'd worked in the fields planting potatoes with the baby strapped to her back as she had done with the boys as babies. Yet, he'd been insistent that she take extra special care of Ava.

Ellen was adamant to travel to Louisburgh before it became too cold on the property. She felt that spending a couple of weeks in Louisburgh and then returning to Emmerson Park for the winter a perfect solution. 'Ava handled the journey from Sydney just fine. She'll handle the two days to Louisburgh as well.'

'Can't we leave Ava and Lily here and you and I just go to Louisburgh?' Bridget asked.

'That's not fair on them though, is it? And I will miss them.'

'But they are only babies. Rachel and Lettie can take care of them and Aunty Riona and Miss Lewis.'

Ellen chuckled. 'I can't leave Ava while I'm feeding her, you know that. Now go and find Miss Lewis.'

In the drawing room, Riona was surveying the maid's

cleaning with a critical eye. 'Miss Augusta Ashford and Mrs Pippa Ashford will be arriving soon.'

Ellen paused. 'Oh, I forgot about their visit.'

'And then this afternoon, Mrs Riddle is calling.' Riona nodded at her diary. 'Tomorrow morning, we need to return Mr Taylor's call and we have to call on Mrs Connelly at the mill. She was kind to invite us for tea and I know she's not the *elite* society of the area, but she is very nice.'

Ellen rolled her eyes. Once the district knew they were home from Sydney, friends were paying their calls once more.

'We have a dinner party on Tuesday at the Riddles' and then the garden party at the Ashfords' on Friday.'

'Friday? I wanted to go to Louisburgh on Wednesday.'

'You'll have to travel on Saturday.' Riona closed her diary. 'On Wednesday I have a meeting with the church committee and Thursday night is the fund-raising dance at the Victoria Inn.'

'What are we raising funds for again?' Ellen sat and prodded the fire with the iron poker.

'Old Mrs Finch. Her house burned down, remember?'

'I shan't go to the dance, Riona. Take Miss Lewis with you instead. I'll just give money.'

'Why can't you go?'

'I want to go to Louisburgh.' Ellen sighed and sat back in the chair. 'And I don't feel like it.'

'Alistair is arriving next week. You'll be in Louisburgh when he gets here?' Riona gave her a sharp look. 'He'll not be happy about that.'

Ellen shrugged. 'Not much makes him happy these days. He wasn't grateful for my time I spent in Sydney. He barely took any notice of us being there.'

'You have to fix this distance between you, Ellen. It's not good for you.'

'How? Alistair refuses to talk to me about anything important. We've both changed. I wish I knew how to bridge the gap between us.' She smoothed down her skirts, sad with facing the truth about her marriage.

'Living in separate houses isn't helping. If you go to Louisburgh while Alistair is here then your relationship will grow worse, not better. He's forbidden you to take Ava, anyway, so if you went, he'd be irate and, to be honest with you, I don't want to have to live with him like that. He's your husband, not mine. You should be here.'

She rubbed a hand wearily over her eyes. 'Fine. I'll not travel to Louisburgh then. I'll stay while Alistair is here.'

'Good.' Riona peered at her. 'Are you sleeping?'

'Are you implying I look tired?' She tried to joke, but it fell flat.

'Ava sleeps through the night now, but you look exhausted. You don't rest enough during the day. The only time you sit down is when you're feeding Ava, or if someone is here and even then, you can barely do that for more than five minutes before you're making your excuses.'

'The women that come here are your friends, not mine.' Ellen stared into the flames.

'Whist, you're talking nonsense. They come to see you. You're the mistress of the house. They are friends of both of ours, especially if you put more effort into it.' Riona placed her diary in the drawer of a fine walnut console table by the window. 'Seriously, Ellen, you have to do more socialising for Alistair's and the children's sake. You are good at it when you put your mind to it. I always feel I'm not good enough to mix with these people.'

'Twaddle. You're better than me!' Ellen admired. 'I can't make small talk, you can. Social talk bores me unless it's to do with land and farming.'

'I've had to learn quickly because of all the times we've had callers both here and in Sydney and you disappear!'

Ellen chuckled. 'I am getting rather good at *that*.'

Riona grinned. 'You're impossible. Bridget is becoming just as bad. The girl vanishes the minute Miss Lewis calls her.'

A knock interrupted them and Honor Duffy entered the drawing room.

'Yes, Honor?'

'Sorry to disturb, but Moira has had a bit of a turn.'

'What?' Ellen and Riona rushed from the room and across the hall and along the corridor into the kitchen.

Moira sat at the large cedar table, head bowed. The room was hot with the ovens burning. Fresh bread lay on the sideboard cooling and on the table was the beginnings of tea trays being set for their visitors.

'Moira.' Ellen knelt beside her. 'What happened?'

'Nothing. I'm fine, so I am.'

'You look pale.' Ellen felt her forehead. 'You're not hot.'

'I'm fine I tell you.' Moira waved Ellen away.

'Come outside and get some fresh air.' Ellen helped her up. 'Honor, can you take over in here?'

Honor raised her chin. 'Aye, of course I can.'

Ellen glanced at Riona. 'Mrs and Miss Ashford. I can hear a carriage coming down the drive.'

Riona rubbed her hands together, worriedly. 'You see to Moira. I'll greet our guests and give your excuses.'

'I'll be in as soon as I can,' Ellen said.

'Stop making a fuss, will you, Ellen?' Moira sighed. 'Sure, and I ain't an invalid.'

'Don't argue with me, Moira.' Ellen took her elbow and walked with her outside into the cool air. They sat on a wooden bench Seamus Duffy had made that was placed near the herb garden. 'You gave me a fright. Are you sure you're all right?'

Moira sighed, her face drawn. There was no banter, no jesting or dismissive laughter.

Ellen stared at her friend. 'Are you ill? Tell me.'

'I must be sick in the head for getting myself into such a state.'

'What do you mean?'

For several minutes Moira stared out over the garden. 'Oh, Ellen. A fool is what I am.'

'Why?'

'I think I'm with child, so I am.'

Nothing Moira could have said would have made Ellen more shocked. 'With child?'

'Aye. Isn't it the funniest joke, to be sure?'

'I didn't even know you were... were keen on someone, or courting.' Ellen tried not to act as shocked as she felt.

'Well, hasn't it all been a bit of laugh, so it has? Until now.'

'Are you sure you're with child?'

'It's either that or the change of life, but at forty, aren't I a bit too young for such a thing? Me mam was in her fifties before she stopped her monthly bleeds.'

'I don't know. Maybe we should ask a doctor?'

'A man? As if he'd know the answer,' Moira mocked.

'Of course, they would. They are trained.'

'No. I don't think seeing a doctor is the answer.'

'Who is the father then?'

Moira blushed. 'Now don't be mad.'

'Mad? Why would I be?' Ellen tensed, ready for the answer.

It took a moment for Moira to speak and the birds chirping in the trees seemed louder because of it. Moira gripped her hands together in her lap. 'Because it's Mr Thwaite.'

'Mr Thwaite?' Again, shock made Ellen's eyes widen.

'I know how much you like him. He's your man. The one you depend on above all others, even your husband at times.'

'That is true. I don't know what I would do without Mr Thwaite,' Ellen replied. Mr Thwaite was one of the finest men she knew. They had a special understanding, a working relationship and friendship that meant a great deal to them both.

'He thinks the world of you, so he does, and would do anything to make you happy. If I was a jealous woman, I would have an anger on me night and day about how much he goes on about you.'

'I think highly of him, too. But as much as I depend on him, there is nothing romantic about it.'

'Aye, I know.'

'I feel as though I've let you down, Moira,' Ellen suddenly said.

'How so?'

'Because you've been courting a good man right under my nose and I haven't been aware of it. I didn't realise how self-absorbed I've become.'

'I wouldn't call it that, Ellen. You're a busy woman, owner of properties, beasts, staff and a mother and a wife.'

'That's no excuse. You are my friend.'

'Aye, I am and Mr Thwaite and me have been hiding our close friendship, so we have. Secret night visits and so on have only been a bit of fun. We've not been open about it. Our chats in the garden or in the kitchen are in front of everyone.' Moira gazed over the gardens. 'No one would suspect. You've been away for months, so how would you have had an inkling about it all?'

'Will you marry?'

'We've no choice now, have we? Fools that we are.' Moira smiled wryly.

'We shall build you a cottage.'

'That would be grand, so it would. Thank you.' Moira wasn't one for displaying her emotions or touches of affection so when she took Ellen's hand, Ellen knew it meant something. 'You know, Ellen, I can't remember being this happy. I never thought I'd be a mother. For years I've been on my own. My first husband was sent away in chains and I crossed the seas to find him, only for him to die shortly after I arrived in Sydney. I thought that was the end of any chance to be happy or to have a family. I'm not a looker, and I'm getting old. I've done things I'm not proud of... Yet, Mr Thwaite saw past all that. He is a good man.'

'He is. You'd be hard to find a better one.'

'And I'm scared witless.'

'There's no need to be.' Ellen squeezed her hand. 'You're allowed to be happy.'

'Aye, I've a family here with you all. A good position and now a man and a baby. I feel it's too much, you know?'

Ellen nodded. 'I know exactly. I still wake up some mornings and think I'm back in the cottage in Mayo, smelling the rotten stench of potatoes, or listening to the crying of my children because they are hungry or cold. We managed through the famine better than so many others. Yet, death stalked us, and I had to be so vigilant to make sure we didn't get sick and die.'

'And look at you now,' Moira murmured.

Gazing around at the gardens and buildings, sitting in the fresh breeze knowing she had food and shelter still felt surreal. 'Some days I don't feel all this is true. I live the life of a lady. I used to watch in envy the ladies of the parish back in Mayo. They'd pass me in their fine carriages while I walked in the mud with holes in my shoes, the cold seeping through my clothes, my stomach empty, and I used to imagine what their life might be like. Never in my wildest dreams did I think I would be one of them one day. A lady in a carriage wearing fine clothes and shiny boots. I was Ellen Kittrick, wife of a cottager, a mother to small children. My days were spent doing backbreaking toil on the land, walking the roads to sell my goods at the market. Then the blight came and changed everything. I had to work for an English gentleman to try and keep a roof over our heads while my husband lost his way and turned to drink. Life was never the same again.'

'But you also survived, lass. You weren't buried in a pauper's grave or worse in a ditch by the road with your children. You worked and stayed strong in your mind, so you did. By not giving up and going into the workhouse, you managed to make it *here*.'

Ellen shivered in the cool breeze. 'I got to be a lady by marrying Alistair.'

'Aye and what's wrong with that?' Moira scowled at her.

'I married him for security.'

'Sure, and there's nothing wrong with that. Marriages have been made on less.' Moira tucked a loose strand of hair behind her ear that the wind tugged from her cap.

'Yes, and that doesn't always mean it'll be a success.'

'Sure, and who can ever say they know the success to a happy marriage? It's luck, lass. Pure and simple.'

'Do you love Mr Thwaite?' Ellen wondered.

'I respect him, and we get along well, so we do. I don't know if that's love though. I'm no longer a girl to have foolish dreams.' Moira sighed. 'It's all such a shock, so it is. Me, at this age, having a kid. Mad it is.'

Ellen smiled. 'It's a wonderful thing. A baby for you to love.'

'And worry over as you worry over your lot. I've been fine on my own all these years.'

The sound of a horse trotting down the drive carried on the wind. Another visitor? Ellen and Moira stood and turned for the house.

'Do you feel better now?' Ellen asked.

'Aye.'

'Take more rests. Don't overdo it. Give Honor more duties. I shall hire more maids to help you.'

'Whist, now. I'll be grand, so I will.'

In the kitchen, Moira went straight back to work in preparing the family's next meal, while Honor entered from the hallway, carrying a tray full of used teacups and plates.

Ellen hurried to the drawing room to speak with their guests. Mrs Pippa Ashford and Miss Augusta Ashford were just saying their goodbyes on the front verandah as Alistair climbed down from a shiny black carriage, which had Higgins in the driver's seat.

Hiding her surprise at Alistair's arrival, she smiled at the women. 'Forgive me for not being available to have tea with you.'

Pippa Ashford, a beautiful woman with poise and elegance waved away her apology. 'We fully understand. Sometimes, especially when running a large household, our time is not our own, is it?'

'Yes,' Augusta agreed with a smile, 'we have all been there when plans go awry.'

'Thank you for coming anyway,' Ellen said.

'You will come to the garden party on Friday?' Pippa Ashford asked.

'Yes, of course.'

'What is this?' Alistair said, coming to the verandah and bowing to the women.

'A garden party at our home on Friday,' Pippa told him. 'It might be the last party we have outside for months. Once the weather turns cold, we are cooped up inside until at least September when spring arrives.'

'We shall look forward to it.' Alistair gave them his dazzling dimpled smile. 'I have not spoken to Gil for some time. It will be nice to speak with him.'

They all walked to the Ashfords' carriage and Alistair handed the ladies up into it.

Waving them off, Ellen glanced at Alistair. 'You have arrived earlier than expected.'

He kissed her cheek and then Riona's. 'Once you had gone, I missed you all. How is Ava? Has Rachel been looking after her satisfactorily?'

'Ava is doing very well, and Rachel is good with her.' Ellen hid her disappointment that he focused only on the baby. 'Whose carriage is that?'

'Ours, my dear.'

'You bought a carriage?' She frowned, for he had spoken of their need not to spend unnecessary money.

'I did. And I have hired Higgins fulltime, too. He has given up working for himself and has agreed to be our carriage driver, though I will have him in Sydney with me most of the time. The city is expanding, and I need to be able to travel freely. It will be such an asset to have a carriage and Higgins at our disposal.' He grinned and walked away. 'I shall go and wash off the travelling dust and visit the nursery.'

'How long are you staying for?' Ellen halted him in the doorway.

'Not sure, dearest, not sure.'

Ellen nibbled her bottom lip in irritation. His odd behaviour kept surprising her, and she didn't like it.

When Alistair finally joined them in the dining room for luncheon an hour later, he was all smiles. 'I swear she has grown, and it's only been just over a week since I saw her. I am sure she smiled at me and knew who I was. Rachel is good with her, you are correct. Ava fell asleep in my arms content as can be. I must have tired her out. She's such a sweet thing, such a beautiful baby.'

'All my babies are beautiful,' Ellen murmured, sipping her turnip soup.

'Indeed.' Alistair beamed. 'And perhaps our next child will be a handsome son.'

'You seem very happy,' Riona said, giving Ellen a quick glance.

'I am.' Alistair grinned.

'Can we ask why?' Riona buttered a slice of bread.

'It just so happens that I have done a brilliant business deal. All our problems will be solved.'

Ellen jerked to attention after mulling over Alistair's want for a son. 'Problems? We have problems?'

Alistair blinked rapidly for a moment then shook his head. 'A figure of speech, dearest. We have no problems at all, especially now.'

She didn't believe him. 'What is this deal?'

'I have invested in a trade agreement with a company in Hobart. They are in want of English tools and machinery, which

Rafe and I can get for them, and in return I'll import their timber. I have invested in the pine company.'

Ellen's heart did a little flip as it always did at the mention of Rafe. Would it ever stop doing that? Would she ever stop wanting a man she couldn't have? She concentrated on Alistair's conversation.

'Do we not have enough timber on the mainland?' Riona asked. 'We're surrounded by trees.'

'Yes, but there are great Huon Pine plantations in Van Diemen's Land. The pine is in great demand. I may travel to the Davey River settlement and take a tour of the operation myself.'

'Go to Van Diemen's Land?' Ellen asked. 'That is a long way.'

'Yes. Winter is not the ideal time to go. The crossing from Melbourne over the Bass Strait is dangerous in rough seas and the island itself gets terribly cold. But I shall venture there in the spring.'

'I thought you wanted us to curb our spending? Yet you've bought a carriage and plan to travel.'

Alistair stared at Ellen. 'This is a business venture, dearest. Extremely worth the expenditure if it is to make us more money.' His smile was tight. 'Enough talk of business, tell me your plans for the week. What invitations do we have?'

Ellen inwardly fumed at Alistair's dismissal. Slowly he was distancing her from his business deals. Unlike when they were first married, and he was laid up with his injured leg, she had known exactly what his transactions were and helped to keep his company running and prospering. But in the last year or so, perhaps longer, Alistair had been giving little away and pushing her more into the role of wife and mother than business partner, despite him knowing that Ellen was clever with business, canny and wise in making money. Something that had surprised them both.

Since she had bought Louisburgh, he'd refused to let her buy any more land. Her love for that property had given him ammunition to curtail her spending. Yet, he felt the need to invest in a company so far away without any discussion with her. It was frustrating and deeply concerning that he was keeping her out of his business deals.

Annoyed, Ellen wiped her mouth and pushed her bowl away. Alistair refused to spend money on Louisburgh, but yet was willing to invest in other projects. She'd have to talk to him about it all, but it was a conversation she wasn't looking forward to having.

While Riona filled him in on their social diary, Ellen couldn't bear to stay in the room and left the table to go and feed Ava. She secretly hoped Alistair wouldn't stay in Berrima long.

CHAPTER 12

*I*n the chilly night air, Ellen strolled the verandah after having fed Ava for the night. The baby was indeed good and had begun sleeping through until morning. It was as though she knew Ellen needed her to be undemanding in her busy life.

Shivering, Ellen opened the French doors to her bedroom, her mind on the garden party tomorrow. Pippa and Gil Ashford were charming, their home beautiful. Ellen felt a little intimidated by the family, not that they were unkind to her or paid any attention to her past, yet the Ashfords, like some of the other wealthy families in the area, had an easy way about them being content in their status and class. Ellen, although treated as one of them, still remained a little distant, aloof from becoming too close, too friendly. Riona said she behaved as though she wore a suit of armour around her, especially her heart, not wanting to let anyone in should they turn on her. Ellen couldn't help it. Deep down she knew she was an imposter in this society.

Walking into the dressing room, she stopped on seeing Alistair holding numerous letters in his hand, but the one that he read was the private note Rafe had sent her and which usually Ellen kept on her body but with feeding Ava, and undressing so much to do so, she'd hidden the note in a leather wallet in the bottom of her drawer, covering it over with stockings.

Shock, revulsion and anger at Alistair not only rifling through her things, but reading her private correspondence raged in her. 'What are you doing!' she yelled.

Alistair jumped guiltily, and spun around, his face lost all colour. 'This...' He held up Rafe's note. 'I... you and he...' His face twisted in agony.

'How dare you read my private letters!' She jerked forward and tried to grab the letter, but Alistair was faster and taller, and held it above her head.

Alistair glared at her with utter contempt. 'You and Rafe?'

'It is nothing. Give me my letter.'

'Nothing you say?' Alistair read from the page. *'How I wish you had been on the ship with them. I still love you desperately. With my fondest and most sincere love and devotion...'* He swallowed, colour returning to his face in a fit of resentment and loathing. *'I still love you desperately!'*

Ellen faced him. Hurt and furious yet knowing Alistair was in distress and pain and it was her fault.

She stepped back. 'There is nothing between Rafe and me, Alistair. It was a moment of madness that has gone.'

'Really? Just a moment of madness? Yet he still loves you as of only months ago when he wrote that letter?'

'I do not write to him.'

'Do you still *love* him?' he ground the words out between clenched teeth.

'We will never see each other again. It does not matter. I'm married to you. We have a family.'

'When did this all happen? Before you came to this country?'

'In Liverpool? No...'

'But something happened in Liverpool?'

'No.' Her heart thumped erratically. How was she to explain all this? 'In Liverpool we became friends. I was attracted to him.'

'And he was obviously attracted to you.'

'I didn't know of it at the time.'

Alistair walked to the other side of the dressing room, the note crunched in his fist. 'Did you have an affair with Rafe when he came to Sydney?'

'Alistair, it is all in the past.'

He lunged for her and grabbed her shoulders, his fingers biting into her flesh painfully. 'Tell me the truth, damn you!'

'Yes! Yes, we had one time together, just one!' she shouted back, sick of keeping the secret, of hiding the love she felt for a man who was on the other side of the world.

He slapped her face hard, snapping her head back. In revulsion, he threw her from him.

Ellen staggered back, holding her stinging cheek. That he'd hit her was unforgivable. Whatever fondness she had for him withered and died.

'You disgust me,' Alistair sneered. 'I saved you from the bottom of the heap. I could have had anyone!'

'Then why didn't you!' she screamed back. 'Why did you pick me?'

'Because your beauty dazzled me. You were different, a challenge, a woman I thought would be interesting and different.'

'No,' Ellen scoffed. 'You wanted to be the talking point of Sydney. You wanted to create a scandal, to have men pay attention to you and through that improve your business. You wanted to flout the social rules, be a rebel, be noticed!'

'And it worked!'

Ellen gasped, her inner thoughts proving to be true. She'd been an experiment.

Alistair laughed mockingly. 'Did you think I did it only for love? More fool you.'

Ellen stiffened, putting a brave face on in front of him when inside she felt used and deceived. 'Then you are a fine actor, Alistair, for you fooled not only me but everyone around you.'

His shoulders sagged a little, and he wiped a hand over his eyes. 'I do love you, Ellen. It was a thrill for me to marry outside of my class, to have society gossip about us, about me, but I did want you, and I did fall in love with you. I was in love, and that's the truth. I wanted a family of my own like other men of my acquaintance had. In you I got a family instantly. I was no longer alone.'

The mention of her children brought her head up higher. 'You using me, I can understand, but using my children to make yourself feel better is another matter.'

'I did not use them. I adore the children, you know that.'

'Do you or are you simply acting as though you do?'

His lips tightened. 'Do not dare to question my feelings on the children. I would do anything for them. Have I not shown you that? I took on your three and cared for them as my own. I did not pretend my joy when you became with child, it was real. To be a father in my own right was the happiest day of my life. When Lily was born, I wrote to Rafe and told him how wonderful it felt to be a father. I told everyone. I did not care that she was not a boy...' Then suddenly, he groaned and stared at her. 'Lily... Oh my God. Lily.'

Ellen's heart flipped and her stomach clenched.

'She is Rafe's...' His green eyes widened as the knowledge dawned on him. 'She is his image. I see it now... She has his eyes and his smile...'

'Alistair.' The blood drained from her face.

'It is true, is it not?'

Ellen swallowed, fear of his rejection of Lily overwhelming her. 'I believe so.'

'*You believe so!* Do not take me for a fool, Ellen. I can see it as clear as day now I am aware.' He swore harshly. 'Christ almighty!

I feel ridiculous I never saw it before. She looks nothing like Ava.'

'Lily looks like me,' she defended, knowing it was a lie. The child was Rafe's double.

He slumped down on the chair in the corner of the room. 'What a fool I have been. Hoodwinked by my wife and best friend.'

'We didn't mean for it to happen. It just did. You knew I didn't love you when we married, but I never set out to hurt you.'

'But you have done.' He gazed up at her.

'I'm sorry.' She couldn't go to him. A wall was between them now so great it couldn't be breeched.

'It is not enough.' Tears reddened his eyes. 'To be betrayed by you and Rafe cannot be borne.'

'It was one time, Alistair.'

He shook his head. 'Maybe physically, but in your heart, you are his and he is yours. I do not count.'

She swallowed back her tears. 'My feelings for Rafe were there before I met you. I'm truly sorry.'

'Sorry you've hurt me or sorry that I found out?'

'Both.' She faced him. 'The truth didn't benefit anyone. Rafe doesn't know, and neither did you. We were able to get on with our lives. Ava was born, we continued on.'

'Living a lie!'

'I lived with the lie, Alistair, not you, not Rafe, *me*. I took it on to save you both from being hurt and destroying your friendship.'

'Am I supposed to thank you for it?' he asked incredulously.

'No, of course not.'

'Good!' His nostrils flared in his anger.

Ellen took a deep breath. 'I know this is difficult, but Rafe will be devastated to learn you've suffered because of our one mistake. He does value your friendship.'

'Friendship? If he valued it, he would never have taken my wife to his bed!'

'It was a moment of madness!'

'I have no friendship now with that man. He betrayed me with my own wife!'

'And we are desperately sorry.'

'Are you?' Alistair's eyebrows rose mockingly. 'I believe you are only sorry I found out.' He strode into the bedroom and threw the letter into the fire. He watched it burn. 'Ava is the only one that is mine. The only one I will care about from this day forward.'

Ellen leaned against the doorjamb as Rafe's words blackened and turned to ash. 'I beg you not to treat Lily differently. None of this is her fault.'

'No, it is yours.'

'Yes. Despise me, not her.'

Alistair's fists clenched. He strode to the door. 'I am going to the study. Do not disturb me.'

'We need to talk about the future.'

He laughed, a jarring sound full of hate. 'Our future? What a good joke.' He slammed the door behind him.

Sitting on the bed, Ellen didn't know what to do or think. A part of her was relieved the truth about Lily was out. Yet, she also knew that her marriage was dead. She didn't expect Alistair to forgive her. She had done wrong. Now she just had to work out how to make it up to him.

* * *

DESPITE THE SEASONS changing and winter on their doorstep, the day of the Ashfords' garden party was one of soft sunshine. Heavy frost coated the land, but it had melted by the time Ellen drove Riona and Bridget in the buggy through the gates of the Ashfords' stunning home in Sutton Forest.

Alistair rode Pepper beside the buggy. For days he hadn't spoken to her.

Ellen had told Riona what had happened, and her sister had kept Bridget and Lily out of Alistair's sight as much as possible. For twenty-four hours, Alistair had locked himself in the study and drank. He'd ignored all of Ellen's attempts to talk and so she'd left him to sulk and drink himself into a stupor.

Even now as they halted before the Ashfords' mansion, Alistair looked tired and swayed in the saddle. He'd cut himself shaving and although suitably dressed, he'd not washed and reeked of spirits.

After being greeted by the butler, the four of them walked around the side of the house and down the lawn to where the gathering was taking place amidst the lush gardens.

Feeling anything but happy and social, Ellen plastered on a smile and chatted to Pippa and Augusta and Gil's parents. Pippa's mother, Mrs Noble was seated at one of the tables with some other women, including Mrs Riddle. Ellen went to talk to them, moving as far away from Alistair as possible.

As the day wore on, Ellen became more concerned for Alistair who was drinking steadily. She had offered him a cup of tea, but he'd turned away from her with a sneer.

After a couple of hours talking polite chat about nothing very interesting, Ellen was desperate to make her excuses and head home. She looked around for Bridget, who'd gone to play with some of the other children.

'Your daughter is drawing with the other children,' Mrs Riddle said. 'Augusta has organised children's entertainments on the west lawn.'

'Lovely. I shall go and watch them for a while.' Ellen rose from her chair just as Riona hurried up to her. 'What is it?'

Riona pulled Ellen away from the others. 'Gil has arranged a horse race for the men.'

'So?'

'Alistair is among them, and he is terribly drunk, I'm sure of it.'

Ellen, not wanting to draw attention to them, walked quickly with Riona to the stable block where the male guests had gathered and were laughing and jesting with each other as they mounted their horses.

'Alistair?' Ellen stepped closer to him as he sat upon Pepper.

'What do you want?' Bloodshot eyes glared down at her.

'I don't think you're fit to ride,' she whispered up at him.

'Do not presume to tell me what to do, woman.' He kicked his heels into Pepper's side and trotted off with the others.

Angry, she strode back to Riona and gripped her sister's arm. 'The foolish eejit!'

Riona frowned. 'What is he trying to prove? He'll not be able to stay in the saddle and will fall off and everyone will laugh at him.'

Glaring at Alistair's back, Ellen was torn between concern and annoyance. 'He's going to humiliate himself and be even more irate. We need to go home.'

'Yes, and when we do, you and he need to talk, Ellen. The house has been an awful place to be lately. Bridget is asking questions. Alistair ignored her this morning when she spoke to him.'

Ellen chewed her bottom lip in worry. 'If he won't talk to me, we'll all go to Louisburgh until he returns to Sydney.'

They followed the mounted men to the edge of the field where the women had gathered to cheer and wave handkerchiefs.

'Men can be such children,' Pippa laughed. 'Always trying to better the other. They've taken bets on who will win, would you believe?'

Ellen simply smiled, though inside she was angry. Was Alistair going to always behave in such a way now, being reckless and irresponsible? And was he to snap and snarl at her forever more? She didn't think she could handle it. If this was a taste of their future, she would move to Louisburgh permanently and be done with him and their marriage.

An older man, Gil's father Mr Ashford, set the men off and to a loud cheer the horses sprang forward and pounded along the grassy field.

'How far are they going?' Riona asked Augusta.

'Up to the bottom of the hill out there and then around the clump of trees, over the creek, and back to us. The first rider past Father wins a bottle of Gil's finest port.'

Ellen wished to go back to the refreshments or to join Bridget rather than watch the race. Alistair was in the middle of the pack as the men rode out of sight behind the hill.

As the women chatted and made assumptions on who'd win, Ellen started walking back to the gardens.

'Here they come!' Augusta shouted.

Ellen turned on the path at the edge of the gardens and glanced back at the wide brown fields. She couldn't see which rider was coming first and didn't care. She wanted to go home.

A scream rent the air.

Then another.

The thundering hooves mixed with the cries of the women.

Standing on the path, Ellen couldn't see what the commotion was about. Had a snake come out of the grass and scared the women, or horses?

In surprise, she watched as one of the young ladies fainted. Lifting her skirts, she darted back to the group of women who were all talking at once.

'Riona?' Ellen got to her sister's side, but Riona's gaze was fixed on the riders who were quickly dismounting and hurrying to the fallen man and horse.

'Ellen... Is that Pepper?' Riona pointed at the horse, which was trying desperately to get up but was lashing out at the men assisting her.

'It's Pepper!' Ellen slipped through the rails of the fence and holding her skirts high ran across the field to the narrow creek at the base of the hill.

Pepper's neighing sounded tortuous.

'Dear Mother of Jesus,' Riona prayed running behind Ellen. 'That poor horse!'

Ellen, puffing, slowed as she neared Pepper. The whites of her eyes showed in fear or pain, Ellen didn't know which. Then she noticed the broken bone jutting out of the foreleg. Ellen gasped. 'Oh no!'

'Sweet Jesus,' Riona cried and crossed herself.

'Turn away, ladies.' One of the men ushered them away. 'We'll have to shoot her.'

'Alistair?' Ellen searched for him. 'He'll be heartbroken about Pepper.'

Another group of men stood or knelt by the side of the creek's bank. Ellen raced over to them, searching for Alistair. Then she slowed, her heart sinking, her breath short. Alistair lay on the grass at the edge of the bank. Gil had taken off his coat and placed it under Alistair's head.

Falling to her knees beside Alistair, she cradled his hand to her chest. 'Alistair! Where are you hurt?'

'Nowhere,' he grimaced. 'There is no pain at all. Help me up...'

As Ellen eased him up, Gil restrained her and shook his head. She stared at him wordlessly.

'He's taken a blow to the head.' Gil showed Ellen the wide deep gash at the back of Alistair's head. Blood seeped like a small river turning Alistair's blond hair dark and staining the grass beneath red.

'A doctor.' Ellen turned, ready to run for a doctor.

'He's been sent for.' Gil took a coat offered by another man and laid it over Alistair. 'I've asked for one of the men to go and get the farm cart from the stables. We'll take him to the house on that.' Gil tried to stem the blood from the head wound.

Riona and another man knelt to help him staunch it with handkerchiefs that turned red within seconds.

'Ellen,' Alistair croaked, a trickle of blood ran out of his nose.

'Yes, I'm here, right here.' She smiled down at him, using a handkerchief Riona gave her to wipe away the blood. 'Rest now. We'll have you seen by a doctor very soon, then get you home.'

'I am sorry.'

'Whist now,' she soothed. 'Lie still. Don't talk.'

Men and woman gathered around them. Ellen was vaguely aware of Gil and Pippa issuing orders, of Riona sitting right beside Ellen holding a cloth to Alistair's head. The scene seemed surreal, yet she kept her focus on Alistair, gripping his hand tightly, smiling down into his face.

'I forgive you...' he whispered, his green eyes staring at her.

'Don't talk. Rest.'

'I do love you...'

She kissed his forehead. 'Please stop talking. Save your strength.' She kissed him again. 'We must get you well...'

'Ava... Do not let her forget me...' His eyes closed, and his body went limp.

'Alistair?' She shook him gently. 'Alistair!' She leaned nearer, waiting for his green eyes to open, for him to say something to her. 'Alistair.'

Ellen looked up at Riona, who instantly started praying. Ellen stared at Gil, who knelt and checked Alistair's pulse in his neck. He checked his breathing, ripped open his waistcoat and shirt and put his ear to Alistair's chest.

In utter shock, Ellen stared at Gil as he knelt back on his heels and shook his head.

Ellen grabbed Alistair's shoulders and shook him. 'Alistair, wake up. Wake up now, do you hear me?'

'Ellen,' Riona cried, easing her away. 'He's gone.'

'No. He's fainted. We must take him to the house.' Even as she said the words, the truth seeped into her brain, shutting down her emotions, her speech.

A gunshot made her jump. Someone had put Pepper out of her misery. Ellen swayed at the suddenness of it all.

Riona helped her to her feet, and she stared down at the handsome man she'd married for security, the man she had betrayed, but who she had cared for in her own way. She should have told him she loved him...

CHAPTER 13

*R*afe slipped into the coolness of the house after riding in a stuffy carriage in the warm June sunshine. He bounded up the stairs to Patrick's room and after a brief knock walked in. He grinned at the boy sitting in a chair by the open window. 'You are looking well.'

'I am. I'm glad you're back,' Patrick said, looking thin but with a healthy colour in his cheeks.

'I told you I would only be away a few days to sort out a few things in Liverpool.' Rafe ruffled the boy's hair and sat on the window seat. 'How have you been?'

'Grand. Though a little bored now. The doctor said he'll only be coming once a day now I'm improving so much.'

'Ah, well, that must mean you are recovering well.' Rafe winked, gladness filling him. 'Shall we go for a walk then?'

'Can we?' The boy perked up.

'Yes, and if you are not too tired tomorrow, we might go fishing?'

'Champion!'

Rafe laughed at Patrick's enthusiasm. 'Have you written to your mother?'

'Yes, every day for the last week.'

'Good. I have, too. Now you are well again I have told her the situation of your recent illness. I posted the letter last week. She should have it by August.'

A look of longing entered Patrick's eyes. 'Such a long time.'

'Indeed, it is.' Knowing the depression the boy suffered from missing home, Rafe quickly stood. 'Right let us get you outdoors and in the sunshine. A walk around the gardens will lighten your spirits.'

Rafe helped him pull on his socks and boots for Patrick was still rather weak. The fever had kept him bedridden for weeks as it came and left with varying degrees of severity. It wasn't until the middle of May that the doctor declared Patrick out of danger, yet the road to recovery was long. Some days Patrick thrived, then other days he didn't have the energy of a newborn kitten.

Downstairs, Rafe paused in the hall as the front door opened and Iris and his mother entered the house.

'Oh, you are home?' Iris kissed Rafe's cheek.

'I am pleased to see you, my son.' His mother also kissed him.

'You'll stay for a while?' Iris asked, handing her parasol to a footman.

'Yes, I have worked hard the last two days to sort the office issues and leave instructions to Pollard. I shall return to Liverpool next week.'

'And look at you, young man.' His mother smiled at Patrick. 'You're looking better every day, doesn't he, Rafe?'

'He does. Which is why we are going for a walk.'

'Lovely.' Iris sailed into the drawing room. 'I shall have a tea tray sent out onto the terrace in half an hour and we can all have tea and cake together.'

Rafe and Patrick strolled the white-gravelled path snaking through the pretty and well-tended formal gardens. A peacock called from atop a wall bordering the gardens from the service areas.

'He is a pretty boy,' Patrick said, indicating the male peacock. 'I see him from my bedroom window a lot. His tail is magnificent, but the lady peacocks will have nothing to do with him despite his displays.'

Rafe laughed. 'That is the want of women sometimes. No matter what a man does they ignore him.'

'Why aren't you married?' Patrick suddenly asked.

'Because… Because the woman I love is unavailable to me.'

'That is sad.'

'Life can be brutal at times.'

Patrick stopped at the gate that led to the deer park. 'I nearly died, didn't I?'

Rafe took a breath. 'Yes.'

'If I am to die, I would like to do that with my mammy near me.'

'You have recovered now. You shan't die.' Rafe frowned at the boy's morbid thoughts. 'Look how well you are.'

'I heard the doctor say to Iris that I could have recurring bouts of fever at any time. Some days I can't get out of bed.'

'When did he say that?'

'Yesterday when he called to check on me. They were talking by the door thinking I was napping. But I heard them. If I get ill again, I might not be so lucky is what he said.'

Placing his hand on the boy's thin shoulder Rafe squeezed gently. 'What we need to do then is to fatten you up and make you so healthy the fever cannot take hold again.'

Patrick smiled one of his rare smiles, but it faded just as quickly. 'Can I go home, please?'

Rafe's heart twisted in his chest. The boy would never be happy in England, he knew that instinctively. 'I cannot send you home on such a long voyage until you have fully regained your health.'

Patrick straightened, hope in his grey-blue eyes. 'But I can go home once I'm well enough to travel?'

Rafe nodded, his throat tight. He couldn't keep the boy here. It wasn't fair to him. He'd pulled through a near-death experience and Rafe knew if he became ill again while in England, he might not have the will to survive it a second time. He wanted to go home, to be with his family and who could blame him?

Patrick hugged him around the waist. 'Thank you, Rafe, thank you!'

Patting the boy's back, Rafe felt a swirl of emotions flow through him. He was defying Alistair's orders to have him educated at Harrow and keep him in England for his own safety, but if Patrick did not return home he would pine away, Rafe was sure of it. And as much as he would miss the boy, who he had grown so close to, he knew the right thing to do was send him back to Australia, to Ellen.

* * *

IN THE POURING cold June rain, Ellen stood by the grave of Alistair Emmerson in the churchyard in Berrima. The stonemason had completed his headstone, and it had been erected just that morning before the heavens opened and sent down torrential rain.

She watched in strange fascination as the rain created small rivulets on the mounded dirt and splattered the dried, dead flowers that had been placed on top.

In the three weeks since his death, Ellen had tried to deal with the grief suffered by Bridget, who had taken the news of not only Alistair's death, but also Pepper's, badly. Lily was too little to understand and the same with Ava. The estate had plunged into mourning with Mr Thwaite taking control of the running of the day-to-day issues, while Ellen had organised the funeral and wrote the numerous letters to people that mattered. Writing to Rafe, the boys, and Alistair's parents had been the hardest of all.

It seemed the whole district had turned out for Alistair's

funeral. People travelled from Sydney for Ellen had placed an announcement in the Sydney newspapers. She'd written to Robin in Melbourne, Alistair's cousin, but he'd been struck with a bout of fever and unable to make the journey.

Alistair would have been proud of his funeral. Ellen had ordered the best for him. It was the least she could do. She had to honour him, the man who had given her a grand life, even if it had been for his own reasons. However, all that aside, they had enjoyed good times and created a family. He hadn't deserved to die so young. Despite everything, she would miss him.

'Ellen.' Riona walked through the graves towards her. 'Come along before you catch a chill.'

'It looks grand, don't you think?' Ellen nodded to the headstone.

'Aye, so it does.' Riona smiled sadly at the carved piece of sandstone denoting Alistair as a good husband and loving father. 'You've done him proud, so you have. Come now.'

Heading back to the road where the carriage waited with Higgins up in the driver's seat, Ellen stepped over the muddy puddles not wanting to splash her black mourning skirt.

On the drive back to Emmerson Park, Riona handed Ellen a bundle of letters. 'From the boys.'

'How wonderful.' She hugged the precious bundle to her chest. 'Of course, they will not yet know of Alistair's death. It will be months before they do.'

'I've read my letter from Patrick while waiting for you.' Riona passed the single sheet of paper to Ellen. 'It was posted in March.'

DEAR AUNTY RIONA,

I am writing this letter instead of copying out text from a book. I do not like Latin. I do not like this school. I do not see Austin that much. He is with the older boys. We cannot go horse riding here. The village is

*nice. We are able to buy things on Saturday afternoons from the shops
there. Rafe has given us money to do so. I miss you all.*

Your nephew,
Patrick Kittrick.
1ˢᵗ March 1854
Harrow, England.

ELLEN REREAD THE SAD NOTE, fighting the tears. 'He sounds
terribly unhappy.'

'Aye, he does.' Riona took back the note and folded it.

'I shall write to Rafe and ask him to send the boys home,' Ellen
decided. 'Now Alistair is gone, I feel I can do it. I wanted to send
for them once Colm was no longer a threat, but Alistair wouldn't
hear of it.'

Riona let out a long breath. 'And what of Rafe Hamilton?'

'What of him?' Ellen ignored the way her heart thumped at
the mere mention of his name.

'You still love him?'

Ellen glanced out of the window. 'What does it matter? Rafe
lives in England and I here.'

'So? Sure, and can't you sell everything and sail to England to
be with him in Liverpool?'

Ellen digested Riona's comment as she waited for Higgins to
halt the carriage before the house.

Seamus came from around the side of the house to help them
down the step and take their packages and shopping they'd done
before going to the churchyard.

Once inside the hall, Riona turned to Ellen as they divested
their coats and gloves. 'Well? Is that what you are thinking? Sell
up? I'd like to know, so I would.'

Entering the drawing room feeling chilled, Ellen placed the
letters on the sofa and stood by the fire, holding her hands out to
the warmth. 'I honestly don't want to do that.'

'That surprises me. I thought you'd be on the first ship to Liverpool.'

Ellen had surprised herself with her thoughts since Alistair's death. 'I have no wish to live in Liverpool.'

'I'm sure Mr Hamilton would buy a beautiful house somewhere in the English countryside for you.' Riona's eyes widened. 'You could even buy property back home in Mayo.'

'I have a beautiful house in the country right here, and then there's Louisburgh. I don't want to leave it.'

'Not even for Ireland?'

Ellen sighed, long nights of not sleeping well were weighing her down. 'No, not even for Ireland. There is no future for us in Ireland, only memories and ghosts.'

'Then what will you do?'

'Stay in this country.'

'I'm glad.'

'You are?' This surprised her.

Riona joined her by the fire. 'This is our home now. I'm happy here.'

'Then it is settled.' Ellen sat down on the sofa.

'And what about Rafe Hamilton?'

'I don't know.' And she didn't. She felt she still loved him, but she also felt the need for some time on her own. Since she was sixteen, she'd been married twice and within each marriage she'd grown to feel trapped, contained by her husbands' wishes and wants. It was time for her to have some space to do the things she wanted to do without asking for permission first or needing to consider a husband's opinion and desires.

'Well, there is time for all that, so there is. Right now, Rafe and the boys don't even know Alistair has died and they won't do until August.'

Ellen untied the string of twine from around the bundle of letters. She sorted the letters from the boys to one side to be read later when Bridget had finished her lessons so she could hear.

The bills and business letters were put into another pile. She opened one envelope and read the letter inside.

'I've received a letter from Alistair's solicitor,' she told Riona. 'In the morning, I'll have to leave for Sydney. There is the business to contend with, the will to be read.'

'Do you want me to go with you?'

'No, I'd rather you stayed here as I don't want to take the girls in this cold weather.'

'But you're still feeding Ava.'

'No, not anymore. I've decided she'll have to take cow's milk from now on.'

'Why? She's only nine weeks old.'

'I'm too busy to be tied to the nursery. I don't know what I'm going to have to deal with once I'm in Sydney.' Ellen stood. 'I'll go speak to Rachel and sort it. Perhaps there is a wet nurse in the village we can hire.' She paused by the door about to speak when Caroline Duffy raced into the room. 'You are to come, quickly!'

'What is it, Caroline?' Ellen asked.

'It's Moira. She's collapsed.' The girl looked close to tears.

Ellen and Riona rushed to the kitchen where Honor was kneeling on the floor beside Moira.

'God in heaven.' Riona murmured as they spotted the pool of blood spreading across Moira's skirts.

Moira moaned.

'Honor,' Ellen snapped. 'Send for the doctor and for Mr Thwaite. Hurry now! Riona, find a blanket to cover Moira.'

For several minutes, the kitchen buzzed with people coming and going. The kitchen maids were sent back to the ovens and boiling pots, while Mr Thwaite came in, scooped up Moira and carried her to her room on the other side of the kitchen.

Here, he laid her gently down on the bed. 'There now, lass. Take it easy,' he crooned.

'It's the baby,' Moira mumbled. 'It's coming out of me.'

'Lie still, Moira.' Ellen shooed Mr Thwaite from the room and she and Riona attended to Moira, trying to make her comfortable when she squirmed in agony. They undressed her and placed her in a nightgown before covering the sheets with towels.

Honor entered carrying a bowl of warm water and more towels over her arm. She set to work down the end of the bed.

Moira gave an enormous screech and gripping her knees pulled them up as she cried out.

Ellen stared as a tiny baby boy, no bigger than her hand lay between Moira's bloodied thighs. She held him, but he was blue. His eyes fused closed, his chest not moving.

'He's too small,' Honor murmured.

Crying, Riona held Moira to her chest as Ellen helped Honor to clear away the birth.

Carefully, Ellen wrapped the tiny baby in a towel. Not knowing what to do, she went to take the baby from the room then hesitated and returned to Moira's side. 'Do you want to see him?'

Showing no emotion, Moira lifted her head and stared at the miniature baby. She gently touched the top of his head and then kissed him. 'Take him to his father to bury him.'

Covering the baby, Ellen left the room. Mr Thwaite waited outside the door. Silently, he held out his hands and Ellen placed the wrapped bundle in his arms. 'Find a place in the garden,' she said tearfully.

'I know a spot.' With a nod, Mr Thwaite walked away, shoulders slumped.

Ellen watched him walk towards the rose garden. She knew instantly he would bury the baby under the rose tree that was planted in memory of her Thomas, and which nearby was a bench seat where Bridget liked to sit and talk to her dead brother. Now there would be two little boys they could all mourn.

CHAPTER 14

*S*eated in Alistair's wood-panelled office overlooking the circular quay, Ellen counted the figures again. The desk held several ledgers and Alistair's clerk, Mr McCulloch, was at another desk sorting through invoices.

She'd arrived at the Lower Fort Street house in Sydney yesterday. As a house in mourning, she knew she'd receive no callers when acquaintances heard she was in town, and she was grateful.

After eating Mrs Lawson's excellent breakfast this morning, she'd made her way to this office, a place she'd not visited since Alistair hurt his leg when they were first married and Ellen had taken over running the business while he recovered.

Since then, Alistair had expanded the import and export company, but also bought shares in other companies both here in Sydney and in Melbourne.

'Did you find the paperwork for the deal my husband did with the Huon Pine company in Davey River, Mr McCulloch?'

'No, madam, not yet. I know Mr Emmerson was waiting on documents to come from Van Diemen's Land.' McCulloch, aged about forty, spoke with a thick Scottish accent.

Ellen glanced at the clock on the wall. 'I have to go. Mr Baldwin's office is on the other side of town.'

'Very good, madam. I'll continue sorting through the mail and answering Mr Emmerson's correspondence where I can. I'll have them all waiting for you to countersign on your return.'

'Thank you, Mr McCulloch. I'll be back by three, but if I'm not, go home and I'll see you tomorrow.'

Downstairs, the breeze blew straight off the harbour making her shiver as she climbed into the carriage. 'Bent Street, Higgins, Baldwin Solicitors.'

'Right you are, madam.'

Within a short while, Ellen was stepping down from the carriage in Bent Street and entering the terraced house of Mr Baldwin. The front room of the house had been converted into his office.

'Mrs Emmerson. Come in, do.' Mr Baldwin, a grey-haired, bespectacled man in his sixties, took her hand and ushered her to a chair on the other side of his desk. 'What a terrible occasion for us to meet. You have my sincere condolences again.'

'Thank you. Your letter mentioned the reading of the will. When shall that take place and where?'

'Well, right here and now, Mrs Emmerson.'

'Just the two of us?'

'My clerk will be in shortly and will stand witness to my reading, but everything is very straightforward.'

'It is?' Ellen was surprised. 'I was expecting there to be a delay, that perhaps Robin Emmerson, my late husband's cousin would need to be involved, or Mr Hamilton his business partner, who resides in Liverpool, England.'

'No, not at all.' Mr Baldwin waved in his young clerk who brought in a tea tray and poured out cups of tea.

Ellen thanked him but didn't touch the tea and concentrated on Mr Baldwin.

'Right, shall I get straight to it, madam?'

'Please.' She twisted her hands in her lap, not knowing what to expect.

Baldwin read a few lines out to her, declaring Alistair was of sound mind on the writing of the will which was done by Mr Baldwin and witnessed by his clerk, Haberfield, who reddened at the attention, and also witnessed by Mr Baldwin's partner, Mr Friend, who was currently at a court sitting.

'Basically, Mrs Emmerson, your husband has left everything to you.'

'Everything to me?' Ellen repeated, disbelief making her sit forward.

Mr Baldwin read from the will, which was pages long, but the main thing Ellen heard was the most important line. *All properties, monies and assets are bequeathed to my wife, Ellen Emmerson.*

Mr Baldwin adjusted his glasses. 'You understand that a will is most vital when you have such an extensive property and business portfolio? On your husband's death, you have become a wealthy woman with assets. A will of your own is extremely important.'

'I see.'

'I believe on previous meetings with Mr Emmerson that he said the eldest boy, Austin, is not yet of age? That none of the children are of age?'

'No, none are.'

'Then you must nominate a person, or persons, you can trust to be the executor of your will, should your demise come about before your eldest son is of age, but we can discuss that in a little while. First, we shall fully examine your husband's will.' Baldwin took a sip of tea. 'I will give you a copy for you to keep for your own records.'

Ellen's head reeled. Alistair had left everything to her.

'Firstly, Mrs Emmerson, you are now the owner of the house on Lower Fort Street, the row of five terrace houses on Nicholson Street in Balmain, the country estate of Emmerson

Park, a property containing a substantial house, and nine outbuildings and five hundred acres and all animals upon the land.' He paused. 'Shall I read out all the listed animals?'

'No, thank you. I know every animal on the land. Carry on.'

'You also own a sheep station north of the Goulburn Plains, named Louisburgh, containing a hut and two outbuildings and seven hundred acres and two thousand sheep, the farm at Marulan consisting of five hundred acres and a head of cattle numbering two hundred and four beasts, and a smaller concern at Moss Vale consisting of a farmhouse and three acres of land sown with wheat. You are also owner of twenty-five percent of the Hamilton and Emmerson Import and Export business.'

Ellen frowned. 'You forgot the property at Kangaroo Valley.'

'No, madam. That property was sold in March, the twenty-fourth, I believe.'

'Sold?' Alistair had sold the property she bought without telling her? She'd only bought it when she was pregnant with Ava, less than a year ago.

'Indeed. I have the paperwork to testify that it was sold. I believe Mr Emmerson wanted to use the money to pay off some debts.'

'Debts? What debts?' She knew of no debts, only the original small bank loans. One for the construction of Emmerson Park and the other to purchase Louisburgh. Alistair had told her Lower Fort Street was mortgage free.

Mr Baldwin looked uncomfortable. 'It seems Mr Emmerson had invested in some schemes which didn't make a profit. I should also inform you that the five terrace houses in Balmain, the farm at Marulan and Emmerson Park all have second mortgages.'

'Second mortgages?' The air seemed sucked from her lungs.

'Lower Fort Street has also been mortgaged for security against loans.'

She stared at him, wanting to say he was wrong but instinct

warned her that he was not only right, but she knew something like this must have been happening. Why hadn't she asked Alistair more questions?

'Unfortunately, the bank repayments are somewhat behind...'

Ellen stared at him. 'Behind?' She felt stupid repeating his words, but it was all too much to comprehend.

'Yes. I believe Mr Emmerson was trying to bankroll a new investment in Van Diemen's Land and he used the equity in the house on Lower Fort Street to do so. However, the return on that investment has not yet been submitted by that company. Also, I believe your husband...' Mr Baldwin couldn't meet her eyes and shuffled the pages in front of him.

'Yes?'

'Well, let us put it politely, he enjoyed an extravagant lifestyle. One he couldn't really afford. I advised him against many of the schemes he entered into, but he ignored my opinions. Luckily, he was able to cover the losses by mortgaging the properties. The Kangaroo Valley property made a decent profit but Mr Emmerson invested in a gold mine in Ballarat with that profit. It has yet to pay a dividend and I would advise you to sell the gold licence for that mine.'

'I see.' She wilted under the weight of the problems he was outlining to her.

'The banks are wanting payment, Mrs Emmerson. I cannot stress that enough. If you do not satisfy them soon, they will start proceedings against you.'

The blood drained from her face. She could end up in court?

Baldwin consulted his papers on the desk. 'You must know, too, that I have received a letter from Mr Gardner-Hill stating he wishes to buy your remaining shares of the import and export business, should you wish to sell, which considering the current situation it might be wise to do.'

Confused, Ellen tried to understand what he was saying. 'Mr Gardner-Hill?'

Baldwin looked sorry for her. 'I appreciate this is a shock to you having to deal with such matters at this difficult time.'

'Are you telling me Alistair sold some of his shares of the import and export business he owned with Rafe Hamilton to Mr Gardner-Hill?'

'That is correct. He sold twenty-five percent of his fifty percent holding.'

She couldn't imagine it. That business had been his and Rafe's first concern, their joint venture which had proven to be a wise and lucrative investment that meant so much to them both. 'Why?'

Baldwin shifted in his chair. 'As I just mentioned, your husband was under some financial pressure. I received a letter from him that arrived only a day before your letter came informing me of his accident. His death halted me from acting upon his instructions.'

'Which were?'

'To sell Louisburgh.'

'Sell Louisburgh.' She went cold. The one thing Alistair knew she wanted more than anything else.

'Yes. But I didn't get a chance to start speaking to a land agent for the very next day your letter informed me of his sudden death.'

A white-hot rage simmered in her chest, but she reined it in, needing to focus on Mr Baldwin and what he was telling her.

'Do you wish to sell your shares to Mr Gardner-Hill?'

'No!' she said it too loudly such was her anger. 'Forgive me, but no, that will not be happening.'

'Mrs Emmerson, at present your expenditure is outweighing your income. The bank is demanding payments. Your husband understood the need to sell his assets to keep abreast of the repayments or face ruin.'

Ellen rubbed her gloved hands over her face. 'Can we sell other things to pay off the bank debts?'

'Absolutely.' He nodded vigorously. 'I feel that is the best and perhaps the only option open to you.'

'Are you able to do it for me, Mr Baldwin?'

'Yes, madam, if you wish I can be your solicitor and work on your behalf.'

'That is what I wish.' Disillusionment at Alistair fought with the need to be practical. She needed time to think things through, but she didn't have time.

'Very well,' He indicated to the quiet clerk to start taking notes. 'What do you wish to do, Mrs Emmerson?'

Her mind worked quickly. 'Sell the shares in the Van Diemen's Land pine company and the gold licence and whatever else to do with the mine in Ballarat.'

Mr Baldwin also took notes. 'Anything else?'

'Sell the terrace houses in Balmain.' It hurt her to say so for she had created them, worked on the designs and watched them being built from the first sod turned. Her anger turned into a hard knot of fury at Alistair.

Mr Baldwin looked up at her from his notes, waiting.

She took a deep breath. 'Sell the Lower Fort Street house.'

'Lower Fort Street!' He gaped at her. 'It's prime harbour foreshore land, Mrs Emmerson. You do not need to consider going to that extreme just yet. Perhaps sell something else instead? The Moss Vale farm and the land at Marulan? Shares in the import business?'

She'd rather live on the streets than to sell to the Gardner-Hills. Besides, it was a link to Rafe and income.

'All I care about, Mr Baldwin, is Emmerson Park and Louisburgh and the import business. As long as I can keep those, I'll be happy. I need to have something to pass onto my children. If possible, I'd like to keep the Marulan property, too.'

'You do not wish to sell either Marulan or Louisburgh?'

She clenched her teeth to stop from commenting about Alistair wanting to sell Louisburgh behind her back. He had wanted to hurt her. After finding out about Lily he'd written to Mr Baldwin to sell Louisburgh. 'No. Not those two properties.'

Mr Baldwin started writing on a fresh piece of paper. 'I understand. You must get a good price, and I think you will, on the five terrace houses, to pay off that mortgage. You are unlikely to make a profit, but we'll see how it goes. As long as the bank is paid back, then that is the main thing. The same with the shares in the company in Van Diemen's Land. We need to find the right buyer for those shares and with them offloaded, the bank loan can be repaid. That leaves the house on Lower Fort Street. It would fetch a very good price situated on the shore as it is. You would, I imagine have money left over, which you could use to start repaying the mortgage on Emmerson Park.'

'Then do it.'

'Are you completely sure? A Sydney home is must advantageous.'

'It isn't when it's a noose around my neck because I can't afford it. I'll have Emmerson Park, Louisburgh and the Marulan property and the little farm at Moss Vale. If I can keep those, that will be plenty for now.'

'And not forgetting your shares in the import business.'

'And my shares.'

'You will of course need to put in place a manager for the import business. Mr Emmerson did most of it himself having made the contacts around Sydney over the years and then more recently in Melbourne.'

Ellen nodded. 'I'll see to that.'

'And your country properties will have to start earning their keep. I cannot stress that enough. You need an income from them. The expenditure for Emmerson Park alone is rather high, which was all well and good when money was being earned by other ventures, but now it needs to be reassessed or at least find some way of earning income on it?'

'I'll see to that as well.' She stiffened her spine at the over-whelming task before her.

'With the sales of these properties you will gain some sense of order and going forward, you'll know what you need to concentrate on. I know I do not need to tell you, Mrs Emmerson, that economies must begin.'

'Mr Baldwin, I have lived through the famine in Ireland. I know how to live miserly when needed.'

He nodded and finished writing his notes. 'Shall we refresh our tea and then begin on your own will?'

'Yes.' Ellen leaned back in the chair feeling a mixture of emotions. Relieved that Emmerson Park and Louisburgh were safe for now, but irate at Alistair for making bad decisions that meant the sale of their other properties.

What seemed like many hours later, and when she could stand no more of talking, Ellen left Mr Baldwin's office and gratefully stepped out into the fresh air.

'I was beginning to worry, madam,' Higgins called down from his seat.

'I'm sorry, Higgins, it was agonising for me, too.' She gave him a wry smile.

'Home, madam?'

She sighed. The last thing she wanted to do was return to the house that Alistair loved, and which was filled with his belongings. 'No, can we drive to the Domain please? I fancy a walk.'

'Rightio, madam.'

She relaxed in the carriage, her mind still whirling with thoughts of the day's events. How had Alistair managed to keep all that from her? To sell the property in Kangaroo Valley, the one she had travelled to view while pregnant and which she had told him was valuable in cedar forests alone, she'd never understand. But to then mortgage their assets? It astounded her. To take such risks, to invest in schemes that created debts. Why was he playing with their fortunes as though they meant nothing? The very thought gave her a shiver. All those years of suffering in Ireland through the blight and the starvation, only to come here for a better life could easily have been forsaken due to Alistair's whims and blatant investment gambling.

Hadn't she told him repeatedly that land was the best investment? Yet the land she had bought he had mortgaged or sold to cater to his impulses. She couldn't forgive him for not taking her seriously. He knew of her nightmares of being homeless, of the children having nothing, of hunger and death. He had given no thought to the hardship that could have fallen upon them with his reckless ventures. While she had been trying to secure their future with property purchases, he'd been risking money on schemes that nearly sent them bankrupt. If Alistair hadn't died, who knows where they could have ended up. Would he have mortgaged all the properties, or sold them secretly without her knowledge?

She was still reeling from his deceit to sell Louisburgh. After finding out about Lily being Rafe's child, he'd sent the letter to Mr Baldwin, probably the very next morning. Out of spite, pain and anger he would have sold it and likely enjoyed telling her what he had done. How could she forgive him?

Yet, as he lay dying, he'd told her he loved her. He had said he was sorry.

Pain hit her in the chest.

Their marriage had never stood a chance and if he had lived, they would have torn each other apart and ended up hating each other.

As the carriage crawled to a stop, Ellen lifted her gaze and stared out at the extensive grounds of the Domain, an area in the middle of the city where people could walk, and children could play.

Ellen alighted and walked the paths through the wide lawns and snaked between sizeable gardens planted with specimens from the explored parts of the country.

Her black bonnet shielded her face from those strolling the gardens or sitting on benches in the afternoon sunshine. She hoped to not meet anyone she knew. Wearing mourning black might prevent anyone from speaking to her out of respect. She wasn't in the mood to chat about the weather just now. She needed to think, to plan.

Economies must begin, Mr Baldwin had told her.

Well, she had done it before, she could do it again, and it wouldn't be as bad as Ireland. A ship's horn carried on the slight breeze from the harbour. Ellen lifted her head to stare out at the ships and small boats sailing on the waterfront. One looked similar to the *Blue Maid* that had brought her and her family out to this country. She remembered sailing into the harbour and being nervous and excited. Her dreams of giving her children a better life were forefront to everything else. She was determined to make a success of her new life.

Marrying Alistair had seen that dream become a reality, yet now she was faced with the prospect it could all be gone if the banks weren't repaid. In marrying Alistair, she thought she would be secure, safe, and she had relaxed a little, believing she had their future protected. How foolish of her to trust another with her children's future? Hadn't she learned that lesson in Ireland?

No one could look after her and her family better than herself. She had let her guard down, and the consequences were extreme. She could lose everything if she wasn't careful.

She wouldn't let that happen.

She'd gone through too much to let it all slip through her fingers now.

She had no time to lose.

If the property sales didn't make the amounts to pay off the bank loans she could be in serious debt. She had to make money fast. The Louisburgh lambs and the wool clip couldn't be sold until the spring, months away.

That left the import and export business, but money from that depended on ship arrivals and auctions sales for the goods. For a moment, she was overwhelmed with the task in front of her.

A ship horn blew again, and she took a deep breath. It was all up to her now.

Quickly, she returned to the carriage. 'Higgins, take me back to the office, please.'

Dusk sent long shadows across the city. Once more in the docks area, Ellen headed up the stairs to the office above the Hamilton and Emmerson warehouse. She met Mr McCulloch locking the door at the top.

'Mrs Emmerson. I didn't expect you back.'

'Sorry, I took longer than I thought.' She waited for him to unlock the door and open it for her. 'You needn't stay. Good evening to you, Mr McCulloch.' She dismissed him and sat behind Alistair's desk. She lit the lamp on the desk and another by the window.

'You're staying on a bit, Mrs Emmerson?'

'I am. The news from the solicitor wasn't good.'

Mr McCulloch paled. 'I thought as much.' He took off his coat and hung it up. 'I'll stay and help you, madam.'

Ellen untied her bonnet. 'We may be here for some time, Mr McCulloch. Perhaps all night.'

'I'm a single man, madam. My time is my own.'

'Thank you.' His kind smile made her want to cry, but she had no time to waste on tears. She had to fight for her children's security once more.

CHAPTER 15

*I*n the blazing summer heat of August, Rafe gently
lobbed the cricket ball to Patrick, who hit it well and
the ball sailed over the lawn to land in the hydrangea bushes.

'Oh, I say, excellent shot, young man.' Edgar clapped from his
seat near the picnic blanket where baby Edmund played.

Rafe laughed as Austin ran to retrieve the ball and Iris's little
dog yapped and chased him.

'Hasn't it been lovely to have the boys here for the summer,'
Olive, Rafe's mother, said. 'Especially after the worry over
Patrick and his illness.'

'I can't find the ball,' Austin shouted.

'I'll help you.' Patrick dropped the bat and jogged over to help
his brother.

Taking a moment to rest out of the sun, Rafe laid on the
picnic blanket beside Iris, who poured him a glass of elderflower
cordial. 'I keep forgetting I'm not as young as I once was.'

Edgar chuckled. 'That comes to us all. Lord knows how I am
to keep up with young sir there.' He tickled his son's tummy. 'I'll
be ancient by the time this little man is at school and hitting a
cricket ball.'

'Speaking of school, it will soon be time for Austin to return to Harrow,' Rafe murmured, watching the boys hunt for the illusive ball.

'Then you are sending Patrick home,' Iris murmured. 'The dear boy does nothing but talk about it.'

'You should not send him home to his mother, Rafe.' His mother gently waved her fan in front of her face. 'He was sent here under his stepfather's orders.'

'I shall not argue with you again over the decision, Mama.' Rafe sighed, sipping his drink. 'I have made my decision and as soon as Captain Leonards is in port again, I shall put Patrick into his care for the journey back to Sydney.'

'And what if he is ill on the journey? Who will care for him?' his mother snapped. 'All the hard work we have done to keep the boy alive could go to waste and if he dies, I shall not forgive you, Rafe.'

'Mama!' Iris admonished their mother. 'It is hardly Rafe's fault. He is doing this to make Patrick happy.'

'He is a child. We are the adults and Rafe is responsible for him. Patrick should go to Harrow with Austin and continue his education.'

Rafe gazed at his mother. 'You have become too fond of him, Mama.'

'Is that a crime?' She waved her fan rapidly.

'No. I am pleased you have all taken to the boys so well.'

'We have enjoyed having them,' Edgar said, chewing a buttered slice of bread. 'This house is large and needs filling.'

'I am doing my best,' Iris laughed, patting her belly, which was growing another child.

Edgar kissed her hand, tenderness in his eyes. 'After years of being here at Cherrybank alone, it brings me such joy to see a family within its walls.'

'I cannot thank you enough for allowing me and the boys to

stay the summer, Edgar,' Rafe said, leaping to his feet. The boys had found the ball much to the little dog's excitement.

A footman walked towards them carrying a silver platter.

Olive glanced at it. 'I hope it is not a letter from your father announcing his intentions to come here,' she whispered.

Rafe hoped the same. Having his irritating father living back in London at the expense of Edgar, saved them all the annoyance of having him with them. Thankfully, Drew had been posted with the army, which was another sense of relief to Rafe that they didn't have to put up with him and his reckless ways.

Without either his brother or father at Cherrybank, his mother had regained some semblance of her old self and the stress of being married to a gambler had lessened somewhat knowing she had a home forever with Iris and Edgar. Her health had improved and her general wellbeing. It had surprised and pleased Rafe how quickly his mother had gravitated towards Patrick and Austin. It was as though having young people around her brought her out of her miseries.

The footman bowed next to Rafe. 'For you, sir.'

'Thank you.' Rafe took the letter and instantly recognised Ellen's handwriting. He stepped away from the picnic, going across the terrace and into the conservatory.

His hands shaking, he opened the envelope and pulled out a single sheet of paper.

DARLING RAFE,

I am writing to you in haste for I have many letters to write, and I need to make the post.

Alistair died today. He was thrown from his horse and died at the scene from a head wound.

It is a great shock. One I still feel unable to accept at the moment. I am sorry it falls to you to tell Austin and Patrick this tragic news.

However, with this accident, I wish to have my boys home with me. I beg you to send them to me as soon as possible.

I will employ someone to keep the business continuing until I hear further from you.

In January, I received the letter you sent in October, and your sentiments gladden my heart and are returned entirely. Do believe me when I declare you are always in my heart.

Thank you for taking care of my boys. It gladdens my heart to know they are under your protection and guidance.

With deepest affection,

Ellen.

Emmerson Park

25th May 1854

HE RE-READ THE LETTER. The words sinking in. Alistair dead. He couldn't believe it. His friend and business partner no longer alive? Sorrow filled him. Poor Alistair didn't deserve to die so young. He had so much, a good life, a family, Ellen...

This changed so many things. He shied away from the heart-leaping thought of Ellen being free. He could not think of that right now. He had no right to be selfish at this time.

He glanced through the window at the picnic, steeling himself to tell the boys. Slowly, he walked over to them. 'Austin. Patrick. I need to speak with you both.'

He kept walking, taking the path to the fountain behind a high hedge.

'Has something happened?' Austin asked, frowning.

'Yes. I have just received this letter from your mother.'

Patrick's eyes lit up.

Rafe looked away, then focused on Austin, who thought greatly of Alistair. 'There has been some terribly sad news. A tragic accident has occurred. Alistair has died from a horse-riding incident. I am truly sorry.'

'Dead?' Austin stared in shock.

Rafe nodded.

'Mammy will need us at home,' Patrick declared.

Austin rounded on him. 'Is that all you care about? Going home? What could you possibly do to help Mama now? You're not a man.'

Patrick, always a quiet shy kind of lad, narrowed his eyes. 'No, I'm not a man yet but I soon will be and if I am at home, I can comfort Mammy.'

'Do not call her that!' Austin yelled. 'Mammy is the Irish to say and for babies. It is *Mama*.'

'Why is it? Just because you say so?' Patrick scorned. 'You and your posh friends?'

'Papa wanted us to speak properly, not like Irish peasants!'

'Alistair wasn't my papa! My da is dead!' Patrick bellowed.

'Our da was a pathetic wastrel!' Austin shouted in anger.

'And I'm Irish!' Patrick yelled back. 'I don't want to be English. I'm Irish.'

'You're an idiot!' Austin lunged for his brother.

'Boys. Enough!' Rafe separated them. 'That is no way to behave. I am ashamed of both of you. Stop it.' Rafe shook them by the shoulders as they grabbed for each other again. 'I said *enough!*'

'Rafe!' Iris came rushing down the path. 'What is going on?'

'Alistair is dead,' Rafe said quietly, keeping an eye on each boy.

'That is terrible.' She put her arm around Austin. 'I know how much you admired him. He was a fine man, though I only met him on a few occasions, I did like him.'

Austin nodded, head bent.

Rafe thrust his hands into his pockets. 'Your mother wants you to be sent home.'

Patrick sagged with such relief Rafe thought he would fall.

However, Austin straightened his back. 'No. I shan't go back. Not yet. I have my schooling to finish.'

'Mammy needs us!' Patrick implored him. 'Don't you want to see her and Aunty Riona and Bridget?'

'I do want to see them, but...' Austin's sad gaze lingered on Rafe. 'I want to continue at Harrow. Please allow me to, Rafe, please.'

His begging tone cut through Rafe. 'I must think about it, Austin. It would be going against your mother's wishes.'

'She will be happy having Patrick home and if you explain that I really wanted to finish my education, then she will understand. She will need me to be properly educated now she is alone.'

'You can attend King's in Parramatta,' Rafe reminded him. 'It is a fine school.'

'It is not Harrow.' A stubborn lift to Austin's chin reminded Rafe of Ellen.

'I shall think on it.'

Iris smiled. 'Both of you go inside and wash your face and hands.' When the boys had walked away, she turned to Rafe and linked her arm through his. 'This day started off so pleasantly. Who would have thought it would end so sadly.'

Rafe sighed. 'Agreed. I never expected Alistair to die.'

'I am not talking of Alistair, as awful as that is.'

'What are you talking about then?' He frowned, his thoughts on Alistair and his tragic end.

'Today has been the day I learn that I will lose my brother.'

Rafe stopped and scowled at her. 'What are you talking about?'

'Mrs Emmerson is free, and my brother loves her. Mrs Emmerson lives on the other side of the world and my brother will go to her.'

'Iris—'

'Just like you did last time.' She squeezed his arm. 'Only this time it'll be you who she'll be marrying.'

'I cannot dare to hope...' His heart twisted at the thought of finally being free to love Ellen.

'Take Patrick home, Rafe, and be with the woman you love. We shall take care of Austin.'

His stomach somersaulted at the thought of seeing Ellen again. If she would have him, he'd marry her as soon as possible. 'First, I must visit Alistair's parents.'

* * *

COUGHING INTO A HANDKERCHIEF, Ellen paused to catch her breath. A chest cold she'd caught last week refused to ease. And the chilly August winter winds blowing off the harbour didn't help her when she had to be out in all weathers dealing with cargo merchants.

Outside the warehouse, rain teemed down. The slippery and dangerous conditions were hazardous for the men unloading the cargo off the wagons. The cavernous space was stacked high with crates of household items. In the neighbouring warehouse sacks of wheat waited to be loaded. All were ready to be loaded on to the ships she'd hired, which would sail on the evening tide to Melbourne.

'Mrs Emmerson.' Mr McCulloch came to her side, carrying a ledger. 'The ship, *Snow Cloud*, has been cleared by quarantine and is coming into dock.'

'She is carrying the tobacco.' Ellen nodded, heading for the large open doors. 'Thank the fates for your tip off, Mr McCulloch!'

'I have Higgins waiting for you.' He rushed after her out into the rain. 'Donaldson is the captain. I've sent a runner to him with a note of your arrival. You must beat the other merchants,' he called after her as she climbed into the carriage.

Sitting back in the seat as Higgins sent the horses off into a fast trot to the other side of the quay, Ellen shivered from the dampness of her cloak and bonnet. Tiredly, she closed her eyes for a second.

Weeks of constant battles to beat other merchants and traders for cargo to buy and sell were taking their toll. She'd not been home to Emmerson Park since June when she arrived for the will reading. Now it was the end of August, and she was dreadfully missing the girls and home.

Thankfully, Mr Baldwin had proven to be a valuable solicitor and had speedily sold Lower Fort Street and the five terrace houses. The money from those sales had paid off two loans and given her enough to make some repayments on the loans for Emmerson Park and the Marulan property. The sale of the gold licence had cleared more debt, but for all his hard work, Mr Baldwin had yet to sell the shares in the pine company in Van Diemen's Land.

However, she still needed to make money to keep the properties afloat. Since June she'd begun to expand on her knowledge of buying and selling. She attended auctions and sales, negotiating with men who either laughed at her or despised her. In the end, her money was as good as anyone else's and although she had to work harder than the men to be taken seriously, they soon realised she was not giving up.

Her name was once more the talk of Sydney's society. Alistair's friends helped her at first until she started to beat them at their own game. When that happened, they and their wives shunned her. Not that she cared. Too much was riding on her success now. Before, she'd made the effort to fit in for the children's sake, but now it was for survival. She didn't care if she undercut the price of the cargo other companies sold, she was selling to win a deal.

Nor was she bothered when she bought cargo that was ignored by others. Spoilt goods, often rejected by other businesses were the kind Ellen snapped up. She would have it taken to the warehouse and she and Mr McCulloch would sort through it, extracting what was still worth money, and the rest that was too far damaged was sent to smaller concerns who paid for lesser lots as that was all they could afford.

It had happened by accident this way of trading. Ellen had unknowingly bought crates of bolts of material from a newly arrived ship. When opened the crates revealed they had been water stained from leakage in the ship's hold. Reeling that she'd paid for a cargo of unusable material, she had been close to having the whole lot incinerated when she realised that some rolls in the middle of the crates were untouched by water.

Salvaging those bolts, which she could then sell at full price, she had also appreciated that not every merchant wanted bulk material. She visited her dressmaker, Mrs Haggerty's salon, and after conversing with the seamstress, she learned that damaged bolts could be sold at a lesser price on market stalls to the working class, who would ingeniously sew and create garments where the stains didn't show, or if they did, they could be covered.

With this in mind, Ellen bought more sullied cargo cheaply. Broken candles and soap bars were sold at a reduced rate and the buyer simply melted the candles and soap down and remoulded them. Damaged shoes were taken apart and remade, food no longer suitable for human consumption was sold to farmers for their beasts, and so on.

Ellen learned she didn't have to just import and export expensive wool and delicate China, wheat and other consumables that were high in value but also high in risk if the cargo was damaged or lost in a shipping accident. She could earn money by working the lower sectors. She cut out the middleman and went straight to the shops and factories, the farmers and markets.

Although it was constant hard work, always thinking and planning ahead, she was slowly building a network of traders and customers who came to her for what they needed. Her name was spreading. Her cattle from Marulan went to the markets where she knew the buyers, instead of going through agents, and she would do the same when her lambs were ready to be sold from Louisburgh. She'd send the wool clip to Rafe in Liverpool for him to sell and in return request him to send farm and industry machinery, which was becoming the most wanted commodities.

All over Sydney, factories were springing up, as the population grew from the gold rush. Industries couldn't keep up with the demands of consumers and had to expand with modern machinery. Ellen wanted to be a part of it.

Everywhere she ventured she saw the rise of more and larger manufacturing plants. Sawmills, brickworks, coach works, iron foundries, cordial works, flour mills, breweries and so on were growing in importance and machinery was making it happen. Sydney was outgrowing its confines and spilling into the country areas faster than the roads could be built to travel on to get there.

In the two years since she'd arrived, the sprawl of the city outwards had grown beyond belief and Ellen wanted a piece of it. Alistair had spent too much time on sending goods to Melbourne to feed the needs of the gold rush, and in doing so he'd forgotten about the city he lived in.

She wouldn't be so complacent. Sydney and its growing population needed meat and meat works. Wool and wheat was exported by the shiploads, but not meat which would spoil within days. Ellen had a belief that with the growth of the population, food would be paramount. Land and food went together. She had to buy more land.

Alighting at the wharf, Ellen strode up the gangway and onto the ship's deck. She searched for a sailor who might be in charge and instead found a familiar face. 'Mr Donaldson!' She smiled at the man who had been the first mate on the *Blue Maid*, the ship she'd travelled on to Australia.

'Mrs Kittrick. What a pleasant surprise.'

'I'm Mrs Emmerson now, though my husband has recently died.'

'I am sorry to hear it. How is the rest of the family? Your sister and your children?'

'They are all very well. You would have seen Austin and Patrick when they sailed to England last year on the *Blue Maid*?'

'Alas, I did not. I left the *Blue Maid* the same time you did. I had a better offer to captain my own ship around the coasts of India.' He spread his arms out wide. 'This is my ship.'

'Well done you. What an achievement.'

'I am very happy.' He beamed at the accomplishment. 'So, why is it that you are here on my deck, Mrs Emmerson?'

'I've come to purchase your cargo of tobacco.'

He smiled. 'Direct from the West Indies.'

'Is the cargo bought all ready?' she asked.

'No, it is going to market next week.'

'I can give you fair a price for it today.'

He frowned. 'Forgive me, but why would I do that when I might be able to get a higher price at auction?'

'Because, Captain Donaldson, I have a proposition for you.'

'Which is?'

'Do you have your next consignment?'

'Not yet. I have only just docked.'

Ellen smiled. 'I have a warehouse full of the most beautiful Australian hard wood timber, that I know will sell in Liverpool through my contacts. In return, I am in need of machinery made in England. You and I could have a business relationship the same as my late husband and Mr Hamilton have with Captain Leonards. A constant agreement. No more will you have to compete with other ships for cargo.'

Donaldson bowed his head, his fingers tapping his chin, thinking about her suggestion. 'The Liverpool and Sydney route. They are longer voyages than the ones I've been doing to India.'

'Is that a problem?'

'No... Am I in competition with Captain Leonards?'

She shook her head. 'There is enough cargo to go around. Mr

Hamilton and my late husband invested in another ship. You will be the third captain to carry our goods. Unless you prefer the inconsistent auctioning for cargo lots? Our agreement would mean you continually have your holds full.'

Donaldson grinned. 'I always did like you. Shall we retire to my cabin and talk some more over a pot of tea?'

She took his arm. 'What an excellent idea.'

CHAPTER 16

*E*llen pulled the shawl around her shoulders, fighting the chill from the draft under the door. Winter seemed to be lingering into September and she longed for the warmth of spring. The poky little cottage she rented in Surry Hills was cheap and unpleasant but since she spent so little time in it, she didn't care.

On her desk, she tallied up the figures in the red ledger, corresponding them with the figures in the green ledger. Painstakingly, she was making enough money to keep the banks off her back and creating a savings hoard towards her next venture.

From outside the window, she heard Bridget laugh at something Lily had done. The two girls were playing under an apple tree, gathering the spring blossom to make posies. Miss Lewis's voice often warned Bridget to not climb so high.

Riona came in carrying a tea tray. 'I know it is spring, but September can be chilly. I insisted the girls wear their woolly hats.' She bent to the small fireplace and stirred the burning logs to send out more heat. 'Stop that now and have something to eat and a cup of tea. Rachel is feeding Ava milk sops and the girls are busy outside with Miss Lewis.'

'Yes, I can hear them.' Ellen closed the ledger.

'Aye well, sure and you can take a moment to have a break from those figures?'

Ellen nodded and tiredly pushed herself up from the chair. A pain in her back made her wince, and she coughed.

Riona glared at her. 'What have I told you? You need to slow down and rest. Will you not come back to Emmerson Park for a few weeks?'

'I can't, you know that. I need to stay here in Sydney and make money.'

'You sound just like Alistair used to,' Riona scoffed.

'No, I don't.' Ellen sipped her tea, enjoying the warm sweet taste. 'Besides, I am making money not debts, that's the difference.'

'And half killing yourself in doing it, so you are. Will you not come home for a while, please? Moira is asking after you. Even Honor wondered when you were returning and I'm sure Mr Thwaite is counting the days you've been gone and wondering if he'll ever see you again!'

'I'll think about it.' In truth she longed for her home in Berrima and for Louisburgh.

'Good.' Riona added another log and then sat back down.

'I have a meeting at four,' Ellen reminded her.

'What is it for this time?'

'A shareholders' meeting for the pine company in Van Diemen's Land. More money is needed to buy equipment for the logging.'

'I thought you wanted to sell it?'

'I do, but no one wants to buy my shares. I even offered Mr Gardner-Hill a chance to buy them, but he refused. He is still annoyed with me for not selling the shares of the import business to him.'

'As if you would. Look how well it is doing.' Riona cut slices of fruit cake and handed a thick wedge to Ellen. 'Eat it all. You're nothing but skin and bones. Why you had to let go of Mrs Lawson and Dilly, I don't know. At least you would eat properly with Mrs Lawson in the house.'

'Mrs Lawson wanted to retire to join her sister and I have no need of a cook or a maid here. I don't entertain and I'm barely here more than to sleep. I'm perfectly fine.'

'Fine? I've seen more meat on a bone after a dog's chewed it. And that cough! You're not looking after yourself. Now I'm here, you will eat more, I'll make sure of it.'

'I said I'm fine and I am.' Ellen took a bite of the cake to please her sister. Having Riona and the girls here made her so happy. They had arrived unannounced two days ago and Ellen cried in sheer joy of hugging them all.

'Mama!' Bridget ran into the tiny room. 'Miss Lewis says we can go for a walk to Hyde Park. Ava and Lily can go in the perambulator. Will you come, too?'

She hesitated, she had more figures to work on and her appointment was in an hour, but she needed to spend time with the girls, too. 'How about I walk with you to the park and then I can go from there to my appointment?'

Bridget clapped and raced out to tell Miss Lewis.

'She has missed you,' Riona said. 'Three months is too long, Ellen. Lily barely remembers you and Ava has no idea who you are.'

'Ava is a baby and knows no different. Lily is warming to me. I think she is starting to remember me.' The one hardship of being in Sydney was not being with the girls, especially as Lily had acted so shyly around Ellen, as though she had forgotten her mother. It had hurt Ellen to the core. She couldn't let that happen again, but she also needed to work and make money. It was difficult to find a balance.

'If this house was bigger, you could all stay longer,' she said to Riona. 'But I rented it for the cheap price not to house us all.'

'So, what is wrong sharing a few rooms?' Riona grinned. 'We've slept in worse in Ireland.'

'That is what I'm trying to avoid going back to.' Ellen laughed wryly.

'And are you? Are you working all these hours and seeing a benefit? Because as I'm looking at you now, you're half the woman you were. You're pale, and too thin, with dark shadows under your eyes. Your hair is lank and that cough near sends you to your knees. You look like you did in Ireland.' Riona sat forward and took Ellen's hands. 'Is it worth it, Sister? Can you not let it all go and sell everything? We can be happy at Emmerson Park, we need no more than that.'

'I told you in my letters, Emmerson Park has a mortgage on it. If I don't make the repayments, it will be sold. We need income.'

'But the other properties can you not sell them?'

'Louisburgh pays its own way with the lambs and the wool clip. I will never sell it.'

'Right then. Let us all move to Louisburgh. Sell everything else. We can make Louisburgh our home.'

Ellen sighed, exhaustion creeping up on her. 'I have thought of it.'

'Then why not do it? I'd rather have you with us in one place, than killing yourself trying to keep the others.'

'Because it isn't enough for the children. I have to think of their futures. The boys need properties to raise their own families.'

'The boys can see to themselves when they are men!' Riona snapped. 'They might not even want the properties and do something else entirely. Have you thought of that?'

'I have and if that is the case then the girls will have them.'

'Ellen, please. This empire you want to build will destroy you if you're not careful.'

'This *empire* as you call it, keeps us from living in a place like *this* forever.' Ellen waved around the bare room.

Riona sighed and sat back. 'So, you are to remain in Sydney for years driving yourself into an early grave? When will it all be enough?'

'No, I shan't stay in Sydney for years.' Ellen sipped her tea. 'I have plans which hopefully will pay off very soon.'

'Such as?'

'I intended to buy more land.'

'You and your insatiable need for land!' Riona fumed. 'It's mad that you are.'

'Listen to me. I want to annexe the land at Marulan with Louisburgh by buying the range of hills between them. Then if I buy land on the other side of Louisburgh, stretching the run northwest into unclaimed territory, the whole property will be able to hold larger flocks of sheep. I heard reports that some of that land was once granted to the likes of the Macarthur family and others are becoming available. One section,' she searched through paperwork on her desk to find a piece of paper and held it up, 'this section on the Tarlo River was an original grant to one of the early explorers and extends over the mountain ranges. The man's family have either died or no longer want it and it's up for sale. It's going cheap because some of the land is on the hilly ranges and farmers think that's a waste because there aren't enough grass pastures to feed stock.'

'Then why do you want it?'

'Because sheep will feed between trees on hills better than cattle and we can clear some of the slopes of trees for we'll need the timber to build a house and outbuildings. There are still seven hundred acres of pasture besides the acres covering the range. Many new arrivals in this country don't want to risk being so far from civilisation and the cities and ports. Because of this, I may be able to acquire it cheaper. I've made inquiries to the appropriate offices and asked for all the details. It goes on sale next month.'

'We are to live there?'

'No, but a manager will want decent accommodation.'

'Can you afford it?'

'Yes, if I can sell these shares in the pine company and I've been building a fund to buy more land, but I'm not there just yet, but I will be in the next few weeks. I've not been working all these hours for nothing you know. Sheep and lots of them will help us survive.' Ellen stood. 'Soon I'll be turning my attention to all our lands. I'll make Mr McCulloch manager of the import business and only have to come to Sydney a few times a year.'

'You wear me out just by talking of your plans. I don't know how you manage to do it all, so I don't.'

'I do it for us.' Ellen walked to the door as Bridget came in dressed in a pretty bonnet and coat for their walk. Ellen kissed her cheek. 'Fetch my bonnet, darling, while I put on my coat.'

On the walk through the streets leading to Hyde Park, Ellen linked her arm though Riona's. Bridget ran ahead only to come back again to chatter about the things she saw. Being in the city with sights and sounds not found in Berrima assailed the little family. Stallholders harked their wares, while an omnibus rumbled past filled with passengers, horse drawn vehicles of all shapes and sizes clogged the streets while boys on street corners offered newspapers for sale. A woman sold flowers from her handcart, while factory whistles blew and the noise of hundreds of builders working to create new shops, hotels and better-paved roadways echoed.

The green lawn of Hyde Park sat amongst the industry of a growing city. Bridget ran to a small drinking fountain on the edge of the path, laughing as two young boys splashed each other.

'Don't get wet, Bridget. It's not warm enough,' Ellen warned. She turned to the pram and bent to give Lily and Ava a kiss on their cheeks.

'You heading off now?' Riona asked.

'Yes, or I'll be late.' She strode off along Bathurst Street and then turned into Pitt Street. Another hundred yards brought her to the offices where the meeting was to be held.

A little nervous as she always was when entering a room full of businessmen, Ellen kept her head held high and made for the table in the middle of the room.

'Mrs Emmerson.' One of the main shareholders, Mr Triverton, shook her hand. 'I am pleased you could make it.'

'I wouldn't miss a meeting that is important to me.' She nodded to several other men standing nearby.

The meeting got under way once everyone was seated. For a few minutes, Mr Triverton spoke of the company and the inroads they were making to build the company's growth. He forecasted profits in the next quarter for the first time, which brought a cheer to the room.

Ellen sat quietly, listening but also gaining the reaction of the other men. The only other time she had been to this company's meeting was last month when shareholders demanded to know what was happening in Davey River and when would they start to see a profit. That meeting had been full of shouting and angry insults before Mr Triverton managed to control the men and promise returns very soon.

Although Ellen liked the older man, she felt he only humoured her. Her questions had been rebuffed or side-lined in favour of other shareholders who had more at stake.

When finally the meeting came to an end, Ellen stood and made her way to Mr Triverton.

'Ah, Mrs Emmerson.' He handed her a cup of tea.

Holding the saucer, Ellen looked around. 'You said many positive things, Mr Triverton.'

'Indeed, the future is looking bright, madam.'

'I'm pleased, truly, for it will make my shares easier to sell.'

Mr Triverton sighed. 'We spoke of this last month, madam. Now is not the time to sell. We need investors to remain strong.

If word leaked out that people were selling their shares, then it could affect the company's reputation.'

'Then why don't you buy my shares, and we keep it between us.'

He rubbed his bald patch. 'I do not have the extra capital to buy more, Mrs Emmerson. I have sunk every penny I have into his company.'

'But I have not,' a voice said from behind them.

Ellen turned and faced a tall man, suited in a tailored suit of black and grey stripe. He had a short well-trimmed beard that didn't detract from his handsome face.

He held out his hand. 'Maxwell Duncan. Pleased to meet you, Mrs Emmerson.'

She took his hand.

Mr Triverton glared at the newcomer. 'Duncan, you are not welcome here. This is a meeting for shareholders only.'

'Forgive my late arrival. My ship has only just docked this morning.' Maxwell Duncan grinned. 'And as of four days ago, Triverton, I am a shareholder due to my buying five percent shares from Mr Hoddle in Melbourne.'

'That is outrageous.' Triverton huffed. 'Hoddle is on his deathbed. He couldn't possibly make a deal with you.'

'Yet he did. I visited his house, and we summoned our solicitors. It is all done and sealed with signatures. Mrs Hoddle can now bury her husband in a manner he deserves and be kept in comfort herself in her old age.'

'You won't get away with this.'

'I just did.'

'Scoundrel!' Triverton's cheeks blazed red. 'If you'll excuse me, Mrs Emmerson.' Mr Triverton bowed and stepped away to immediately talk to the man behind them.

Ellen glanced at Maxwell Duncan. 'How easily you upset him.'

'He deserves it, Mrs Emmerson.' He shrugged as if it meant nothing.

'You know my name.'

Maxwell Duncan smiled. 'How could a man in his right mind not find out the name of a beautiful woman when he enters a room?'

She chuckled at the flattery for she felt anything but beautiful in black mourning. 'So, Mr Duncan, you are interested in my shares?'

'I am.' His dark eyes seemed to stare right through her. 'But it is not something we should discuss over tea.' He took the cup and saucer out of her hand. 'Shall we find a table in a pleasant restaurant and order wine and fine roast beef?'

'Why not?' She'd do anything to sell the shares and if that meant spending an hour drinking and eating to do so, more the better for her.

Outside, in the chilly breeze whistling through the streets from the harbour, Ellen had to stop to cough. When she regained her breath, they walked along Pitt Street until they reached Market Street where they turned left and soon were seated at a white-clothed table in a small elegant restaurant.

'Here's to a successful dinner.' Mr Duncan raised his wine glass to hers, his gaze roaming over her face and down to her bodice.

Ellen sipped the white wine and leaned back in her chair. 'Are you really interested in my shares, Mr Duncan?'

He grinned. 'Indeed. But I am also interested in you. Is that very forward of me to say so on our first acquaintance?'

'I believe it is.'

'Good. I like to surprise people.'

'Why are you interested in me?' she asked, aware of other diners who were of the high social class. She knew some of the faces from parties and balls she had attended with Alistair.

'Because you are different. Fascinating.'

'You don't know me.'

'I know of you. I know you are the widow of Alistair Emmerson. I know you have been spending the months since his death reclaiming some sense of financial security that your husband was rather lax with and—'

'How do you know that?' She leaned forward, alarmed he'd learned all that about her and she knew nothing of him.

He bent closer to her. 'I make it my business to know other people's business, especially where money is involved,' he spoke in a low tone that held a hint of warning.

Ellen sat back, goosebumps rising on her skin. 'What do you want?'

'You.'

She stared at him.

He laughed at her shocked face. 'But I shall wait for that. In the meantime, I think we should do business together.'

'Do you want to purchase my shares?'

'Indeed, yes, but aside from that I think we would work well together.'

'How so?' She couldn't take her eyes off him.

He lounged in his chair and sipped his wine. 'Your background. Irish peasantry, is that correct?'

Ellen stiffened. She immediately grabbed her reticule and made to rise.

His hand clamped down on her wrist and held her still. 'Sit down.'

She glared at him. 'Let go of me.'

'Let me finish what I was going to say.' He relaxed his pressure. 'Please?'

Teeth clenched in irritation, she slowly sat down.

'I mentioned your origins because mine are similar.'

She frowned. 'You're Irish?'

'No. Scottish. That is my grandparents were Scottish. I was born here in this country...' He tilted his head boldly. 'My grandparents came here in chains. They'd been thrown off the land in Scotland and ventured to England to find work. They were starving. My grandfather stole some bread and gave it to my grandmother who was with child. They were both caught and sentenced to life in Van Diemen's Land.'

Ellen heard the bitterness in his voice.

'They served seven years each before my grandfather was sent to work for a gentleman north of Hobart. That man was kind, decent. He liked my grandfather and he sent for my grandmother to work in his house so they could be together.' Mr Duncan sipped his wine. 'That gentleman encouraged my grandfather to send his son to school, which was my father, who the gentleman also took an interest in. My grandparents died from fever when my father was twelve. The gentleman made my father his ward and brought him up to be a gentleman.'

'Why are you telling me this?' Ellen asked, ignoring the first course of oysters that was delivered to the table.

'My father had to fight to be taken seriously in a class he wasn't born into. He was shunned and secretly laughed at when he attended social functions.' Mr Duncan swirled the wine in his glass. 'My father wasn't accepted in Hobart. When the old gentleman died, he left half of his fortune to my father. The other half was left to his nephew.' Mr Duncan looked up at Ellen. 'Mr Triverton is his nephew.'

'This is all very fascinating but again, why are you telling me?'

'Because, dear Mrs Emmerson. Mr Triverton made my father's life hell. He contested the will in court, which he lost, so then he blocked every attempt my father made to get on with his life.' Duncan took a large gulp of his wine. 'My father killed himself because of Triverton.'

'Oh, that is tragic.' Ellen watched the emotions flitter across his face.

Duncan refilled his glass. 'My mother died seven months later of a broken heart. I was away at school, just a child. Triverton caused me to lose both my parents. I aim to make Triverton pay.'

'And how will you do that?'

'Triverton's success rises and falls on the pine company at Davey River. I plan to buy enough shares to become the major shareholder.'

'How will you do that when Mr Triverton holds fifty-one percent?'

'I have my ways.'

'Starting with buying my shares?'

'Indeed.' He raised his glass to her.

'I am happy to sell them at the going rate.'

'Thank you, but that's not all.'

'No?' She turned her head away to cough into a handkerchief.

Mr Duncan waited until she'd composed herself. 'I would like you to accompany me to a ball tomorrow night.'

Her eyes widened at the suggestion. 'Why?' she gasped, fighting the tickly sensation in her throat.

'Why not?' He took a sip of wine, his eyes laughing at her over the rim.

'I don't think so.' She looked away, meeting the gazes of some women at another table. She couldn't remember their names but knew their faces. She coughed again.

'I heard talk that Mr Gardner-Hill wants your shares in your import business, and you won't sell despite you needing the money.'

Her head snapped back to him. 'How did you know that?'

'I know many things, Mrs Emmerson. I know the financial state your husband left you in and I know how well you are doing climbing back out of that deep hole.'

She felt exposed as his gaze raked over her again. He knew too much about her, as though he was a snake in the grass, and she was his prey. 'I don't wish to be a player in your game with Mr Triverton. If you wish to buy my shares, then have your solicitor contact mine. Mr Baldwin on Bent Street.'

He ate an oyster, taking a moment to savour the taste. 'Forgive me. I am making you feel uncomfortable, and I do not wish to do that at all.' He added more wine to her glass despite that she'd hardly touched it. 'Mrs Emmerson, I like you. I like that we have things in common. We are pariahs in this closed society. We are not one of *them*. Do you not wish to beat them at their own game?'

'I am doing that in my own way.' She drank some wine to ease her throat.

'Buy undercutting them on the odd cargo deal.'

She stared at him. He really did know her business. Was he friend or foe?

'What are your ultimate goals, Mrs Emmerson?'

'I feel you already might know them, Mr Duncan,' she said sarcastically.

He laughed uproariously at that. He leaned forward, his voice dropping to a whisper. 'I would sincerely like you to share your desires with me.'

She swallowed. A wave of sexual awareness heightened her senses. This man was indeed exciting, if not a little mysterious and dangerous.

Mr Duncan sat back in his chair, his dark eyes watching her. 'You have land in the country.'

'Yes.'

'Do you want more?'

'Yes.'

'I can get you more.'

'How?'

'I will buy your shares of the pine company and with that money you are to buy more shares from other investors who will not sell to me because they are friends with Triverton. Buy the shares in a different name.'

'You are using me?'

'No, it is a mutual benefit. You keep buying shares with my money and in return I will sell to you at a discounted rate land I own and do not want.'

'Land you don't want? Why wouldn't you want land?' That seemed ridiculous to her.

'I live in Van Diemen's Land. It is where I want to spend my money and show them all that they did wrong to reject my father.'

His need for revenge radiated out from him like a force. Ellen shivered, feeling the tickle of another cough forming in her throat. She took a sip of wine.

'So, what do you say? Shall we shake hands on this deal?'

She held up a finger, stopping him. 'What if I don't want your land? It might be somewhere too difficult for me to visit often, or it might be useless and unsuitable for crops or beasts.'

A sly smile spread across his handsome face. 'You already know this land.'

'I do?'

'I bought the land on the Tarlo River you have been enquiring about.' He'd played his trump card.

Ellen felt the breath taken from her and started coughing, gasping for air.

Concerned, Maxwell Duncan tried to soothe her with pats on the back and ordered her a glass of water.

When she finally caught her breath, embarrassed for causing a scene, she turned to him with watery eyes. 'You have a deal.'

CHAPTER 17

*E*llen descended the carriage. 'See you in the morning, Higgins.'

'Right you are, Mrs Emmerson.'

She walked to the gate leading to the little cottage and paused for a moment to steady herself. The light-headedness receded a little, and she straightened, ready to face Riona and the children.

The front door opened, and Bridget raced out to her. 'Mama, Mrs Stein said I did excellently on the piano today.'

'Wonderful.' Ellen kissed the raven black hair on top of Bridget's head.

'Mrs Stein says that you are welcome to come and listen to me play at any of my lessons. Will you come?'

'I will.' Ellen walked with her to the door. 'How fortunate we are to have a piano teacher just down the road.'

'Can you come to my next lesson?'

'I will try.' Ellen untied her bonnet and hung it up on the hook in the hallway.

'Mama.' Lily toddled towards her, and Ellen bent to hug the child to her. Lily was resembling Rafe more the older she became, though she had the chestnut colouring of Ellen in her hair as it grew longer.

Riona came out of the front room with Ava in her arms, looking a little harassed. 'I swear this one is nearly about to crawl. She's only six months and can't stay still on the rug for a minute.' Riona gave Ava to Rachel and Lettie, who came to gather the girls into the tiny kitchen for their supper.

'You look worn out,' Riona said as she followed Ellen into the bedroom, which was not large enough for two grown women and three children. The lean-to out the back was even smaller for Miss Lewis, Rachel and Lettie.

'I am feeling tired.'

'Is it any wonder? You've been out all day working and then at night you're with Mr Duncan attending dinners and balls.' Riona knelt to help Ellen pull off her boots and replace them with house slippers.

'I am home tonight.' Ellen longed to just sit. Her head pounded.

'Good.' Riona stood and placed the boots at the end of the bed. 'This can't go on, Ellen. You look ill.'

'I'm just tired from too many late nights.'

'Then stop going out. Tell Mr Duncan to leave you in peace for a few weeks.'

'I can't do that.' Ellen poured water from the jug into the basin to wash the city dust off her face.

'Are you falling for him?'

Ellen snapped her head around to Riona. 'Are you mad?'

'Well, people must be talking. The two of you are forever together. I expect they are waiting on a proposal any minute.'

'I've known Mr Duncan a month and a half. Hardly proposal worthy.'

'Would you say yes if he did propose?'

Ellen paused in drying her face. Maxwell was surprisingly

good company. He made her laugh a lot. They talked for hours, but he could also plunge into dark moods where he snapped and walked away from her no matter where they were. He'd done that a few times, and she'd hated him for it. He would always apologise the next day and send her numerous bouquets of flowers and she'd forgive him. She enjoyed his company, and he was happy to go for walks with the family, treating Bridget to toffee apples and races across the park lawns.

'You're taking a long time to answer,' Riona prompted.

Ellen folded the towel. 'Maxwell Duncan is a friend. A business associate as I explained to you.'

Riona clasped her hands together in front of her. 'Then can we return to Emmerson Park?'

'I thought you liked being in the city with me?'

'I did, but not any longer. I have met up with friends we had in Lower Fort Street but living in this little cottage makes it difficult to return invitations, especially when we have no staff, and I am cooking.'

Ellen couldn't help but smile. 'Listen to you, complaining about cooking and not receiving callers. How different you are from the Irish peasant woman who landed here two years ago.'

Riona chuckled. 'True. I hardly recognise myself, but it's your fault for turning me into a lady of leisure, so I am.'

'That you are gives me such pleasure. I want only the best for you and the children.'

'The best for us is being with you and having you healthy. For the last six weeks you've spent all your time with Mr Duncan and this house is too tiny for us all. If I'm not seeing you, then I might as well do it in the comfort of Emmerson Park.'

Tidying her hair, Ellen nodded. 'I understand. This cottage isn't ideal for us all.'

'Please come back with us. You need to rest, Ellen.'

A longing for Emmerson Park and more so for Louisburgh

overwhelmed her for several seconds. She was so tired of the city, of the business, the dealings and always trying to be one step ahead of the men who had more contacts and more wealth than her. Maxwell Duncan had taken her to parties, dinners, theatre shows and social entertainments, which had turned heads, and caused gossip just as it done when she was married to Alistair, only this time it was worse because she wasn't married.

She was constantly tired of smiling, chatting, dancing, making an effort to be sociable to people who didn't like her as Alistair's wife and certainly didn't like her as his widow being escorted about town by a stranger, no matter how handsome and sophisticated he was. Maxwell Duncan wasn't one of them. He was an outsider, a convict descendant.

But the plan Maxwell set out for them to achieve was working. Ellen had bought thirty-five percent of the pine company with Maxwell's money under Riona's name. Tomorrow night she was to have dinner with a wealthy gentleman, George Evans, who held ten percent of the shares and make him an offer he hopefully couldn't refuse.

'Ellen?'

She snapped back to Riona's questioning face. 'What did you say?'

'I asked if you were coming home with us to Emmerson Park?'

Suddenly she wanted nothing more than that. 'If the dinner goes well tomorrow night, then yes, we'll pack up and head home next week.'

Riona clapped her hands. 'Thank the Holy Virgin you've come to your senses.'

Ellen gave her a wry look, but a fit of coughing overcame her and she spent the next few minutes trying to get her breath back.

'I think you should see another doctor, Ellen,' Riona said, wrapping a shawl around her shoulders and forcing her to lie on the bed.

'I'm much better than I was before. The warmer weather is helping.' She laid on the bed, eager for sleep even though it was only six in the evening.

'You have a nap.' Riona threw a blanket over her.

'Only a short one,' she yawned. 'Wake me for supper.'

When Ellen woke, she heard rain beating on the tin roof. The light was murky and grey as though dawn was breaking. She felt hot and pulled the blanket off her.

Next to her, Riona turned and leant up on her elbow to tuck the blanket back over her.

'I'm too hot!'

'Aye, you've been sweating and then shivering all night. I think you have a fever.' Getting out of bed, Riona pulled on her dressing gown. 'I'll make you some tea,' she whispered not wanting to wake Bridget.

'What time is it?'

'Early morning. You've slept since yesterday evening.' Riona stood by the door. 'Do not get out of bed. I'll send for the doctor.'

'I'm fine, it's just a chill.'

'Whist, the doctor will be the judge of that, so he will.'

Two hours later the doctor, a kind young man, who lived a few streets away proclaimed Ellen had a slight fever and should stay in bed for the next couple of days.

Once he had gone, Ellen dressed and went into the front room where Riona and Miss Lewis entertained the girls while rain continued to fall outside.

'What are you doing up?' Riona queried, annoyed.

'I have too much to do, Riona, so don't start on me. I must attend this dinner tonight.'

'Why?'

'You know why. I need the shares for Mr Duncan then he will sell me the Tarlo land.'

Riona's lips thinned in anger. 'I'm tired of all this worry, Ellen.

Enough is enough. We don't want you dead for the sake of more land!'

Bridget swung her head from Riona to Ellen. 'Mama?' her worried voice made the sisters instantly regret speaking out in front of her.

'It's nothing, darling.' Ellen smiled. 'A silly joke.'

Riona smiled falsely. 'Yes, a silly quarrel. Keep drawing. You're doing a grand picture, so you are.'

Ellen went back to the bedroom with Riona on her heels.

'Send a note to Mr Duncan. Tell him you can't make it tonight. You're ill.' Riona stood over Ellen as she lay down on the bed.

'The sooner I see this deal finished the sooner I can leave the city.'

'Is that what you want? To leave the city? To leave Mr Duncan? Because I feel he is the one keeping you here and nothing else.'

Wearily, Ellen closed her eyes. 'This is the last deal and then we'll go home.'

But as the hours passed, Ellen began to feel worse rather than better. Riona forced her to sip at some beef broth, but the effort was too much.

When the sun began to slip beyond the hills, Ellen knew she had to bathe and dress. Getting out of bed, she stumbled, the objects in the room wavered before her eyes.

'Mama?' Bridget came into the room and ran to steady her. 'Aunt Riona!' she yelled.

Riona raced into the bedroom and took one look at Ellen. 'Get back into bed or I'll not be responsible for my actions, so I won't.'

Ellen reached for the bed, but it all turned black and the last thing she remembered was Bridget screaming.

* * *

For three days, Ellen sweated and shivered and slept. She heard the doctor and Riona speaking in hushed tones, not understanding what they were saying and not caring. She had no energy, no desire to do anything, to not even move.

By the morning of the fourth day, she woke when Riona entered the room and felt the need to relieve herself. She tried to move and found it incredibly difficult.

'Ellen!' Riona hurried to the bed. 'Steady now.' She smiled lovingly at her. 'How do you feel?'

'I need the pot.'

'Oh, right. Yes, of course.'

After Riona helped her to use the pot, Ellen laid back, exhausted from that slight activity.

'The doctor will be here in an hour.' Riona adjusted the blankets. 'He'll be happy to see you awake and speaking. He's been so worried. We all have. I... I...' Tears filled Riona's eyes and trickled over her cheeks. 'I've been so scared,' she whispered, kneeling down beside the bed and taking Ellen's hand. 'I never want to go through that again. I thought you were dying and... and... I didn't know what to do!'

'I'm sorry.' Ellen squeezed Riona's hand gently. Vases of colourful flowers caught her attention. The bedroom was full of them. 'The flowers...'

Riona dashed her eyes with the back of her hand. 'Mr Duncan. He's been twice a day for the last three days. The poor man has been beside himself, so he has.'

It came back to her that she had meant to have gone to dinner, the shares, the deal with Maxwell. Suddenly none of it mattered. She didn't have the energy to care about the Tarlo land. 'I want to go home, Riona.'

'Aye.' Riona smiled tearily. 'We will. As soon as you are well enough.'

'The girls?'

'They're fine, so they are. Bridget is worried, but she's being brave and behaving the best she's ever done to help Miss Lewis, Rachel and Lettie with Lily and Ava. She's even been wanting to help me cook, so she has.'

Relieved, Ellen rested and closed her eyes. 'I need to go home... to Louisburgh...'

Later when Ellen woke, she heard voices outside the door. Expecting to see Riona bring in the doctor she was surprised to see Maxwell Duncan enter behind her sister, his face full of worry.

'Mrs Emmerson.'

She gave a brief smile for everything took so much effort.

He sat on the wooden chair beside her bed. 'I cannot begin to tell you how happy I am to see you awake and over the worst.'

'Thank you for coming to see me.'

'Nothing would keep me away, though your sister has tried hard enough to prevent me from getting through the door.' He chuckled. 'You gave us all quite a scare.'

'I'm sorry about the dinner... the shares...'

'Nonsense. That is not for you to be concerned about at all. Regaining your health is the most important matter. When you are well, I shall take you on gentle walks in the fresh air. Perhaps, even a trip on the harbour, and a picnic on one of the beaches.'

'I'm going home...'

His face paled. 'Home?'

'I've grown weary of the city, of business.'

'Of me?' he joked half-heartedly.

'No...' Her throat was dry, and she reached for a glass of water, but he got there before her and helped her to sip at it.

'May I offer my assistance to you and your family to help you return to the country?'

She shook her head. 'Thank you, but no.'

'Ellen.' He took her hand in both of his. 'It has taken me utterly by surprise, but I care for you.'

'Maxwell...' She felt his emotion but couldn't answer it with her own. She had nothing to give him. Her heart was already taken by another, even though she doubted she'd ever see Rafe again.

'Say nothing now. I'll call again in a few days, when you're feeling more your old self.' He kissed her hand and quickly left the room.

Riona came in, a question in her expression. 'He left in a hurry. Didn't even say goodbye.'

'He says he cares for me.'

Riona clenched her hands in front of her. 'Do you care for him?'

'Not in that way, no.'

'I'm selfish enough to say I'm pleased. Mr Duncan would be a complication. He wants to return to Hobart.'

Ellen gazed at her sister. 'We aren't going to Hobart.'

'So, I can start to pack for home and end the lease on this cottage?'

'The sooner the better,' Ellen replied tiredly.

A few days later, Ellen took her first walk outside. Higgins had taken her, Riona and Bridget in the carriage to the Botanical Gardens down on the foreshore.

The day was beautiful, with a clear blue October sky and a warm breeze coming off the water. Being a Sunday, the paths through the gardens were packed with people strolling after the morning church services, all wearing the best clothes in summer shades.

Although Ellen still wore her black mourning and Riona wore dark grey in respect of Alistair, she still felt lighter of heart than she had for some time.

'You mustn't tire yourself out,' Riona warned, holding a parasol for them both to share.

'I'll stop in a bit.' Ellen, her arm linked through Riona's, watched as Bridget skipped about, smelling the flowers bursting from the buds and admiring the ships and boats on the harbour.

They walked for another ten minutes before Ellen felt the need to sit down on one of the bench seats.

'There's a talking parrot on a man's shoulder down there.' Bridget pointed to the small crowd gathered around an old man and his bird.

'Take her to see it,' Ellen said, adjusting her skirts on the bench. 'I'll wait here and enjoy the sun on me.'

From her seat, Ellen waved to Bridget as her daughter sat on the grass to listen to the old man and the talking parrot.

'Mrs Emmerson.' Mrs Gardner-Hill stopped before her. 'I heard you were ill. I am pleased to see you are recovered.'

'Thank you.' Ellen inclined her head, expecting the older woman to move on.

Instead, she sat down beside her and for several moments didn't speak. Then, the society matron twisted the wedding ring on her finger and glanced at Ellen. 'I am sorry we did not start our friendship very well. I apologise for any offence I may have caused you.'

Taken aback by the admission, Ellen stared at her. 'Really?'

'Indeed. I acted abominably towards you. I saw only your past, not the person you are, and I allowed narrow-mindedness to cloud my judgement. I regret that.'

Ellen was stunned. 'Forgive me if I find your admission shocking. I never expected you to speak so honestly to me.'

Mrs Gardner-Hill continued to twist the ring on her finger. 'It is... difficult to be a woman in this colonial city. We are always judged. Us women of the higher class must set such an example to erase the stain of the convict history, to extract the town and its people from a murky past that is distasteful. I am afraid it has made us very great snobs, and our behaviour is such which would shame our counterparts in England. Charity and generosity seems to have been stripped from us the minute when we step ashore here.'

'I don't agree. I believe we make a choice, Mrs Gardner-Hill. We can be civil and kind or we can be objectionable and mean-spirited. We are not slaves to do the bidding of others who are vicious. We have a choice.'

'Indeed, you are correct. My actions shame me. Your arrival in our midst shook us. We all thought ourselves more superior to you. Yet, you fascinated us. When Alistair married you, we all thought him stupid.'

'Perhaps he was.'

'No.' The older woman stared out over the park. 'We were the stupid ones for allowing our prejudices to rule common sense. You are very different to us, it is true, and it was that difference which upset us. Our husbands admire you, Mrs Emmerson, for not being the same as us dull wives. You enjoy business, exploring that great unknown world, which most females have no wish to delve into. Add to that, you excelled in creating estates in the country, of speaking your mind, of breaking the rules, of wanting to do whatever you wanted without thought or care of what society expected from you.'

'I never did any of that to make others feel uncomfortable. I did it because that is who I am.'

'I know that now. But when you first married Alistair and you scorned everything we held up as true and good, you made us feel inferior and weak. We felt as though we were less than we should be, and we blamed you for feeling that way instead of changing our mindset. Others, of course, will never change, will never consider it. A certain behaviour taught since birth cannot be changed in a matter of months, or even years, and sometimes never. But I will change. I have. You, Ellen Kittrick Emmerson have shown me that wealth and status does not make a person decent. It just makes it easier to hide the flaws.'

Ellen didn't know what to say.

'I spoke to Mrs Haggerty in her salon yesterday,' Mrs Gardner-Hill continued. 'She told me that your sister said you were recovering, and that you were heading back to the country to fully recuperate.'

'Yes.'

'I also understand my husband has shares in your import business.'

'That is also true.'

'Then we have a connection you and I.' The older woman rose to her feet, walking stick in hand. 'Take it from me, Mrs Emmerson, unless you bring scandal to your name, I will never speak ill of you again. You have my word.'

'Thank you.' Ellen inclined her head in acknowledgement.

'Good day and be well.' Mrs Gardner-Hill strode away, and Ellen realised that was the first time she had seen the woman alone and not with her swarm of society friends.

The entire conversation surprised Ellen. Why had Mrs Gardner-Hill changed her opinion, even her behaviour towards her? What had caused the sudden alteration in her attitude? Did it matter? As long as the other woman meant it, that was all that concerned Ellen. Time would tell.

'Mama!' Bridget came running up to her. 'The parrot said a bad word.'

'It did? Well, don't you repeat it then.'

'It said *damn*!' Bridget declared with a giggle.

Ellen laughed. Her eldest daughter also broke all the rules. 'Come on, let's go back we have to pack for home.'

When they arrived at the cottage, Mr Duncan was standing at the gate. He helped them down from the carriage.

'Come in,' Ellen invited, her stomach turning. Maxwell looked devilishly handsome in a tan-coloured suit.

Riona steered Bridget out to the kitchen to wash and Ellen waved Mr Duncan to a seat.

Ellen was pleased he hadn't brought another flower bouquet for they didn't have any more space to place them. 'Tea?'

'No, not yet, thank you.' He looked a little nervous. 'Are you well? You seem so much better than when I last visited.'

'Thank you, yes. I am feeling more myself today. We've been for a walk.'

'Excellent.' His smile didn't reach his dark eyes.

He was making her nervous, but before she could speak, he leaned forward.

'Have you thought about what I said when I last came?'

'I have.'

'My feelings haven't changed. I care for you, Ellen. I would consider it a great pleasure if you would become my wife.'

'Maxwell, I admire you. You are good and kind, but—'

He held up a hand. 'But you do not love me.'

She shook her head. 'I'm sorry. I don't. I married Alistair without loving him and I wouldn't do it again. It's too hard. Besides, I quite enjoy my independence.'

His expression softened, a wry smile lifted his lips. 'I thought as much. It was worth a try though.'

'We can be friends? I would like that very much if we could.'

'You'll always be my friend, Ellen.' He took from his coat pocket a rolled piece of paper tied with red ribbon. 'This is yours. I wanted to give it to you before I returned to Hobart.'

'You're leaving?'

'Yes. Like you, my time here is done.'

'What about the pine company shares?'

'Oh, I'll get them, eventually.' He winked. 'Because of you I now own more stakes in the company than when I came to Sydney, so it's all been worth it, even if it meant my heart was slightly bruised in the process.'

She grinned. 'It's better to be bruised than broken.'

'Agreed.' He kissed her cheek. 'Never change, Ellen.' He pulled his coat straight. 'Open that later. Goodbye.'

She held the rolled paper and through the window watched him leave the cottage and stride down the street. Once he had gone from view, she untied the ribbon and rolled out the paper. She gasped as she read the deeds to the land on the Tarlo River were in her name.

CHAPTER 18

*E*llen walked the riverbank in the late afternoon sunshine, which as the days stretched closer to Christmas became longer and hotter. Ahead, Bridget galloped Princess as though she'd been born in the saddle. Her daughter kept to the fields, but Ellen edged into the trees seeking the shade. She took long walks each day to rebuild her strength. They'd been home for two months and she was eager to travel to Louisburgh and on to Tarlo River, but Riona forbid it until Ellen was stronger.

In truth, Ellen felt able to travel, but she owed it to her sister to stay for Christmas and make the occasion a happy one. The girls were growing up and she needed to devote some time to them before she threw herself into managing the land. Also, she enjoyed being home with Moira and even Honor, who even after eight weeks, had yet to get on her nerves.

Mr Thwaite spent hours with her each day, as they discussed the properties and future plans. He and Moira wanted to marry quietly after Christmas and that was another reason why Ellen would stay at Emmerson Park until the New Year.

A twig snapped behind her and Ellen jumped and spun around. She couldn't see anything. Was it an animal in the long grass? A snake? She'd taken one step when a figure appeared from behind a tree.

She jumped in surprise. 'Eddie Patterson.'

'Ellen.' He touched the rim of his hat to her, but the movement was slow. He looked starved, dirty and dishevelled.

'I didn't expect to see you again.'

'I...' He stumbled.

She rushed to help stay upright. 'Are you ill?'

'No.' He slid down the trunk and she crouched beside him. 'I've not eaten for days. The police have hounded us these last few weeks. Nowhere is safe.'

'Then go to Louisburgh. I told you to hide there if needed.'

'I don't think I could make it. My horse broke its leg. The others have managed to scarper. Dan's dead, may the Blessed Mother care and protect him.' He crossed himself.

The sound of hoofbeats and the creak of leather sounded behind them, and Ellen twisted in fright, scared of Eddie being found.

Bridget sat on Princess staring at Eddie.

'Bridget, sweetheart.' Ellen stood. 'You remember Mr Patterson who saved you from Uncle Colm?'

'Yes. Is he hurt?' Bridget looked concerned and not the least frightened.

'He's hungry, that's all, and it's made him weak.'

'I'll go up to the house and get some food.' Bridget gathered up the reins.

'No one must see you,' Ellen warned, astounded at the maturity of her nine-year-old daughter.

Bridget gave her a look of someone much older. 'I know that, Mama.' She rode away and Eddie chuckled.

'What a girl she is.' Eddie swatted away a fly. 'You should be proud of her.'

'I am, though she'll be a handful when she's older. There are times when I wonder if she is really nine or twenty.'

Eddie grinned lopsidedly. 'She'll have all the men around her like flies on shi—' He stopped speaking and grinned. 'Forgive me, I am uncouth, so I am. Too many years living with men in the bush away from polite society.'

She peered at him, seeing the ingrained dirt, the long straggly beard. 'We'll get you some food and then I'll try and sneak you up to the outbuildings where you can spend the night.'

'No, it's too risky.' Eddie shifted wearily against the trunk. 'I've been sleeping around here for two nights and noticed your men don't patrol at night.'

'No, we have no need to.'

'No dogs?'

'No.'

'Sure, and that's music to my ears.' He scratched his beard. 'I'll stay here tonight and once I've eaten, I'll be able to walk a few miles, so I will.'

'You can't walk far in your condition,' Ellen scoffed. 'Tonight, take one of the farm horses in the field behind the stables. I'll leave a bridle on the fence post once its dark. I doubt I can get a saddle without it being noticed though.'

'A bridle will be enough. I can ride bareback.'

'Douglas, our groom, sleeps in the barn next to the stables. You'll need to be quiet.'

He laughed. 'I'm a wanted man, sneaking about is what I do, so it is.'

She ignored that comment. 'Leave the gate open, so it looks like a mistake that someone hasn't secured it. The other horses won't wander far.'

Eddie took her hand in his dirty one. 'Thank you for giving me a horse. You're a good woman.'

'You gave me back my daughter.' She slipped her hand away from his, not wanting him to assume she enjoyed his touch. 'Where will you go?'

'Into hiding, naturally. The police are searching for me.'

'Oh, Eddie.' She wished he was anything other than a bushranger. If he'd been a normal man, she could have given him work and a home.

Twenty minutes later, they watched Bridget come thundering down the slope and across the fields.

'She knows how to ride that one,' Eddie admired.

Panting a little, Bridget dismounted and unhooked a large hessian sack.

'Heavens what have you brought, child?' Ellen helped her to bring the sack to Eddie.

'Lots of food and a bottle of wine from the cellar, and a blanket, and matches. I also grabbed one of Papa's old coats.'

'What a glorious girl you are, Bridget me darlin'. So clever!' Eddie praised her, biting into a leg of roast chicken.

'No one saw you?' Ellen asked anxiously, helping Eddie to take off his filthy and torn brown jacket and replace it with Alistair's long black riding coat.

'No one.' Bridget beamed triumphantly.

'Go now, both of you.' Eddie waved them away. 'And thank ye kindly.'

'It's nothing compared to what you did for me.' Ellen paused. 'Go to Tarlo River Ranges. I own land there on the west side of the range and south of the river. Hide there.'

His eyes widened, but he simply nodded. 'Thank you and goodbye, Ellen. Bridget, be a good lass for your mammy.'

Walking out of the trees, Ellen waited for Bridget to remount and together they headed up the slope to the house.

'I like Mr Patterson,' Bridget murmured.

Ellen glanced back over her shoulder but there was no sign of Eddie Patterson. She wondered if she'd ever see him again. 'Remember, you must never mention his name.'

'I never have, Mama. I'm not silly.'

'No, you're not. You're a grand girl, so you are, and I'm proud of you.'

At the top of the slope, Ellen walked the path through the gardens while Bridget steered Princess around the back of the outbuildings to the stables.

On the verandah, Ellen heard excited voices and wondered at them. Did they have visitors she wasn't aware of?

Going through the French doors, she was hit by a body lunging at her and she stumbled back with a squeal.

'Mammy!' Patrick cried, hugging her so tight Ellen could barely breathe never mind take in the sudden appearance of her beloved son.

'Patrick?' Ellen pulled away so she could see clearly into her cherished boy's face, a boy who was now the same height as her and who could easily look into her eyes as she did his. He'd grown and changed and looked like her father. She burst into tears, hugging him as though she'd never let him go.

'Oh, my darling, darling boy.' She couldn't stop the tears, her heart bursting with such love it was overwhelming.

Patrick hugged her just as tight, swearing to never leave her again.

Over his shoulder, Ellen saw Riona wiping her tears, but behind her stood Rafe and Ellen's heart twisted and somersaulted against her chest so hard she thought she would die from it.

'Rafe…' She gulped back her tears.

His own face was washed with emotion, but he stayed where he was, and she felt uncertain to go forward. Then, like a whisper of dread filtered through her happiness, she glanced around for Austin.

'Now, Ellen,' Riona murmured, half in warning, half in pain.

'Austin?' Ellen focused on Rafe, knowing he had the answers but not wanting to hear them.

Rafe stepped around Riona, his hands held out to her, the anxiety in his brilliant blue eyes. 'Ellen, my love.'

'Where is my son?' she demanded, her chest tight. Was he dead? God no! She couldn't bear it if he was. 'Where is he?'

'He stayed in England. At school.' Rafe was a few feet from her, hands out as though pleading.

'England?' She caved, bent over as the relief of him not being dead sank into her brain.

'Yes, he wanted to stay at school, Mammy.' Patrick was beside her, looking worried.

'But he's all right?' She turned to Patrick, not wanting to look at Rafe.

'Yes. He was well when we left. And I am well now, too.'

Ellen frowned. 'You've been ill?'

He nodded. 'I nearly died, but I'm fine now. Much better.'

'You nearly died?' A fear gripped Ellen. She spun to Rafe. 'He nearly died?'

'Yes, a fever.'

'Rafe saved me, Mammy. He took me from school to Cherry-bank and he and Iris and Mrs Hamilton looked after me. They made me well again. I begged Rafe to bring me home.' A look of uncertainty crossed his sun-tanned face. 'I wanted to come home.'

She hugged him to her. 'I wanted you home, too, darling. I wanted you both home.'

'Austin refused to come,' Rafe said quietly.

'So, you allowed him to stay in a place where fever raged and nearly killed Patrick?' she snarled, full of disappointment and hurt.

'I thought it best to let him stay and finish his education.'

'You *thought*?' Ellen rounded on him. '*You* thought? It wasn't *your* decision to make! He is my son. *My son*. Not Alistair's and not yours but *mine* and I want him *home*!' She grabbed Patrick's hand and pulled him from the room, the tears flowing again at the heartache of not being able to see Austin for years.

'Don't blame Rafe, Mammy,' Patrick said when Ellen finally stopped walking and they sat on a seat in the middle of the rose garden.

She took a deep breath. 'Austin is a child to do adult's bidding, not to go his own way. I wanted you both to come home.'

Patrick gazed down at the gravel beneath his boots. 'I know you'll miss Austin, but are you happy that I am here though?'

'Oh yes, darling.' She hugged him to her. 'So very happy.'

'I've missed everyone, but especially you.'

She kissed his cheek. 'And I've missed you, my son. We have a lot to catch up on. So much to talk about.'

'You won't send me away again?'

'No, not at all.'

'Rafe said I could be tutored if I can't get a place at King's School.'

'We'll decide all that later.' She kissed his cheek. 'For now, let us enjoy you being back with us.'

'I'm home for Christmas.' He grinned.

'Patrick!' Bridget's scream echoed around the garden.

'Bridget!' Patrick ran to embrace his sister. 'You're so big.'

'You are too. Look, Mama, look how tall Patrick is.'

'I can see.' Ellen cried again at the joy in their faces at being reunited.

'Have you met Miss Lewis?' Bridget asked him. 'She is my governess. She's very nice but doesn't like to ride. We'll have to go riding tomorrow. You need a horse of your own, doesn't he, Mama? Did you want to see Princess?'

'More importantly than visiting Princess, have you seen Lily and Ava?' Ellen asked, coming to stand beside them.

'No, they were napping when we arrived.'

'Come along then. Let us go to the nursery and spend some time with them before dinner.'

For some time, Ellen remained in the nursery watching Patrick get to know his two little sisters. Lily had been a tiny baby when he left, and Ava not even conceived. But he took to them straight away and they to him and the laughter filled the room as they tumbled about on the rug.

Riona came in, all smiles and watery eyes watching them play, but after a moment she dragged Ellen to one side. 'Go to Mr Hamilton.'

Ellen stiffened. 'No. I can't.'

'Why? You can't blame him for Austin.'

'I can and I will. Austin isn't an adult. He was to do as he was told. Rafe was to bring both boys home. Rafe should have insisted on Austin coming too.'

'And you know from Austin's letters how much he is enjoying school. Ever since the day we went to Alistair's house, Austin has wanted to be like him. He's always wanted to go to a gentleman's school like Alistair. He would have put up a good argument to Rafe to not get on the ship, so he would!'

Ellen clenched her teeth. It hurt to think Austin was still on the other side of the world, especially when seeing Patrick with his sisters gave her so much joy. She couldn't forgive Rafe. He knew she wanted them both home. Why didn't he bring them to her?

'You're a stubborn fool,' Riona whispered. 'Mr Hamilton is a guest in our house. Are you to ignore him the entire time? The man loves you and I thought you loved him.'

Tormented, Ellen hurried from the room and across the hall into her own bedroom. She paced the floor, not knowing what to think, what to do. It was all such a mess. Every time she looked at Rafe she felt such pain that he'd not brought Austin home.

Yet he was here, at long last, here within reach. Her heart twisted, and a sob broke from her. She loved him. God, how she loved him. From the first moment she met him years ago in Mr Wilton's house, she had held him in her heart and mind.

A note was slid under her door. She stared at it for a second before picking it up.

My love,

I shall stay in my room tonight to give you time with the children and to save you from the embarrassment of being in my presence which seems to conflict you and cause you heartache. I'm sorry I did not insist on Austin coming with us. I made a mistake that I deeply regret.

Tomorrow, hopefully, we can talk. Then if you still feel unable to forgive me, I shall return to Sydney and sail home to England.

I love you,

Rafe.

INSTINCT TOLD her to go to him, but she couldn't. Instead, she began pacing, her mind in a whirl. What were Rafe's long-term plans? What had he expected when he arrived? Had he left everything behind to come to her? He said he loved her. She loved him. Why couldn't she go to him? She didn't understand what was stopping her. Was it too late for them? Had too much happened?

A knock on the door made her jump. 'Come in.'

Patrick entered shyly. 'Mammy.'

'Yes, darling.'

'Don't be angry at Rafe. He loves you very much.'

Hot tears stung her eyes. 'How do you know that?'

'He told me. Please don't send him back to England.'

Ellen wiped her eyes. Gazing at Patrick, seeing the change in him, how tall, how grown up he had become caused her heart to ache for Austin even more. But her eldest son hadn't wanted to come home when he had the opportunity to do so. He'd decided to stay on the other side of the world, away from his family. He had chosen his own way, and it reminded Ellen that it is something she had also done when leaving Ireland. She had gone her own way. Austin was very much like her. Strong-willed and independent. Nor was he a child any longer.

Going to the dressing table, she splashed her face with cold water and tidied her hair. Her dress of green and white stripe needed to be changed for dinner but today that could wait.

With a smile at Patrick, she left the room and went to the nursery. She picked up Lily and kissed the little girl's cheek.

Ellen took a deep breath. She had made a decision. Now it was time to act on it.

Carrying Lily, she walked to the bedroom Riona had given Rafe and knocked.

He opened the door instantly and stared at her then at Lily. His dark blue eyes looked pained.

'This is your daughter, Lily. She'll be two in two months. She's named after a flower like your sister,' Ellen's voice broke on the last word.

Rafe's face crumbled. Tears filled his eyes as he smiled at his daughter. 'Lily…'

Ellen's heart swelled with love at the similar faces staring at each other. 'Would you like to hold her?'

He nodded and she passed the little girl to him. Lily gazed up at him and touched his chin. Rafe sucked in a breath. 'I cannot believe she is mine. She is beautiful.'

'And your image.'

The light of pure joy lit up his eyes. 'She is.'

Ellen watched the emotions play across his face. 'Thank you for bringing Patrick home.'

His expression fell. 'I am sorry about Austin.'

She shook head. 'You are not to blame. It was wrong of me to behave as I did. You did the right thing. Austin has made his choice just as I have made my choice.'

Rafe frowned. 'Your choice?'

'To marry the man I love and adore.' She smiled tenderly at him. 'If you'll have me?'

He crushed her to his side with one arm while holding Lily in the other.

Ellen welcomed his kiss like someone starved. Desire and longing rose in her, needing this man's love as much as she needed air.

When Lily's little hands touched their faces, they reluctantly broke apart, but smiled happily and tearfully at each other, not daring to believe it was all true and real.

Ellen wiped the tears from her eyes and then his. 'I hope you want to become a sheep farmer?' she teased him.

Rafe kissed her softly. 'As long as we are together and a family, I do not care what we do or where we are. I simply want to love you forever and be in the same country as you.'

'No more partings,' she vowed.

'You have me for life now, my love. I never want to be away from you again.' He kissed her to seal his promise. 'We do everything together. We are a partnership in every aspect, family and business, yes?'

'Sounds perfect.'

'No secrets between us.'

'No, none. I will tell you everything.' She thought briefly of her part in Colm's death and aiding Eddie Patterson. All of it would be discussed. She leaned into him, and his arm tightened around her. Ellen closed her eyes and for the first time in many years felt safe and secure and loved.

AFTERWORD

Hello readers!

I hope you enjoyed more of Ellen's story. Right from the beginning I felt Ellen had more of a story than just one book. Beyond the Distant Hills formed in my mind while I was writing the first book, and while writing the sequel I had thoughts of a third book. So, I'm sure I'll write about Ellen's children in the next book. They have such personalities that I'd like to know them when they are adults. We'll see!

My own Irish ancestors were called Kittrick and came from the area around Louisburgh, County Mayo. Researching my family is fascinating, and time consuming and never-ending! I read about my Irish ancestors who lived through the famine and, quite often, were in front of the local magistrate in the petty sessions for slight misdemeanours such as drinking, trespassing, etc. I based Colm and Malachy in book 1 on them. My ancestors were a little naughty, but they had to be tough to survive those times.

Thank you for joining me on this ride. I truly appreciate all your reviews and messages. Your support means a lot to me and gives me the drive to keep writing entertaining stories. I love being a storyteller and knowing that people have received a few hours of pleasure from reading one of my books is very humbling.

Best wishes,
AnneMarie Brear
September 2021

ABOUT THE AUTHOR

Australian born award winning & Amazon UK Bestseller Anne-Marie Brear has been a life-long reader and started writing in 1997 when her children were small. AnneMarie has a love of history, of grand old English houses and a fascination of what might have happened beyond their walls. AnneMarie's interests include reading, travelling, watching movies, spending time with family and eating chocolate - not always in that order! Anne-Marie is the author of historical family saga novels.